ONCE UPON A STAR

Gajra Kottary is a multimedia writer. Her first collection of women-centric short stories, *Fragile Victories,* was published in 1996. It was followed by another collection, *The Last Laugh*, in 2003. Her debut novel, *Broken Melodies*, was published by HarperCollins Publishers India in 2011 to critical acclaim, simultaneously with its Hindi translation *Bikhre Sur*. Gajra has written television serials like *Hamare Tumhare*, *Astitva—Ek Prem Kahani*, the nation's most popular daily soap *Balika Vadhu*, and more recently, *Buddha* and *Veera*. She has won many awards for her TV scripts/stories; among them are the Indian Television Academy's Best Teleplay Award, the Indian Telly Award, the Apsara Award and the Global Indian Television Award. She was also a script associate with Mahesh Bhatt on the film *Yeh Zindagi Ka Safar* directed by Tanuja Chandra. This is her second novel.

Praise for the Book

'Behind Bollywood, beyond Bollywood ... a compelling page-turner that looks at celebrity lives and the costs and collateral damage of stardom.'

—Namita Gokhale, writer and co-director of the Jaipur Literature Festival

'Over the years, Gajra has sensitively, and realistically, portrayed women and their issues. In *Once Upon a Star* too, she displays her fine writing style in detailing the trials and tribulations of the protagonist. A great read.'

—Anupam Kher, actor, teacher and motivational speaker

'I can't stop marvelling at this story told with grace, warmth, nuance and unrelenting self-belief. It is immensely inspiring and deeply moving. A saga of resilience, redemption, compassion and hope, it is also a timely reminder that women have stopped being mere spectators who let the men in their lives trample their dignity and sense of self-worth. They realize their talent and pursue their dreams; they know they can win.'

—Feroz Abbas Khan, Theatre and Film Director

ONCE UPON A STAR

Gajra Kottary

HarperCollins *Publishers* India

First published in India in 2014 by
HarperCollins *Publishers* India

Building 10, Tower A, 4th Floor, DLF Cyber City, Phase II,
Gurugram Haryana – 122002, India
www.harpercollins.co.in

P-ISBN: 978-93-5136-334-7
E-ISBN: 978-93-5136-335-4

2 4 6 8 10 9 7 5 3 1

Typeset in 11/14.2 Linux Libertine
Saanvi Graphics Noida

Printed and bound at
MicroPrints India, New Delhi

For my mother, Maya, whose blessings and prayers I can feel long after she has gone away from my world ...

1

When Simran looked back, she realized everything turned from this point, this day.

Her worries had been burgeoning: her hair, Trishala's dress, what to wear, the tone of her makeup. Was the table set? Would Raj come on time? The air conditioning, the nick on her finger ... and something unexplained. Something that was gnawing at her but she couldn't put a finger on. Was it a premonition?

Just twenty minutes to get ready. Simran looked at the clock. Trishala was fussing. *What is it about birthdays and children?* Trishala, her baby, nine now. Fussing over every errant strand of hair, already conscious about her weight. *When did you grow up?*

The Mehras loved their chicken tikkas and aloo parathas. Trishala did not have any reason to worry about weight for now. *You're nine, baby. We'll worry about that in a bit, when you grow up and decide to get married. Maybe to someone in the film industry?*

Simran sighed as she switched on the air conditioning in her large walk-in wardrobe. There she went, day-dreaming again. She glanced at the clock. Less than 20 minutes to get ready! Should she wear the Tarun Vahiani sari or her latest

Prabal Gurung gown? The rows of saris glimmered. All the brands in the world at an arm's length.

Simran knew that accessorizing would take up another ten minutes. *I'm going to get late and everyone's going to think ...* As the wife of the reigning superstar of Bollywood, she could not afford to have anything less than impeccable manners and perfection at every touch, especially as the hostess.

'Life's tough, but someone's gotta live it!' she said, as she lifted the Prabal Gurung in beautiful pink and shaded grey. It would set off her grey eyes. Simran wore the gown and then opened her jewellery box. Her largest solitaire drops and diamond-crusted bangles were all she needed to complete the statement.

Ex-actress Simran Tiwari, you do look good even if I may say so myself. She twirled in front of the full-length mirror in the wardrobe but then frowned. Was that a new tyre around her waist? When did this appear?

She glanced at the Tissot on her wrist. Too late to worry about it now. Too late to change into something that will hide it. She took one last look at herself in the mirror. A tall, fair woman with chiselled features stared back at her. The industry had compared her to Madhubala following her debut. She had the same infectious smile, the same cascade of wavy, long hair, the same innocence ... Simran sighed. *I'm happy.* She looked at the tyre again. *Maybe I do need to take Divya and Mouli's advice seriously and hire a personal trainer soon.*

And with that thought in mind and a smile on her face, Simran aka Mrs Raj Mehra was ready to take on the world.

It was a fairy tale romance. The press had gone gooey over them. The beautiful Simran Tiwari was going to marry the heartthrob of Hindi films, the man who romanced a million beautiful women, the man who generated mass hysteria among girls. She was the one he came back to every night. Yes, Simran was the envy of a lot of people.

Of course, stardom came with a price. The cutting remarks when she chose to stop working hurt. Later, those fashion magazines and websites that damned her choice of clothes at parties hurt. When the media mocked her shape, that hurt too. It was like they were telling her that she did not deserve a demi-god like Raj.

Nowadays, Simran found herself looking at her husband. Staring at his perfect profile, the curl of his hair, the mole near his ear, the way his cheek creased into a dimple by his famous lopsided smile, she felt a rush of adoration. Raj was hers. He would catch her staring and cock his eyebrows at her in his beautiful way, and she would find herself blushing with happiness. He could still do it to her. Make her go weak in the knees.

I must lose some weight.

But then, all those parties, late nights and the occasional beer were to blame. Still, Raj came back to her, to their children, every day that he was in town. Which was saying a lot for 'Bollywood men'.

In the balancing act of life, Simran was Raj's real world. She, her presence, meant sanity.

After a gruelling day on the sets, Raj went back to a picture-perfect home. His kids were doing the right things, his parents were able to relax and enjoy being grandparents, his brother and wife looked up to him ... everything was organized with clockwork precision and simplicity. Some women made careers for themselves, but Simran had crafted a career for Raj. She was the real strength behind his success, his back-bone.

Lifting her chin in unconscious pride, Simran left for the party.

As with everything else in Simran's life, even her home was designed to look like a sprawling movie set. As she walked down the carpeted stairs, Simran looked at the gleaming leather upholstery, the massive Raza painting that dominated their glittering dining room and the Swarovski chandelier at the centre of the high ceiling. Soft lounge music was already playing and she knew that the maids were readying the cutlery.

Vardaan was sold for a song by a hard-pressed actor. Simran had heard the story many times over. How her father-in-law saw the place and fell in love with it, how after his film had sunk he didn't have too much left. How Raj signed a film simply to put in money and how young Karan gave away his car and Raj's mother sold all her jewellery, all for this house. But they had never regretted it, never looked back.

When Raj and Simran were dating, Simran realized that she meant something more than a colleague to him on the day he took her to Vardaan to show her his home.

And his parents had instantly liked her. *Mori. Mine.* They had named her that instant, and that was the name that had stayed. At home she was Mori, not her. And it meant so many things to her: acceptance, love, simplicity and responsibility.

She hurried into the kitchen. No traces of cooking showed.

Good. The dessert-of-the-day was usually her creation. She wanted to check the consistency of the tarts, too. The menu for today's party had plenty of finger food for the kids and cocktails and barbeque food for the adults. The Mehras loved eating.

People had already begun to trickle in, and Simran mixed with them with practised ease. 'Congratulations, Mrs Raj,' almost everyone wished her. The Cinefare Popular Awards had just been announced. News travelled fast.

'We need another party for that. This won't do!' Responding, smiling, pausing for the right words, Simran was on auto-pilot mode.

The kids were out in the front garden, participating in games that had been organized by a popular television host whom Simran had hired especially for Trishala's big day. Shrieks of laughter came from that part of the house. Simran felt her muscles relax. These were the perks of being a superstar's wife. And she no longer flinched from these words. *There was a time when 'superstar' meant me, Simran.* Simran shook off those memories. *It's been good,* she told herself. *Everything is perfect. I couldn't have asked for more.*

Or could I?

Simran shrugged. Today, she was the woman behind one of the biggest names in Bollywood. And she had a bank balance to match.

Simran glanced up towards the ceiling to check if her latest purchase, a gigantic Lalique chandelier, placed in the entrance of the house, was indeed looking as glamourous as had been promised to her by the salesgirl.

'It looks beautiful, beta, and so do you,' said a kind voice. Simran turned around.

'Thank you, Mummy. You are always such a sweetheart!' said Simran, her heart lifting. A compliment from Kamla Mehra, her mother-in-law, had the power to make her happy.

'Come now, Mori. We have more people coming in,' said Kamla as she manoeuvred Simran towards the guests.

Where's Tarun? Her eyes scanned the room for the elder of her two children. Her eleven-year-old was supposed to keep an eye on Trishala. She found him sitting in a corner, busy with his phone. Another of Raj's guilt-ridden indulgences of being an absent parent. Simran felt mildly irritated as she made her way towards him.

'What are you doing in the middle of a party?'

Tarun looked up. 'Just trying to break Nitin's score in Angry Birds.'

'We have guests! And here you are playing games! This is why your dad should not have given you an iPhone ...'

'Save it, Mamma. Not today at least!' said Tarun before he walked off.

Simran sighed aloud. Whoever said money makes life easier must have simply been a complete pauper.

The kids who ran into her arms and wouldn't sleep unless she read them a bedtime story, the fingers that clung to her on the first day of school, seemed to have disappeared with the growing years. Now, Trishala had her friends; Tarun had his games. 'I-need-space', 'I'm-stressed' were part of their everyday vocabulary now. Suddenly, Raj, his gifts and his star aura were very cool to them. While Simran was the quintessential party pooper.

Raj and his gifts. All his statements in the press that he spent quality time with his kids ... She did not remember the last time Raj and she had a day entirely to themselves. Work and more commitments. But he gave her gifts too. Expensive stuff that she couldn't help but flaunt. *Why wouldn't they delight the kids?* 'Wait a minute with those angsty thoughts,' she said aloud to herself.

'Talking to yourself?' said a husky voice. 'Nice chandelier, Simran,' added Kavita, Karan's wife. Kavita was—Simran thought—everything Simran would never be. Slim and tall; self-confident to the point of being overpowering. She had two kids but was still reed-thin.

Recognized as one of the upcoming fashion designers in the country, Kavita was wearing one of her own creations, a gown that enhanced her slim figure.

'Thank you,' mumbled Simran. Kavita always had the power to fluster her. But Kavita had barely stopped to hear her. 'But you know what Simran? If I had that kind of a budget at my disposal, I would have picked a Versace chandelier instead. You know, the crystal on those chandeliers is especially polished and cut to pick out the light even in a dark room. They certainly know their stuff.'

Simran felt herself flush. Just like Kavita to fling a barb her way.

Then Karan piped in, 'But I really like it, Bhabhi. In fact, I think it adds grace to the entrance.' Simran exhaled. Kavita looked on coolly. It was so typical of the peace-maker that Karan was, thought Simran. *Just for this, I'll make him his favourite chicken Manchurian for dinner tomorrow.*

Karan was not as successful as Raj, but he had never made it a prestige issue. Easygoing and genial, he did just about decently at the box office and earned fairly well too in the B-grade films. Karan was happy but Kavita grudged Raj's success. Compared to Raj, whose career had long been on a roll and for whom money poured in like water, Karan's earnings seemed paltry to her. Over the years, Kavita had encouraged, cajoled, pushed and even bullied Karan into trying harder. But Raj occupied too much space in the industry, and nothing Karan did seemed to make much of a difference. Then Kavita gave up and began to focus on her career. A successful fashion designer today, she called the shots in her husband's life.

Simran dared not voice it aloud, but she secretly envied Kavita for the fact that she had a career of her own, and that there were never any ugly rumours of link-ups and affairs surrounding Karan and also for the fact that her two children were so gentle and loving. In Simran's eyes, Kavita had it all.

Kavita seemed to sneer at Simran. She made it a point to snub her whenever she could. *She must laugh at me all the time.* Whenever she saw Kavita she wished she had not left work. She could have been a brand in herself.

She quickly shrugged the thought off.

I have a loving husband. I have two amazing kids. I am happy. I am the centre of Raj's world. He adores me. His parents adore me. Over and out.

When they had started out, the balance was tilted. Simran was the reigning star and Raj was the promising, budding actor. There was always promise in Raj. But he had to struggle for years. Simran had convinced him that his luck would change one day; he just had to keep plodding on. And sure enough, in a few years, there was a breakthrough—a hit, which was then followed by a string of hits. And Raj never looked back.

But, with Simran, it was different. Each accolade, every milestone, the windfall of money, the spin of success only made her turn back and look. And watch wistfully. It was like watching someone else, another Simran wander in the labyrinth of each day, manoeuvring, sometimes on autopilot.

Celebrity status was like a mirage. Everyone wanted to get there, but it was only when one actually reached there, that the hollowness of it all was truly revealed. And by then, it was too late. One had to put up with the consequences of living with the mirage. And that was exactly what Simran was doing now, burying real feelings away in this illusionary world.

Why did she put up with it all? The answer was very simple. Raj. He was her world. Raj did have many commitments but Simran was convinced that she came first in his list of priorities.

The smutty reports of link-ups that came with stardom would always be there. It was part of the job. The other part was to not let it affect you, or at least to not let anyone know it affected you.

'So where is Bhaisahab by the way?'

Trust you to do everything possible to make me squirm.

Simran smiled even before she turned to answer Kavita. 'Busy as usual with a script hearing,' she responded with a smile. Kavita feigned surprise, 'Doesn't he know we have a party at home?'

'Don't be silly, Kavita. Why would he forget T's birthday? He's up in his study. You know how producers are. They need to be indulged too. They must be done. He will come down any moment now.'

Kavita laughed and said, 'Yes, Bhabhi. Raj Bhaisahab and on time! Right!' Watching Simran flinch, she added, 'You will have to call him at least ten times before he deigns to make an appearance. You know how much he loves a grand entry!'

Gritting her teeth and faking calmness, Simran retorted, 'He really didn't want to sit for the narration today. But you know how insistent Subhash Bhai can be. He said it was a really good script and he only wanted Raj to do it and so, pressed for a narration.'

Stung by Simran's answer and the suggestion hidden in it, Kavita said, arching her brow, 'Well, let's hope to see him soon.' And before Simran could say anything, she walked off.

Relieved, Simran whipped out her phone and called Raj. She knew he was in the middle of work and chances of him answering the phone were minimal. Sure enough, the call was answered by Mahesh, Raj's secretary. He said, 'Madam, sir will be down in five minutes.' Simran was irritated now. 'Mahesh, the party is halfway through. When does he plan to come? Please tell him I called and that he needs to hurry downstairs.'

Simran hung up, knowing Mahesh would not interrupt the reading. Mahesh, Raj's shadow, would move heaven and earth to ensure that his boss's work went on without a hitch.

Raj will not turn up for at least another half an hour. I better do something.

A blast of cool air hit Simran as she entered the study at Vardaan. Mahesh looked a little flustered but she ignored him. This was Raj's escape on the rare occasions that he was at home. The room was very masculine, done up with leather couches and mahogany bookshelves. Raj had an expensive taste, and his study housed an enviable collection of first edition books as well as paintings. Simran often wondered why he took all the trouble when she never saw him reading any of them. It was here that Raj kept his cigar collection too. Some of the finest cigars from the world over were enjoyed here on the evenings they entertained people. Simran heard someone reading. It was not Subhash Bhai.

Now that she was in, Simran tried to be discreet. Raj glanced at her irritably and motioned to Subhash Bhai, indicating that the reading should continue. His young assistant stopped and Subhash Bhai, with a flair for the dramatic, continued in hushed tones, 'So the hero, I mean you, finds this other woman captivating. And, tired of the constant fighting with your wife, one day you decide to do the unthinkable. You leave your wife of seven years for the other woman in your life.' Raj clicked his tongue in impatience. 'Subhash Bhai, how can the hero leave his wife just like that? Think of my image. This won't go down well with the family audiences. If the hero's morals are low, my image will be compromised.'

There was silence as Subhash Bhai considered what was said. 'That's the twist in the story, Raj-ji. It is only after the hero moves in with the other woman that he completely reinvents his life. He tackles the failure and losses in his business and then makes a massive comeback!' But Raj didn't seem convinced.

Subhash Bhai looked anxious. Would Raj reject the film?

'Subhash Bhai, Raj has a point.' Simran's voice seemed to startle everyone.

'Why don't you try this,' said Simran hurriedly as she noticed Raj looking exasperatedly at her. 'Make the hero leave his wife but not move in with the other woman because somewhere deep in his heart, he still loves his wife. Let him continue seeing this other woman. And then, when he joins back his business, his wife works alongside him. In the process, they resolve their differences and realize that they cannot live without each other. The hero thanks the other woman for having made him a new man, and, apologizing to her, returns to his wife.'

Raj's hand moved dismissively. But Subhash Bhai jumped at the idea. 'You are a genius, Simran Bhabhi!' he said, beaming. 'This is a very good idea. What do you say, Raj-ji?'

Raj frowned. *What the hell is she doing here?* He glared at Simran. 'Arrey, Raj-ji, think about it,' cajoled Subhash Bhai. 'This angle is good and it resolves the point you made about family audience-waudience!'

'Umm, okay, it is doable.'

Subhash Bhai exhaled loudly. 'It is decided then. Raj-ji, you are doing this project. And Simran Bhabhi, have you ever considered writing for films?' Simran glanced at Raj. But he was smiling and talking to Subhash Bhai's assistant. 'Subhash Bhai, I am very happy where I am,' she said. 'After so many years of living in this industry, hearing scripts and seeing movies, one tends to pick up a few tricks and ideas. It's no big deal.'

'Subhash Bhai, if she starts working, when will she get the time to spend all my earnings?' said Raj suddenly with a wide grin. Subhash Bhai laughed politely, and so did Simran. Raj continued, 'Simran, don't you have to be downstairs? We will wrap up in five more minutes and I will be down.'

'Yes. Do come soon. Everyone's waiting. Subhash Bhai, you too,' said Simran and, taking it as her cue to leave, exited the room.

As she shut the door, Simran heard Subhash Bhai congratulating him on the award he bagged the previous night. She didn't hear what Raj said as she shut the door softly. *That was a close one.* Simran realized that she should not have butted in. Had the conversation moved in any other angle, Raj would have sulked for days.

Raj smiled and changed the subject tactfully.

It was just so typical of Simran to come and steal his thunder, behaving like the malkin of her estate. The way she waltzed in anywhere and anytime, reprimanded him for being late and generally hogged the family limelight these days! Raj seethed beneath the veneer of geniality. *Why does she have to be Little Miss Perfect? Simran has forgotten to be just my wife.*

He remembered the days when she would walk into the sets and his heart would skip a beat. Her laughter, even now, had the same power ... *I loved her simplicity and her trust.* Now, Simran was perpetually engrossed in running the house, pleasing everyone, worrying about the kids and dictating to the maids. He and Simran had not made love in a really long time. Copulation was the right word for what they did. The tenderness, the love, the passion was a thing of the past.

Raj's mind drifted towards what Subhash Bhai was saying: Shubham. Raj and Shubham. Both had started out at the same time in their careers. Raj couldn't help gloating. While he became a superstar, Shubham, a National School of Drama graduate and a gifted actor, never touched the heights of superstardom. *Sometimes just being great at your work is not all that you need. There's something called instinct.*

Raj knew that Simran did not approve of his behaviour towards other 'less fortunate' actors. The showbiz was a hard world to be in. There was no time for charity. *Charity is never a good thing. Who had said that? Maybe no one.* Raj's star had been on the rise and he had slowly cut himself off from his past. Shubham was just one of the many unfortunate casualties. Being a celebrity is relentlessly addictive. The more you get used to being the centre of attention, the less you are able to tolerate the spotlight focused on someone else. It's like sniffing something that gives you a high. Once you've had too much of it, nothing but that can keep it going.

But he had better things to dwell on. Sia for instance. Raj felt his mouth curve into a smile.

Raj had changed. The transformation had been visible, palpable, rapid. Simran took a deep breath, smoothed out a few strands off her face. Just then the phone rang. She answered it immediately, and sang into the phone, 'So how is my favourite sister-in-law today?'

A playful voice from the other end said, 'Favourite? Better be, since I am your only sister-in-law!' Simran laughed out and said, 'Got me, Ashima! So how are you?' Ashima answered, 'Absolutely great. How is the party going, Bhabhi? Since you've organized it, it must be the best.'

Pleased, Simran said, 'You do know how to keep your Bhabhi happy. The party is great, but it would have been better if you were here. I am sure Tanuj could spare you for a while.' Ashima's voice turned sombre now. 'I am coming to Mumbai soon. And besides, there is something important I want to talk to you about.'

'What's up, Ashima?' asked Simran, alert now and trying to keep the tension out of her voice. 'Oh it's nothing. Relax,' said Ashima, lightly. 'Really, Bhabhi. It can wait until I come.' Simran hesitated, but socialite couple Amir and Sudha Tyagi had sauntered up to her and she had to hang up.

Sometimes, Simran watched herself from the outside, in a detached way. She saw what the world saw: an elegant smile on her face, the easy camaraderie, the poise and the deference. She saw herself answering the most mundane questions with utmost interest, she watched her eyes going wide and mouth softly radiating a smile every now and then. She watched the lights, the people flitting from group to group. Stars, celebrities, people who ruled, faces that one saw on magazines and screens. She saw herself with them, and nothing betrayed the emptiness she sometimes felt.

Everyone told her she looked so pretty and nice. One part of Simran was honest enough to admit this is exactly what she wanted to hear. But they were just words. Words used lightly. The same words could be twisted with a sneer and a cruel laugh.

Tonight, if there was one question on everyone's lips, it was, 'Where's the hero? Where's Raj?'

Kavita had been right. Raj adored the attention. Perhaps it was best that it was he who got it. Simran scanned the crowd, looking for someone she had not greeted yet. Divya and Mouli. Simran smiled happily. Her two 'best friends'.

'Divya! Mouli! Muahh!' As soon as the cheek to cheek greetings were out of the way, Simran got to the point, 'How do I look, girls?' Divya said, 'You look gorgeous as usual, sweetie. Don't you ever doubt that!'

'Really?' Simran asked, sounding unsure. 'Of course! Raj Mehra may be the superstar, but he wouldn't be half as popular as he is without his gorgeous wife!' said Mouli.

Simran couldn't help giving them a hug saying, 'Right back at you girls, right back at you!'

Across the room, watching Simran with a leer, were Tara and Divya, two starlets riding high on the wave of a few successes. Tara, who had been busy piling on praise before Simran just a few seconds ago, said, 'Oh my God, Divya! That latest Spring/Summer Prabal Gurung is such a waste on Simran. She looks soooo fat!'

Divya agreed saying, 'I know! She has on her a million bucks, but she definitely doesn't look it. I wonder what happens to these star wives as soon as their husbands start doing well.'

In another part of the room, a group of young and happening actors and directors were talking about their latest conquests. One said, 'At the outdoor of *Jeevan*, we had three upcoming models wanting to make it in movies. I did them all and none got to know of the other!' The other jokingly asked, 'Oh, and were all of them female?'

More chuckles followed and someone said, 'Speaking of which, guys, is this Raj-Sia thing for real?' The rest of them turned to him and someone answered, 'Which rock have you been living under? Raj and Sia are an item! They can't keep their hands off each other. It's for real, man!' It was followed by another comment, 'Tch, Tch, I wonder how his wife is going to afford her designer gowns if the marriage goes kaput.'

At that, they all broke into laughter.

Oblivious to all this, Simran settled into the company of Mouli and Divya. They themselves were wives of popular stars and Simran could relate to them. God knows it wasn't easy to be in the background when one's spouse was the desire of every woman in the country. And it was even tougher when one knew that there were a lot of people waiting for that one opportunity to bring you down with a thud.

'There you are!'

Simran turned with delight, 'Mamma!' The two hugged. 'How have you been, beta?' Shammi asked. 'I am good. You look radiant, Mamma. How was Nice?' Shammi replied with a chuckle, 'I shall not say Nice was nice, as that is too clichéd. It was lovely. I had the best time ever, just by myself for the first time. And yes, I did try a few spas while I was there, which explains the glow.'

Simran grinned. 'It is great that you are back. We missed you so much while you were away.'

Shammi said, 'You mean *you* missed me so much. That workaholic son-in-law of mine barely has the time to miss you, forget me!' They laughed.

And before Simran could add anything, Raj appeared on the top of the stairs. And as though on cue, Sia too.

2

Bollywood: the informal name given to the Hindi film industry in Mumbai. If you look up the word Bollywood, you will find that it is the largest film producer in India and one of the largest centres of film production in the world. What no website or magazine will ever be able to capture is that Bollywood is not a place; it's a way of living and thinking. Its heroes and heroines dictate how people in India look and feel. Bollywood dicates our moods and moves. It pins down emotions and puts words to what people feel.

Bollywood is immense. It is what makes the dreams of ordinary people. Bollywood is about possibilities. Also, impossibilities. Ordinary people can actually dream of singing or acting, and it can happen. People from remote villages watch a film and pack their bags and head westward—to the island city. Some dreams are fulfilled. Many aren't. But nothing can stop dreams from being churned. Nothing.

Shammi came to Bollywood with stars in her eyes. She had beauty. But in show-business, beauty is just one element. Shammi had started out very young in an industry that was always on the lookout for fresh faces. Things had gone well for Shammi and the dreams of ruling the industry had not seemed so far-fetched for a while. She almost got up there. Then her dream crashed. A few bad choices of films and Shammi was written off. Bollywood, in its many avatars, could be merciless. No matter what she did, no matter the long hours she kept, the work she chose, Shammi could not find a foothold back among the top in the industry.

But the taste of success remained in her mouth. Enough for her to keep stretching, hoping, walking around in her life, blinkered. Films ruined her whole life. Looking back, Shammi realized that they had perhaps ruined her marriage too. Or would it have crumbled anyway? Was she too much in love with herself that there was no room in her heart for anyone else? Perhaps.

Shyam walked off. Shammi was left alone with a little child holding her hand. Simran was dragged from set to set while Shammi hunted for work. Simran grew up on sets. Cinema was in her blood.

By the time she was sixteen, producers started eyeing her. By the time she was nineteen, she was established in Bollywood and had a fan-following to be envied. Shammi didn't have to approach any film-maker for a role for her daughter.

Shammi watched her daughter, at first with a mixture of mild jealousy and much protectiveness. Then, she learnt to enjoy it. Soon she felt relief and pride. Shammi's career was not meant to be, but thank god her fatherless child (because Shyam never showed his face again) would be all right.

Simran, shy, beautiful and reticent, bloomed on a film set. Acting seemed to be her second nature. When Shammi learnt to be comfortable with Simran's success at work, she watched her daughter's career with admiration.

Money started coming again and Shammi could indulge in small pleasures. She saw to it that she managed Simran and her projects. She worried for her daughter. *May she never choose a wrong film. I won't be able to watch my own life happen all over again. Please god!*

That is why, when Raj fell head-over-heels in love with Simran, Shammi did the hard thing of telling Simran to choose marriage over films.

Shammi knew that a career in films came with loads of insecurities and jealousies. And in a space where women mostly played decorative roles and where your status was as unsteady as the stock market, Shammi knew that Raj, with his impeccable family background and money, was the best bet.

Simran had complied, as she did with every decision of Shammi's.

Shammi had been watching Simran socialize. *She's a natural at this. Should she have continued working?* Shammi often wondered if her decision for her daughter was right.

But today, on an evening like this, when she saw her daughter glowing with self-assurance, Shammi felt elated. She had taken the right decision for her daughter all those years ago. *I never had anyone taking care of me.* There was no one to guide me. The Mehras loved Simran. It showed. And Raj was doing better than she had dreamt.

Raj stood on the stairs, waving. *Always the hero.* And then, Sia turned up at the door. Simran stood for a moment, witnessing the silence, the shifting, knowing glances and the hushed restart of conversations. Shammi watched as if in a trance.

She watched her daughter continue to glide from visitor to visitor—still playing her part. Still performing. *At some point we are all always performing.*

Was Raj also performing? It was difficult to not notice

the way his face glowed when his eyes took in Sia. Shammi gritted her teeth, then sighed. The travails of stardom. *If you think you're God and if every woman you meet is ready to fall at your feet, why wouldn't you cheat? A fling here and there is normal.*

Shammi glanced at Simran. She seemed slightly pale. Every time the gossip columns tattled about Raj and his new arm candy, Shammi would reassure her daughter. 'A clingy wife only serves to drive the husband further away,' she would tell Simran.

And even if that failed, a shopping expedition certainly did the trick! Either way, Shammi knew, her daughter ruled Bollywood by default right now. And through her, since she had always lived vicariously through Simran, so did Shammi.

Tonight was a special night. After all, she was going to meet everyone in *his* family for the first time. Sia was very nervous but it didn't show. Standing inside the Mehra house with the family gathered nearby and all those who mattered eyeing her, Sia surveyed the scene in front of her. Everything had to be right. Everyone was looking at her. But Sia was used to that. She smiled and walked towards Raj.

She planned her entry meticulously. She had to look perfect. Twenty outfits from top designers had been viewed and rejected. In the end, she had picked up a simple sari. It made the highlights in her hair shimmer. The makeup was artfully done. She had to look young and fresh. It was a child's birthday party after all. Everyone's eyes would be on her, as usual. Yet she must not look like she cared too much.

'Madam, that's a beautiful sari. It will go very well with your complexion,' Shukla-ji, her personal assistant had said. 'Shukla-ji, do you know what is the best outfit in the whole world?' Sia had replied. 'It's success. A person who wears success will look good in anything.'

The gift was also planned. A beautiful charm bracelet in gold from Tiffany & Co. with the letters of Trishala's name engraved on each charm. Expensive, but not shouting it out. Sia had gazed at it when it came. 'It's beautiful. I hope Trishala will like it.' *And Raj too.*

There he was. He too was looking only at her. Just looking at him made her heart skip. He did feel something for her, didn't he? Was it possible that the star who everyone was crazy about was crazy about her?

It was funny that she had everything she had ever set out to achieve. But the more she achieved, the more she lost out on the simplest pleasures. She couldn't take a stroll out on the streets when she wanted to, she couldn't be seen hanging out at a cafe with a magazine without attracting attention. She couldn't even go and pick her own clothes. Worse, she couldn't have a simple dinner out with the love of her life.

I need a smoke right now.

Sia had taken her time to get ready. She draped the yellow and gold sari around herself with care. She looked at herself and laughed. She had lost more weight. Yoga. She had mentioned this in some interview. After that, all the heroines she met wanted to know who her trainer was. She always gave them the details. *You can stand on your head all day but you'll never look as good as me!*

The blouse would need to be tucked in. Sia called Gracy in. Gracy, who had been doing Sia's hair and makeup ever since the super successful *Raahi*, walked in and immediately knew what had to be done. 'Makeup?' asked Gracy after the blouse was perfected. 'No.' Sia wanted to do it herself today.

Pale gold Jimmy Choos and a green Fendi clutch completed her look. When Shukla-ji came back into the wardrobe, he was all praise. 'Madam, you are looking divine. No other woman in the party will be looking even half as good as you.' Sometimes, it was good to hear what you already knew. Sia smiled at her reflection.

Tonight, she was going to need all the confidence she could muster. The makeup was perfect. Her long, black hair framed her face. Her large, black eyes were rimmed with kajal and lashes were swept with mascara. No eye shadow. Her lips had a hint of translucent gloss and the blue brocade blouse of her sari perfectly complemented her alabaster complexion. Her skin glowed; the result of endless hours in the gym and her wonderful cosmetologist, Dr Rashmi Shetty.

She chose not to wear jewellery, except for a pair of ornate Jadau earrings set with Polki diamonds. She wondered what Simran would say when she saw her. Meeting Simran would be the tough part, and something she was not looking forward to at all. But it was unavoidable. She gathered her clutch in her arms and was inserting the gift in it when her mother stepped in.

It is often said that the mothers of actresses in Bollywood call the shots in the film industry. With Sulochana Devi, this was an understatement. There was not a whiff of air that could reach Sia, without first being examined and approved by Sulochana. Known for her mercurial temper and an unerring eye for the right projects for Sia, she was nothing short of a control freak.

Once Sia was on a project, her mother would uncompromisingly negotiate for the best deal for Sia and she always made sure she got them too. She had such a vigilant eye on her daughter that none of Sia's leading men even dared to show any sort of romantic interest in her. Sulochana Devi was sure of one thing—one day, when the time was right, Sia would leave the film world behind and settle down with a very, very rich man. But until then, she would have to slog.

Raj was the only thorn in Sulochana Devi's side. She had been against him from the very first film they had done together. He had a reputation for being a ladies' man. His success gave him a sort of arrogance that girls found very attractive. And he seemed to have taken a shine to Sia. As far as she could, she ensured Sia stayed away.

But she fell ill and could not accompany Sia on a shoot abroad. Shukla-ji was sent. But Shukla-ji was Shukla-ji. Raj wooed her. By the time the shoot was tied up, Sia had fallen head over heels in love with Raj. By the time Sulochana got her report, threw off her bed clothes and marched to the site, the deed was done. Nothing Sulochana said or did could make a difference to her smitten daughter.

'I have done every single thing you've ordered,' said Sia after one snarling fight. 'Don't stop me now.' And it was not the words. It was the look in Sia's eyes that forced Sulochana to grit her teeth and witness the madness.

Long ago, Sulochana had promised herself that she would make her daughter the reigning queen of show-business. Sia's involvement with a married filmstar was disaster spelt out in capital letters for Sulochana. But she realized that the more she protested, the more she drove Sia into Raj's arms. And so, she swallowed her anger and stood watching helplessly.

When she entered the room and saw Sia all dressed up to go to that man's daughter's birthday party, something seemed to snap inside Sulochana.

There was her divinely beautiful and talented daughter blindly stumbling towards an aging actor with two kids. Her hatred for Raj surged up her throat like bile. Biting back her rage, she said, 'Beta, you are looking exceptionally beautiful today. All those directors who force you to put on loads of makeup should see you now. So natural and yet, so breathtaking.'

Sia, nervous in the presence of her mother, said, 'Thanks, Mamma.'

Sulochana continued, 'We must get you to act in one of those art film type movies now. You know the ones where the heroine goes without makeup and all. It's about time you got a couple of national awards.' Sia was not surprised. All her mother thought was work and how to get Sia up there.

She nodded and got ready to leave. Sulochana asked sharply, 'Where are you going today?'

'Mamma, I told you today morning that I am going to Raj's daughter's birthday party.'

Sulochana said quietly, 'And I told you not to.'

They stood opposite each other, glaring angrily.

'You and Raj are in the news for all the wrong reasons of late,' said Sulochana, hissing with anger. 'Everyone is still gossiping about how you were at his office till 3 in the morning a few days back. Now, you decide to turn up at his house, that too for his daughter's birthday party? What does a kid's birthday party have anything to do with you? What do you want? You think his family will take you in their arms? He's a married man, Sia! Don't be stupid ...' And even as the words spilled out of her lips, Sulochana knew it was the wrong thing to say.

Sia reacted. 'Enough, Mamma, that's enough! No one takes these gossip magazines seriously.'

Sulochana said wryly, 'Really, Sia? Then how come you want these very magazines to take you seriously every time you have a new project to promote? People are not fools. They know there can never be any smoke without fire.'

Sia coolly walked towards the door. She did not want to get into another argument; today of all the days. 'I'm leaving, Mamma. Raj has invited me. He wants me to be there. He wants me to meet his family because very soon I will be a part of it.' And without looking back to see how the words stung her mother, Sia walked off.

But Sulochana's words followed her. 'I curse the day you met him, Sia! This man is never going to give you a legitimate status in society. He cares too much for his reputation to leave his wife. You'll end up like one of those actresses who change their religion in order to be the second wife, and you'll be stuck with that status forever. You'll have to live a lifetime of loneliness, and he'll just turn up as a guest at your own children's weddings!'

Sia saw Simran approach her with a sweet smile. In her head, her mother's words kept ringing. She smiled back and allowed herself to be escorted inside the house. Simran was saying something to her and Sia, thankfully, didn't have to answer because by then, Raj and his entourage had arrived. Raj held out his hand. Sia's heart soared.

She would have good news to give to Mamma tonight, and then there was Subhash Bhai to talk work with. Surely, Mamma would be delighted. Sia cast a surreptitious look around the room. Yes, everyone's eyes were on her. *I look good.* She glanced at Raj and her heart skipped a beat.

Raj said, 'Welcome, Sia. I am so glad you could make it.' Sia read the message in his eyes—his desire.

Simran watched the two from the sidelines. Her heart sank. *So he was having an affair. It's true.* 'Mamma!' Simran looked down at Trishala. Everyone had completely forgotten the birthday girl. She looked at her baby with a heavy heart as another woman stole away the thunder. *I have to pull myself together.* Someone from today's list of guests would call and tell some tabloid tomorrow, anonymously of course, that there was high drama at the Mehra house when 'the other woman' turned up at Trishala's birthday.

'Yes, darling,' she said as she hugged her daughter, 'shall we cut the cake?' Holding Trishala's hand, Simran walked to the centre of the room and clapped her hands. 'It's time to cut the cake!' she announced gaily. 'Gather here, everyone. My princess is ready!' Looking up, Simran smiled at Sia and beckoned to her.

Sia walked towards Trishala. Still aware that everyone was watching her, she bent towards the little girl and said, 'See what I've got you!' Trishala barely smiled as she took the present from her and tossed it casually on the table on top of a pile of presents. Sia was startled.

Raj frowned. He was already annoyed that his parents had stayed behind and had done nothing to welcome Sia. On top of that, here was Simran playing the buffoon, by grinning too much. And to make matters worse, Trishala had decided to throw tantrums. Raj felt angry with Trishala and the rest of his family for not being able to understand. *I must not create a scene.* He quietly took Sia's hand and squeezed it.

Sia felt just a little better. Being with Raj was enough to drive away the hidden stress and depression that threatened to overtake her. When the 'Happy Birthday' chants were loudest, Raj whispered to her, without looking at her, 'Look what you've done?!' Sia was startled. What had she done, now? 'Did you have to look so breathtaking tonight that all I want to do is kiss you right here and right now?' Sia blushed. Keeping a straight face, she played on. 'What's stopping you then? Go ahead and kiss me. I dare you.'

Raj grinned. In Sia, Raj saw an end to his search for the perfect partner. She had it all. Beauty, brains and personality. They were perfectly compatible: physically and mentally. *Look at the cow Simran has become. Worse, such a bore. Constantly instructing me. Actually coming to my office and trying to tell me off in front of Subhash* Bhai. *The nerve! Sia would never do that.* With Sia, Raj felt young again. And strong. Sia knew how to make him feel like a million bucks. *I am in love!* Of late he didn't even want to go through the motions of pretending in front of everyone that she was just a friend.

If there was one thing Sia thrived on, it was attention, and right now, she was getting plenty of it, not just from everyone else, but most importantly from Raj too. She knew her effect on Raj. *I'm liking it. Am I loving it?* She took a deep breath. She felt Raj's hand caress her fingers. Then everyone clapped. Raj and Sia joined in. Trishala was beaming. She had managed to blow her candles without anyone's help.

Sia watched Raj surge back to the centre. Candles that had lit up the huge pink and white tiara-shaped cake had smoked out. Trishala had picked up the knife with a huge ribbon pasted on its handle, and was happily attempting to attack the cake. Sia recognized, from the photos she'd seen, Raj's son Tarun, his parents, his mother-in-law, Kavita and Karan and their kids gathered around the table. Raj was smiling and feeding a slice of the cake to Trishala. Trishala was pulling in her mother. Simran was laughing and pulling *her* mother in for a bite of the birthday cake, too. Sia watched, her mind shifting back to her own mother.

Mamma's got to like him. He comes from a respectable family. They have money. After all isn't that what Mamma worries most about? Sia was tired of the endless flings she had had in life. *I want to settle down.* 'But he's married!' her mother had screamed at her. 'You want to be the other woman all your life? Someone's mistress?'

I've got to keep Mamma out of my head.

Everyone was clapping and Raj—looking smashing in his casual white tee and jeans with a designer jacket thrown on—seemed like he was the best dad in the world. Simran felt tears prick her eyes. A bit of cake had fallen on her new gown and she had noticed Raj's sneer. *How could you do this? Didn't you even think of Trishala? Me?*

As if wallowing in self pity was not enough, Kavita turned up at Simran's side. She placed her arm on Simran's waist and didn't say anything but looked at Simran with a very didn't-I-tell-you-so smile. Simran's heart sank. Yet again, the mighty Kavita's words haunted her. Just like Kavita had predicted, Raj had delayed making an entry into the party till the last minute so that all eyes could be on him. Worse still, this woman ... he had gone straight to her. Simran instead smiled disarmingly at Kavita.

When she turned, she found that Raj had left her side and sidled up to Sia and the producer. And going by the way they were laughing now, it didn't seem like they were talking about work at all.

'You're looking good, Sia,' Subhash Bhai was saying. 'Oh, you are very kind, Subhash Bhai,' said Sia. 'In fact, I was thinking of coming to meet you tomorrow.'

'I am honoured!'

Not wanting to eavesdrop, Simran decided to move away. She wanted to go to her room, lock the door and be alone. She had begun to walk away from the table when Divya and Mouli appeared.

'Why did you call that vixen to this party?' Divya blurted out to Simran in a low tone. 'Look at her, playing the role of the femme fatale and looking so innocent at the same time.'

'Do both of you seriously think I called her here?'

Mouli and Divya stared searchingly at Simran.

'I am not as stupid as that.'

'Okay, so you didn't invite her. Kavita wouldn't call her without running it past you either. Sia is too proud to turn up here on her own. That means only one thing.' Divya looked in Raj's direction. He was laughing, looking poster-perfect. Mouli and Simran follow her gaze.

Sia, who had been personally invited by Raj, was gracefully leaning over Raj's shoulder and laughing. Subhash Bhai, who was with them, also seemed to join in the mirth. But he caught Simran's look and stopped short.

Divya said, 'One would think that after all the trash that is being written about her in the papers and magazines, linking her to a married man, she would have the decency to not turn up at this party.' Mouli joined in and said, 'But she wouldn't be Sia then. After all, why would she turn down an invite from the biggest star in Bollywood? She has no shame I tell you, that woman.'

Then Simran said, 'But it is so surprising. Why would she come here and give the press more opportunity to write about her? Maybe this way she wants to dispel the rumours.'

Divya said, 'Do you really believe that, Simran? If she wanted to dispel the rumours, she wouldn't be clinging to Raj all evening. She would cling to you instead. After all, what better way to prove everyone wrong about her alleged affair with Raj than get along with you, his lawfully wedded wife?'

Simran took a deep breath and squeezed Divya's hand. Divya had gone through a rough patch a year ago when her husband had become involved with the foreign heroine he had signed on for his home production. Things had become so nasty that Divya had moved out of her home with both her kids while her husband was abroad for the shoot. This had given the press a lot of fodder. But when her husband got to know, he immediately returned to the country and begged for her forgiveness. To make it look like everything was okay, they had jointly issued a statement to the press that, due to a bug infestation at home, she had to move out so that the problem could be fixed.

Raj wouldn't do this to me. It's Sia.

'You are right about that, Divya,' Simran said. 'But she really can't help being the way she is. After all, being seen with Raj helps her stay in the news. And any publicity is good publicity, right?'

Mouli, who was quiet all this while, said, 'She is very smart, Simran. Stay wary of her. The way she is behaving right now, I can tell you she is up to no good. She tries to play the helpless, innocent girl, but remember, she hasn't reached the number one position by virtue of innocence. The news doing the rounds is she has her eyes fixed on Raj.'

'If she has her eyes set on Raj, she is barking up the wrong tree this time,' Simran said fiercely. 'This is just gossip. If I took all these rumours seriously, I would have landed in a mental asylum a long time ago. Believe me, she is not going to be able to do anything with Raj. She isn't even his type. He likes intelligence in a woman, and she looks so dumb. Her mother calls the shots. Trust me, she is going to be disappointed this time.'

Divya and Mouli looked at each other, clearly not convinced.

Please, God. I hope I'm right.

Subhash Bhai wandered off to get himself a drink and Raj sighed with relief when his mother came by. The two women hugged each other and Raj watched Sia with pride. *She looks delicious in a sari.* Raj had often asked Simran to wear saris too, but she clearly preferred those hideous gowns instead. *An Indian woman's body is better suited to saris.*

He looked at Simran and found her talking to her friends. He glanced back at Sia. *We look good together.* He could hear her now, giggling with his mother over a song they both liked. Raj felt satisfied.

Sia's cell phone rang. She looked at the cell and, suddenly looking wary, excused herself and moved away to take the call.

She seemed to freeze, eyes wide, phone pressed against her ear. Then a guttural cry escaped her mouth.

3

The ambulance sped through the weekday traffic. Strobes of light sliced through the dark glass of the ambulance window and fell on Sia's face. Sia looked blindly outside the window. Somewhere, at the back of her head, she could hear the wail of the ambulance siren. Her thoughts were muddled. Faces, bewildered expressions, Raj's cold eyes, her rushing back home, her shaky hands, her mother's words to her as she left for the party that evening, the sight of her mother collapsed on the floor with the telephone toppled next to her.

Why didn't I turn back? How could I walk out on her?

She looked at her mother. Drenched in cold sweat, Sulochana looked suddenly shrunken and grey. Tears ran down Sia's face. She checked Sulochana's pulse. Faint. The ambulance was moving as fast as it could. It was the route that seemed long. Sia felt her own chest clench in pain. *Please, God. You'll be okay, Mamma. Trust me.* Even as she focused on the words in her head, Sia felt tears trickle down her face.

Her pallu was trailing in dirt. Why was she dressed in this sari? Raj. Where was he?

'Sia!'

'Mamma ...'

'Sia, Sia ... come ... take me ... hospital ...'

For one second, she had thought her mother was trying her last stunt. In the next fraction of that second, she knew it was not an act. No one could have made the blood-curdling sound that her mother was making.

Then the line seemed to go blank. Sia suddenly couldn't move a single muscle. When her brain seemed to process the information, her first words were, 'Raj!'

Thinking of it made Sia want to cringe. The look on Raj's face when she told him that her mother seemed very unwell. 'Raj, come with me,' she had said, spontaneously, reaching for his hand, like she were drowning.

But no hand was offered back to pull her from the swirling, powerful waters. The cold, angry look that he gave her ... Sia closed her eyes, trying to shut the memory out. To think that hand was caressing her a few minutes ago.

'Raj, I need you!' she had said, uncomprehendingly.

It was his secretary who spoke, who held her gently by the elbow. 'I'll take you, Sia-ji. I'll drive you back. Here, this way, madam.'

She had blindly followed the secretary. She didn't even remember the man's name.

She heard Raj saying, very matter-of-factly, 'Mahesh, see if madam's mother needs medical attention. Get everything arranged and don't leave her side until I tell you.'

I need you. Not your secretary.

Subhash Bhai had made a feeble attempt to accompany her. But she didn't need anyone else.

I'm with you, Mamma. Stay strong.

The ambulance had pulled into the towering hospital. She gripped her mother's limp hand. *We're there. You were right. I was wrong. Please stay strong. I'll never hurt you again.*

In the Mehra house, there was silence. Everyone had left. Only the debris of the party remained. Raj's parents, who would have normally stayed back to gossip and indulge in post-party chatter, had retreated to their room after he had told his father, Bhupinder, that he had to leave.

'It is Sia. Her mother has had a heart attack and it isn't looking good. She is very scared. I need to go, Papa,' Raj told his father. Bhupinder knew something was up between Raj and her. He looked at his son gravely. He knew Simran was staring at him, appeal writ in her eyes. But now was not the time to get into all of that. *Some other day.* He had been lucky that both his sons respected him and sought his approval for everything. He tilted his head in assent. 'Drive safely, beta.'

Simran felt empty. Raj had climbed the stairs and was changing to leave.

They had argued. 'Where are you going?'

'Didn't you hear what I told Papa? I have to go, Simran. Stop treating me like you treat the kids. I'm not a teenager. And Sia is in trouble. If not for our party, I would have left with her.'

He saw her eyes fill up with tears, but chose to be cruel about it. 'Please try those props on someone else.'

The parting shot was, 'And teach your kids to behave better. I would have slapped Trishala if it hadn't been her birthday today. Imagine tossing an expensive gift from someone like Sia. And your son, he was busy with his new toy.'

The toy you gave him. And, isn't Mahesh enough? Didn't she have someone else to cling to? She's only a friend. She's only a friend. She's only a friend!

There was no way out but to remember that. They could meet a hundred, thousand times outside her home and she wouldn't have a clue. After all, they worked together. *I need to exorcise the demons in my head.* Simran fell in a heap on the bed as the door shut.

Raj was irritated on all counts. He was mad at Sia for asking him to come along with her in the middle of his own party. Her mother was unwell, but how tactless of her to want him to walk off in front of everyone. He was stung at Kavita's sneering face and her barbs. He was mad at his father's trying to delay his exit from the house. And at Simran, busy doing her own little drama!

He tried Sia's number. It rang. She was not taking his calls.

Could it be that the old lady kicked the bucket? Poor Sia.

He remembered her smile. The way her eyes crinkled when she laughed. How, when she had walked in, everything around him seemed to dissolve. There was a time when he felt that way about Simran. *Love is also about perspective.* His family took to her immediately. Was it because he had told them, 'I will marry her and no one else'? Simran was beautiful. *Is? Used to be?*

Of course, he had had his share of flings. To be looked at that way all the time. You would have to be God to be tested with temptation all the time and not succumb. But much to his alarm, he was getting old. The swings of boredom, the need to experience highs all the time, to keep testing if he was desired, to constantly need the assurance of lust ... He had never needed those before. He seemed to need them now. In all of this, Simran was an irritant. A need he didn't need any more.

What nonsense am I thinking? A need I didn't need. Yuck!

Sia had also started as a conquest. A point to be proved. Sulochana would not let him near her. Well, he would get right in. And he did. Then it became a habit. Later, it seemed fun. The nervousness was new. The strategy ... the mating game ... all gave him a high.

Raj remembered the flash of anger he saw in Sia's eyes as she left. *I'll make it up to her. How could she think I would hold her hand and run away with her to see her goddamn mother?*

Sia knew what this meant. Sulochana had suffered a massive cardiac arrest and needed angioplasty. 'I'm afraid it doesn't look too good,' the doctor at the Emergency Unit had said gravely. The dregs of hope that Sia was holding onto sank. They had wheeled her immediately for the procedure. 'We're giving it our best, Ms Sia.'

But nothing made sense to her. Everything seemed to be a blur. Thank god Raj's secretary was there. He gently guided her to sit and made rapid phone calls. He seemed to be asking Sia something. Everyone seemed to be asking her something. But all she wanted to do was curl up and sleep.

Back in the house, Simran wiped away all traces of her grief. She thought of her mother; of how she traversed life's travails with dignity. She thought of her aging in-laws. Her in-laws were the picture of grace and contentment. They never let the ups and downs of life disturb their equation. For Papa, even today, Ma came foremost. They did not openly display their affection, yet they subtly let each other know that they still cared and that the other half was still the most important one.

If Papa had allowed Raj to leave like that, maybe it was all right. In any case, she also believed that everyone should be given the space to decide for themselves. What would any of them benefit by coercing someone to do something other than what they wanted to? *Even Kavita and Karan have a better life than me. All this glitter, what is the point?*

She splashed water on her face and went to the children's room. Trishala was sleeping on her stomach, her hair tousled, while Tarun, immaculate as ever, was sleeping on his back like a king. *My poor babies.* Trishala and Tarun craved their father's attention and mostly never got it. Even on her birthday, Trishala had to beseech her mother to make her father come down from the study.

Sia was panicking. She felt she would collapse any minute now. Now the doctors were saying that in addition to a cardiac arrest, her mother had also had some kind of stroke. They even explained it to her in medical terms saying it was a TIA. Salil Rao, the young doctor who was handling Sulochana's case, seemed like a nice man and was being particularly attentive to Sia. 'Please do not panic. The thing is, she must have had a Transient Ischemic Attack for the stroke to hit that violently.' Sia said, 'A what? Doctor, I do not understand.' He then elaborated, 'Did she have stroke-like symptoms earlier, even if for a brief period?'

Sia tried to remember and then it struck her, 'Yes, she had a mild stroke last year when we were abroad. It lasted upto half an hour and then she was fine.' Dr Salil Rao then asked her, 'Did you follow that up with further medical tests to check the cause?' Sia felt guilty now as she stammered, 'Actually, she was fine and then she did not want to make a big deal about it so ... Besides, I was swamped with work ...'

Dr Salil Rao then said, 'A TIA should be followed up on priority. Your mother has cholesterol and diabetes and she's above sixty. These factors makeup a lethal cocktail. She has had a massive stroke and she needs immediate surgery. The more we delay, the faster her brain will die.'

Sia broke down. Mahesh tried to salvage the situation saying, 'So then, if there is no other option, please go ahead with the surgery.'

Dr Rao then asked Mahesh to follow him to get Sia to sign some authorization papers. Sia was left alone. Suddenly, she felt as if she had hit a wall. In her head, someone was chanting 'happy birthday to you' while the ambulance siren throbbed in her brain. *I'm on the verge of a nervous breakdown.*

She heard the sound of heeled boots down the corridor. No, she was not imagining it. It was Raj. She lifted both her arms.

4

One of the most thankless jobs in the world is probably journalism. You cover news and spicy tidbits and put it together, and then you do it over and over again. It's about deadlines and wheeling and dealing with regulars in your beat, only to know that someone else got there before you. With 24-hour news channels on the go, getting the right mix of news, analysis and gossip, and airing it through the day is always a challenge. Journos are like hyenas. Baying at the dying, feeding on the dead.

Who knows who spilled the beans, but within fifteen minutes of Sia getting to the hospital, the security had to be beefed up. One photographer had scaled the walls and by midnight, a large crowd had gathered. TV vans with their equipment were already spreading the news.

Sia was disgusted. She was going through hell and people were asking her for autographs, asking her to speak a few words about anything: her mother, Raj, her new film ...

So this is how it felt. Fame rubbed in your face. She had always wanted people to rush to her for her autograph. And today, it was happening. Ironically, she wanted to get out of it. *Let me go. I want to eat some daal-chawal and go to bed, knowing that Mamma's asleep in the next room.*

Sulochana was in the next room. Asleep. With six tubes weaving in and out of her. They had induced paralysis so that there would be minimum stress on her heart. She was on life-support.

She'll be well.

This was Sia's new chant. *She'll be well.*

'The next twenty-four hours are crucial,' the doctor had said. Sia would have collapsed if Raj had not come. But he had arrived. He had talked to the doctors, made many phone calls, all the while holding her hand.

When Raj arrived, the media went berserk. The hospital turned into a madhouse with flashes going off everywhere. Sia felt like a deer caught in front of headlights. Mercifully, both he and Mahesh were cool. Mahesh efficiently blocked off the scribes and told her 'Madam, people are clicking pictures of you in this state. Please wear your shades.' Sia immediately obeyed.

She kept thinking of her mother. When did she get so old? *Why didn't I notice the veins on her hands? When did her hair go this grey?*

She'll be okay. She'll be okay. She'll be okay. She'll be okay.

'Sia! Are you okay? You've been mumbling.'

Raj. She had already wet his shirt with tears. Thank god Raj came. The minute she had heard his footsteps and seen him ... and let him hold her ... everything seemed slightly more hopeful. Mamma will be better. Raj will move in ... *Maybe this happened so that everyone could get a perspective.*

Sia brushed off the memory of him looking at her coldly at the party. The starkly contrasting behaviour. *Which of the three was the real Raj?* The one who was flirting with her at the party, the one holding her hand now, or the one who looked at her in disdain?

Stop it!

Mamma was important. Everyone knew how important Mamma was to her.

If Sia was a superstar today, it was because of Sulochana. Sia had no memory of her father. He was a lawyer but had passed away when she was just four. Sulochana always spoke very fondly of him. Her parents had had a love marriage. But her mother was never accepted by her grandparents and they always gave her grief. When her father died, her uncle and grandparents took away everything that belonged to her father. But the penniless Sulochana never bowed down to anyone.

Sia was a pretty child and after a few auditions, she began to get commercials down south. A few years later, film offers in Kannada, Telugu and Malayalam came by. Sia did everything that came her way. Sulochana was a determined woman. Every contract that came their way was deftly negotiated by her. Who taught her the business of negotiating was something even she sometimes wondered. But one way or the other, she made her daughter a big star in the south.

Failure is an orphan but success has many relatives. The very grandparents and uncle who had kicked them out appeared at Sulochana's door, asking them to come back. But Sulochana could never forgive them. Sia was very young. Sulochana knew that her next step was not towards relatives who would leach them out, but Bollywood, where you could either get lost in a crowd or you could stand out like a superstar.

Dance, diction, etiquette classes, finishing school, and finally, networking parties. In no time, Sulochana was grooming the princess of Bollywood. 'You'll make it big,' Sulochana would say, looking at Sia with undisguised pride.

'Just do what I tell you. I'll see to it that you have the world wrapped around your fingers.'

And she had kept her word. Hard work, studied moves and a lot of luck helped Sia. Yes, she had to sleep around to get some roles. She also knew there were many who slept around and didn't get anything. Her journey to the top wasn't easy.

A few years ago, she had slipped into depression. She had even hurt herself, tried taking her own life. But Sulochana did not let her give up. She got her counselled, gave her the best treatment money could buy, and ushered her back into films with a vengeance.

Why didn't I remember any of this when I slammed the door in her face and left the house a few hours ago?

Thank god Raj had come when he did. *If he had turned his back, it would mean that Mamma was right. I would have been devastated to know that I had abandoned my mother for a man who didn't have a spine.*

She felt glad she had him—he was the love of her life. *With Mamma and Raj by my side, I will be unstoppable.*

She squeezed Raj's hand. He held her closer.

Get well, Mamma. Get well soon.

5

Simran had just come back from the gym and was headed for a shower when she saw Raj's younger sister, Ashima, sitting at the dining table with Papa and Mummy.

Ashima rose in delight, squealing, 'Simran!' The two hugged. Simran did not remember the last time she had smiled so genuinely. She looked at Ashima and said, 'Not bad, Mrs Khetrapal. You have lost weight and your skin is glowing! What's up?'

Ashima smiled as she said, 'I'm the same old hag, Bhabhi. How have you been? I have missed home so much. It's great to be back.' Before Simran could say anything, Kamla said, 'Enjoy while you are here, but always remember that now your husband's house is your home. That is where you belong.' Ashima's eye clouded momentarily as she looked at her mother. Then, looking back at Simran, she brightly said, 'How are you? Why do you look so tired?'

Simran smiled, squeezed Ashima's hand and said, 'Nothing. I guess I haven't been able to sleep well of late.' Ashima knew Simran too well to take her at face value. 'Come with me,' said Ashima. 'Let me show what I bought you.'

But the minute they went to Ashima's room, which was still kept the way she had left it a year ago, Ashima said, 'I know you too well. I know what is being written and said about Bhaiyya and that woman. And I know it is affecting you. Bhabhi, don't think about it, this is not the first time the media has spread such lies.'

Simran felt tears welling up. 'You know it is not what the media says that hurts me. What really pains me is that your Bhaiyya is not coming out and denying it. Why is he giving them a free rein to say whatever they want to? It is affecting me, our family.'

Two days after her birthday, Trishala came back from school looking upset. 'What is it, beta? But no amount of prodding would make her speak. This was most unlike her chirpy little girl. Simran guessed it must be about the gossip in the newspapers. She did not badger her. But at bedtime, when she went to tuck her children into bed, Trishala clung to her and began to cry.

She asked, 'Mamma, is Papa really going to leave us and go live with Sia now?' Simran was stunned. Feigning calmness, she said, 'Not at all, beta. What makes you think so?' Trishala answered, 'Everyone is talking about it in my class, Mamma. My friends whisper about it and then go quiet when they see me. They laugh behind my back too.'

Tarun, who had been hearing this quietly, now whispered to his mother saying, 'Mamma, my friends say that Papa is lucky to have an affair with such a hottie. They say in front of Sia, you don't stand a chance.'

Simran felt like she had been physically assaulted.

She said, 'Now listen to me very carefully, both of you. Do you know your father is a very famous man?'

The kids nodded.

'Everywhere he goes, everyone he meets and everything he does, becomes news. And he has worked very, very hard to reach this position. Everyone in the film industry respects your father. And so does Sia aunty. She knows your father well because they work together. Her mother is very unwell.'

The kids stared at her, wide-eyed. *My poor babies.*

'Your Papa is helping her out. You know, we are lucky to have such a loving family. But not everyone is so lucky. Sia aunty only has her mom. Now how would you feel if you had no one in the world to call your own except for your Mamma, and she suddenly fell ill?'

'I would like my friends to be with me at such a time,' said Tarun.

'Exactly,' said Simran, 'Similarly, your Papa is by Sia aunty's side because she needs a friend right now. And because he is an important man, the newspapers and magazines feel that maybe he is her boyfriend. But I promise you, your Papa loves your Mamma and you too much to ever think of leaving you. So, the next time your friends tease you about it, tell them to not believe what the papers say. All right?'

Both the kids looked relieved. They nodded eagerly.

Ashima held Simran's hand in hers and said, 'Bhabhi, you do realize that Bhaiyya is a star. If he comes out and denies this affair, it will give people another chance to talk. So I guess he is just going to lie low, because eventually, everything gets buried under the truth, right?'

'Ashima, you're telling me what I told the kids,' said Simran with a sigh. 'I'm not making a mountain of a molehill. I think, this time, it's not just a rumour.'

Ashima's heart ached for Simran. She loved her Bhabhi, sometimes more than her own Bhaiyya. The truth was, that she herself was quite surprised to read about Raj and Sia. She had secretly called up Raj a few days ago and had made her fears known to him. She had asked him to not add fuel to the fire by being seen with Sia. But Raj had uncharacteristically fought with her, asking her to mind her own business.

Ashima was hurt by the way her brother had so easily told her that she was not to express any concern as far as his matters went. She had not said anything to him after that. But looking at Simran's sadness, she resolved yet again to get her brother to see some sense. She said, 'I had spoken to Bhaiyya a few days ago about this matter.'

Simran smiled and said, 'You spoke and he heard you, I am sure. But he did not listen. Ashima, he is not ready to listen to anyone right now. Let him be.'

Ashima was angry now. She said, 'How can I let him be? If his actions are causing you pain, he needs to do something about it. If it requires me to make him realize that, so be it.'

Simran said, 'Ashima, don't do it. Let this whole thing be. Besides, you are here just for a few days. Don't spoil them for yourself.'

As Simran said this, she again noticed a sadness on Ashima's face. She knew now that something was wrong. Why had Ashima suddenly turned up in Mumbai?

'Ashima, what is wrong? Why do you look so sad when I mention you going back? Tanuj is all right, I hope. I mean, everything is fine, isn't it?' Ashima looked silently at Simran. Then, without warning, she began to cry.

Simran was shocked. Ashima buried her face in her hands and kept crying. Finally, she lifted her tear-drenched face and said 'Bhabhi, please don't judge me. I want a divorce from Tanuj.'

'A what?!'

Ashima began, 'It was doomed from the start. I am fed up of the mindless parties, the decadent lifestyle. Do you know what is the most important decision I make in the day over there? It is what I am going to wear to tonight's party. It's the same story with Tanuj. He has no interest in the business. He pays people to run it for him. I wanted to join the business but was refused saying women of the Khetrapal family do not work. I am asked to show an interest only in the kitchen. Tanuj and I fight all the time over this. He just does not want to let me do anything with my life.'

Simran's heart sank. First, there were just her own problems and now, there were Ashima's too. 'Ashima, that's all?' Simran said. 'Baby, just because you are not allowed to work does not mean you should leave your husband. It just means that you need to feel a little more settled in your life. Have you considered having children? It will give you something to do, you will stay occupied and all these useless thoughts will stay miles away from you.'

Ashima did not look convinced and Simran feared for her. It was a given that girls from families like her husband's did not work. The Khetrapals were a very powerful business family in Delhi. A divorce would not just cause a huge scandal but relations between the two families would get very ugly too.

Simran said, 'Ashima, what is wrong with Tanuj wanting you to live a life of comfort and luxury. You have been brought up with so much care; he is just making sure it stays that way. He is a good husband, baby. Don't do this.'

Ashima looked bitter when she said, 'A good husband when he is not drinking. Once he begins drinking, he is a beast. He illtreats me, insults me on a whim and ... and he even forces himself on me despite my protests.' She broke down and began to cry. Simran was stunned.

If she supported Ashima, she was breaking her sister-in-laws home. If she forced her to go back, there was no telling what Ashima would do. What if she tried to harm herself? Simran asked her quietly, 'So suppose you come back. What then?' Ashima's eyes lit up now as she answered, 'If I come back, I will fulfil my life's ambition.'

Simran was completely dismayed now. Ashima had always wanted to act in films. To get this wild notion out of her head, she had been hurriedly married off.

Simran looked searchingly into Ashima's eyes. Ashima looked back pleadingly. 'Okay. For now, keep quiet,' said Simran. 'Let's see how we can work this out.'

Ashima's arrival in the house was always a pleasant occasion for everyone. It was no different this time. Even Kavita would rein in her nasty self. Not because she cared for Ashima, but simply because if she so much as tried to needle her, she had the whole household to answer to. The darling of the house, Ashima, was a happy soul and everyone wanted her smiling. Raj also seemed to come home more often, make excuses less often.

After the birthday fiasco, Raj had been pointedly rude to Simran. He had made it a point to contradict everything she said. Simran, on the other hand, was trying her best: cooking his favourite food, wearing the clothes he liked. But it seemed as if Raj didn't care. Or worse still, didn't notice. Raj not only began to spend more time at the hospital with Sia and her mother, but also late hours of the night at Sia's home.

Simran found a fitness instructor and started on a weight-loss programme. She barely ate and dropped kilos immediately. She felt a surge of hope as she stared at her whittling waist in the mirror. Today, perhaps Raj would come home and once again whisper into her ears as he used to in the early days. Today they would make love.

She longed for him beside her in bed. They had not been close for a while now. At least earlier, when he lay down beside her, she slept under the illusion that he was safe from any other woman.

The door opened and Simran felt herself blush. *Think of the devil.*

He had returned home after three days, yet he barely looked at her. Strangely Simran, who was so upset with Raj just moments ago, was glad he had come. She smiled at him. He looked like he was in a bad mood but gave her a cursory smile. Simran then, more for herself and her peace of mind, decided to talk to Raj. She said, 'Raj, I need to talk to you.' Raj immediately said. 'Not today, Simran! I am too tired tonight.'

Simran, however, could not bear the thought of sleeping beside him, pretending that everything was okay. Being uncharacteristically brave, she said, 'Raj, the kids were very upset today. They are being teased in school about you and Sia. They feel that ...' She broke off, unable to bring herself to even say it. But she had Raj's undivided attention now. She continued, 'That you are going to leave us ... and go to Sia.'

Raj took it all in silently. Then he asked Simran, 'And what did you tell them?'

Simran said, 'I told them that all of it was rubbish; that Sia is a friend and you are helping her out just like they would help their own friends. That's all.'

Raj now looked away and said, 'You did the right thing. This media, it just blows things out of proportion.' He looked weary.

Please tell me that all this is rubbish. Please tell me that you love me and that everything will be okay soon.

Simran pleaded with her eyes. Raj turned away and stood near the window, looking out at the sea. Simran stepped towards him. Raj turned around and walked into the bathroom.

Raj had had flings before. They both knew it. Yet every time it threatened to blow over, Raj cajoled her, talked to her, convinced her about the media and the trash they wrote. Simran shuddered. *Why is he not doing it this time?*

She began to feel suffocated. Covering her face with a pillow, she wept into it.

Simran had barely composed herself the next morning when the next crisis overtook her. The whole family was present at the dining table, chatting and bonding over hot theplas and chaas. Raj seemed relaxed, as if nothing had happened, and Simran went back and forth, not meeting anyone's eye when Raj said teasingly, 'Ashu, it's been a month. Are you planning to go back or not?' Karan joined in, 'Yeah, you better be back otherwise your lovestruck husband will think we've decided to keep you with us.'

Simran's heart sank. Ashima kept quiet. In an attempt to change the topic, Simran said, 'Don't you boys have to get to work? Troubling our little sister first thing in the morning.' Raj and Karan looked at each other and chuckled saying, 'Oh, so Bhabhi to the rescue?' But Ashima said softly, 'Good you noticed, Bhaiyya ...' Then looking at her parents, she said, 'Actually there is something I needed to say to you about going back.' Simran opened her mouth to say something, but Ashima silenced her with her hand. 'Bhabhi, it's time I told everyone. Papa, Mamma, I have decided not to go back. I want a divorce from Tanuj.'

First there was silence. Then Raj was on his feet saying, 'Are you out of your mind? What rubbish is this?'

Simran almost wanted to laugh. Raj, of all the people, defending the sanctity of marriage! Bhupinder was next. 'Ashima, stop talking nonsense.' Kamla was too stricken and Kavita's mouth was agape in surprise.

Karan, as usual, tried to control the situation saying, 'Hold it. Ashima, what is this newfangled idea of yours? Marriage is a big deal, a divorce even bigger.' Ashima had worked herself up now. She said, 'Nonsense, rubbish, newfangled ideas! All of you are quick to brand my opinion. But none of you bothered to ask me why I am saying that. Bhaiyya, a divorce is the last thing that even I want. But do all of you not trust me enough to realize that things must have gotten really bad for me to take such a step? As much of a big deal as it is to you, it affects me a thousand times more. And yet, here I am saying I do not want to go back to that man. I have suffered many indignities. And yet I bore them stoically because of all of you. But I can't go on any more.'

Raj said, 'And I am saying no. You cannot walk out of this marriage. No way. This time Ashima, you are not going to get what you want.'

'Bhaiyya, this is not a toy that I want. I have lived that life, been through hell. How can you send me back where a man does not know how to respect his wife?'

Now Bhupinder spoke up. 'Raj is right. If you want to destroy your life, we can't let you do it. We can work out a solution. You can see counsellors, take therapy, but no, you will not end this marriage, and that is final.'

Ashima looked at her father. Did these people love her? Could they not see they were passing a death sentence on her? Tears streamed down her cheeks as she ran to the sanctuary of her room. Everyone stared after her. Bhupinder said, 'Simran, she listens to you. Talk her out of this crazy idea.' Simran wanted to explain Ashima's stand but thought the better of it. Quietly, she left the dining table and went to Ashima.

Simran had too many things to worry about. Ashima, the kids, her in-laws' state of mind, the stress levels at home and Raj.

She could see that her husband was making a complete fool of himself. For a married actor, getting linked with another woman was bad enough. What was worse was to be seen in the company of the other woman all the time! It damaged the image of a family man. A disconnect with the masses could never be related to a public figure such as an actor. Once a star could not be related to by the masses, he was finished professionally.

She also knew that Sia and Raj's new movie was releasing and that, temporarily speaking, this publicity would be good for the movie. In Bollywood any publicity was good publicity. However, these very publicity stunts eventually tended to backfire.

What was also sad was that, by now, people had begun to believe that Sia's mother's illness was being faked to call more attention to the movie! The ways of Bollywood were strange indeed.

'In the past few days, I feel I have been to hell and back,' said Simran as she sat back at the coffee shop of a five star hotel. Mouli and Divya nodded. 'I know darling, this can't have been easy. We told you that day, her turning up at the party was a bad omen. But you have been brave through it all,' replied Mouli. Divya looked a little uneasy. She said to Simran, 'You need to take a look at this.' She quietly took out a popular tabloid from her bag. The front page had familiar pictures.

They were pictures from Trishala's birthday. She was shocked to see so many of them. But wasn't that the norm of late? Any Tom, Dick or Harry armed with a mobile phone called himself a photographer. A picture caught her attention. It was of Sia and Simran next to each other, talking. Under the picture read the caption: 'The Beauty and the Bloated!'

Tears of humiliation stung her eye. Mouli and Divya who were watching her anxiously wrapped their arms around her. Mouli then gently reminded Simran of her own plight. She said, 'Simran, don't feel so bad about it. You know what they say—a girl can never be too thin or too rich. Right?' Simran nodded. She had known Mouli for the longest time ever. As the wife of a very big star, Mouli had it all. But she too had wanted to make it big on her own once. She had started out as a model and she was very good at what she did. But for every model, the ultimate break was Bollywood. It was just the way the cookie crumbled in this part of the world.

Mouli too had thought she had finally arrived when she got her big break in the world of films. She was launched by a big banner, but one look at the film and Mouli's beautiful but un-emotive face and soon no producer or director wanted her. Somehow, the prospect of going back to modelling after savouring the world of films had seemed very unappealing to her. That was when she had fortuitously met her future husband and they had soon tied the knot. Today, Mouli had it all—a star as a husband and lots of money.

But Mouli never forgot that it was her looks that had made it all possible. And so, she slavishly followed beauty trends and starved herself, just to preserve what she had been born with. Simran realized that she was right. If she really wanted to keep Raj tied to her apron strings—and she really did—she would have to get into action.

Feeling better, she sniffed away her tears and said, 'I have started with my trainer but I guess I'll have to work harder.' The three of them giggled and Divya said, 'I propose a toast then. To the beauty who will no longer remain bloated!' The three of them chuckled as they toasted to Simran.

The next morning, when Simran was wading through a breakfast of much-hated, watery oats, one of the maids came to tell her that someone from the media was on the line. 'Shall

I ...? The maid asked. Simran nodded curtly. The statement to be given to all media was the same: Simran Mehra, wife of Raj Mehra would not be available to give her opinion on the state of affairs between Raj and Sia.

The news running through uniformly was that the frumpy mother of two, Simran, had been dumped for the gorgeous, virginal Sia.

Simran judiciously tried to stay away from such news. She had lost more weight. Soon she would regain her previous figure as well as her glamour. *All I have to do is keep away from negative stuff. Divya was right. The negative eats into you.*

Fortunately for her, she had allies in the form of her mother and mother-in-law. They encouraged her and told her to never look back. Outwardly, through the day, Simran managed to stay afloat. It was the nights she dreaded. When the kids went to sleep and all the chores were taken care of, her self-doubts resurfaced to gnaw at her.

It's just a phase. The film will release and the media and the masses alike would soon forget everything that had happened. Everything will get better.

But somehow nothing got better.

One morning, after days of the Mehras' pretending what Ashima had declared had not really happened, she made a statement. 'I've decided to get into films!'

She said it firmly. She didn't ask.

A Mehra girl going to act! Raj went ballistic. He knew how seedy this line was for a girl. Nowadays, even men were not exempt from being sexually exploited. Moreover, Ashima was a girl, one who was starting out so late in an industry where youth was everything. She would surely make a fool of herself, and therefore, them too. How could he let her destroy herself and their family name?

Raj ranted but Ashima was unmoved. 'Finished, Bhaiyya?' was all she said calmly.

Her parents once again pretended that Ashima was speaking on a whim. But as the days passed, it became evident that Ashima was not only not leaving, she was working towards approaching directors.

Bhupinder began to spend a little more time at home but with his orthodoxy, he made Ashima quite miserable. He constantly fought with her, trying to make her see his point of view. Ashima found him overbearing and suffocating. She also refused to listen to Raj's threats or Karan's gentle persuasion.

Simran felt torn. She knew that Bollywood had no place for women like Ashima. Not only was Ashima older, but she also represented two very powerful families. It would reflect badly on them both. And yet, a part of her kept rooting for Ashima.

One morning, under electric tension in the house, because Ashima had returned after meeting an old producer, Simran spoke. 'I know things have been really bad of late. But Mamma and Papa, please try and listen to what Ashima is trying to tell all of us.'

Kavita pounced on Simran. 'Simran, how can we listen to what she is saying since you are the only one given that privilege?'

Surprised, Simran said, 'In that case, Kavita, allow me to tell all of you what I have heard from her. Papa, Tanuj is not what you think he is and Ashima can't bring herself to describe his atrocities to you all. He subjects Ashima to such levels of humiliation that she cannot call her own mind and body her own.'

Simran knew she had everyone's attention. Ashima came and stood behind her now as Simran continued, 'Papa, we are her family. We want the best for her, but by sending her back we are asking her to kill herself. Even death is better than what she goes through over there. And Mamma, you have taught her your values. She was not allowed to fulfil her dreams before marriage just because she is a girl. Let her fly. She wants a shot at what Raj and Karan have got. Can we not be open-minded enough to give it to her? Let her at least try. Give her some say in her life. Let her prove herself. If she fails, she will know she was given a fair chance. And then she will gladly accept whatever you decide for her. But will all of you ever be able to face yourselves knowing you stifled the wishes of one of the most important people in your lives?'

At this point, Ashima began to weep and rushed to Kamla who hugged her daughter with love. Bhupinder looked like he was caught in a difficult internal conflict. Raj began to say something but his father silenced him.

Of all the phases in his long life, the last few days had been the toughest. Bhupinder was a practical man. He knew that if Ashima was unhappy in her marriage, she should not have to suffer any more. God knew she had suffered more than her share already. But he was scared of her wish to work in films. He knew the industry inside out and he knew it would tear someone as inexperienced as his daughter to shreds. And yet, what could he do? He did not want to meet his Maker knowing he had taken away the freedom of one of his own blood; that he was responsible for never letting Ashima really live her life. No, things would have to change.

Bhupinder spoke up now and everyone listened: 'Simran, without consulting any of us, you have proposed something unheard of in this house.' Simran lowered her head. Then Bhupinder continued, 'But everything you said is valid. Ashima cannot be forced to suffer just so it makes us look good. We will hire the best lawyers and begin divorce proceedings soon.'

Then he said, 'And as far as acting in films is concerned, Ashima, you can try for a year. But if you fail, you must settle down with a boy of our choice.' Ashima rushed to her father, happy beyond words. Raj, on the other hand, looked very angry.

Without another word, he walked out of the room.

6

Raj's presence was like a lifeboat to a drowning person. Sia hugged him tight. She was lost and Raj was the only thing that made sense in her crazy world. Oblivious to the nurses and the doctors, oblivious to the ward boy who had come into the room to change the sheets, Sia clung to Raj. She ached to be held, comforted and kissed.

Sulochana was not doing well. The doctors had thrown another line, this time, through her thigh. Sulochana's body was now a mesh of tubes.

Raj hugged Sia back. He was a worried man. From the back, he heard Mahesh clear his throat discreetly. Mahesh always did that to warn Raj about something. Raj realized that if he did not do something about Sia fast, the whole city would soon be gossiping about the two of them.

Gently, he prised Sia away from himself, saying, 'I have to go and talk to the doctor about the further course of treatment. I'll be right back.' Sia began to protest but knew he was right and so, wiping away her tears, she tried to smile. Then she went and sat beside her mother and tried to collect herself.

Raj walked out of the room. Women! You couldn't do with them and you couldn't do without them. Why did Sia have to make her affection for him so obvious? Couldn't she have waited until it was just the two of them in the room? *But Sulochana means everything to her.*

Raj sighed. Though Sulochana Devi gave Raj the jitters, he respected her for the way she had single-handedly made her daughter the toast of the tinsel world. Ironically, he admired her more for the fact that she disliked him and did everything she could to keep Sia away from him.

Raj loved challenges. After months of flirting with Sia, he had sneaked into her vanity van when her mother was not around, and said all that he wanted to tell her. Fortunately, Sia was equally crazy about him. It felt good. *Romance always feels good.* After the game of acquiring the unattainable, Raj realized that he really looked forward to meeting Sia.

He had warned himself that it had to be just a fling. He had too much at stake. *But so did Sia.* Yet the affair raged. Neither did anything to stop it. It was always carefully done. But people get it. Word leaks. It always did and he always was able to cut off ties, if ever it got to him. In Raj's field, affairs were good for health. It did things to the skin and better still, kept the actor alive in print. Affairs were a must, provided one knew how to handle them.

Is this getting out of hand? Do I want to be here?

He smiled at the thought and then realized he must seem crazy to the doctor who was trying to explain Sulochana's condition to him. He pulled in a worried expression. Again, he found himself drifting. Yes, Sia really did mean the world to him now. But was it Sia or was it his boredom with Simran, which led him to Sia? The doctor was droning about how the vascular system worked. *Simran. Sia. Why did life have to get so complicated?* With the way the doctors in the hospital were looking at him, with the way Sia was clinging to him, this would be splashed all over the tabloids soon.

To hell with the newspapers!

Strangely, this throwing caution to the wind suddenly seemed so liberating. It was what he would have done fifteen years ago, when he was just out of college.

'Sir?'

He realized that the doctor was asking him something.

'Sorry, what did you say?'

'I said, shall we go ahead with the surgery? We need consent from the family.'

An unconscious Sulochana Devi was wheeled into the operation theatre. Sia felt dizzy. But Raj was by her side all the while. Mahesh was told to leave and come back in a few hours.

Now it was just the two of them. Sia shifted closer to Raj and said, 'Thank you.' Raj smiled. 'I love you, jaanu,' he replied. Sia blushed as she answered, 'I know now, and I love you too. I really do.' They held hands and sat together for a long time.

It was after Sia and Raj had their third cup of coffee that they heard some activity in the operating theatre. A couple of nurses stepped out. Sia rushed to them but they did not give any information. In another fifteen minutes, Dr Salil Rao, accompanied by another doctor, stepped out.

He said, 'We've done the operation but we'll have to wait and see. Her brain was deprived of oxygen for a few seconds so we are not sure yet. But let's hope for the best.'

Sia spoke impatiently, trying hard to suppress her panic, 'But doctor, a few seconds ... will that cause so much damage?'

Dr Rao replied, 'Sia-ji, a few seconds are a lifetime for the brain. Look, I do not want to scare you, but I don't want to give you any false hope either. Let's wait, watch and pray. I'll see you in a while.'

Saying so, the doctors left. Sia wrung her hands and then went and clung to Raj. Nothing made sense to her. Her mother who was so full of life, so in control of her life, was lying wasted now.

Sia had been brought up in a world where staying insulated all the time helped. She had developed a thick skin to a lot of things. Nothing worldly really daunted her. But her strength was derived from her mother and so, without her, she felt hollow. She cancelled all her shoots, all work-related assignments, her own appointments with her dentist, cosmetologist, etc. She stayed by her mother's side, praying for a miracle. While Shukla-ji and Mahesh were on standby, Sia only reached out to Raj.

Raj felt stretched. Nothing he did anywhere seemed to be good enough. He was used to being taken care of. Suddenly, it was his turn to look after someone. And after a day, this was turning out to be a drag. He had cancelled his shoots, he stayed by Sia's side in the hospital, he barely went home, earning the wrath of his family. And yet that didn't seem enough.

He was not a man given to impulses. As a superstar, he could not afford to be so either. Every single thing he said and did in pubic, every action, posture, or blink was dissected, analysed and over-analysed.

The *Daily News* got the scoop it had been looking for. The tabloid headlines shouted 'Raj, Sia, why?' jeering that the actor was doing shifts in the hospital with Sia. His 'just friends' explanation did not fit. What was worse, Sulochana's life was hanging by a thin line.

'I don't think this is going to end anytime soon, Sir,' Mahesh said to Raj in a murmur. 'Should I reschedule your next week's shoots too?'

Perhaps for the first time, Mahesh was wrong.

7

Raj turned on the television. Sulochana Devi's death was being covered by every single news channel in the country. Journalists, photographers, incessant phone calls filled his time since Sia's mother had passed away twenty-four hours ago. The surgery had not helped. Raj took a deep breath and turned around to ask the maid to pour him a drink. He froze.

Sia stood there like an apparition, her eyes fixed on the television. Raj was startled to see how haggard she looked. The news began to show images of Sulochana Devi's body being taken from the hospital.

Raj lunged as if to switch the TV off, but Sia screamed. He tried to propel her out of the room but Sia refused to budge. She screamed again.

She had gone into a shock when the doctors came out of surgery and told her that her mother had suffered one more massive cardiac arrest post the surgery, and did not survive. She had blinked, cocked her head to a side and looked at them with a puzzled expression.

Morning slowly turned to afternoon. Sulochana Devi's body was brought home. The cremation was supposed to be held that very evening. Like everything else in Bollywood, even death was an opportunity. Everyone came to pay their condolences, but largely to be seen and heard. Most importantly, celebrities came to pay their respects so that they could show the rest of the world that they too belonged to the A-league.

Sia was a superstar in her own right. And she was clearly favoured by Raj—this made them a very powerful couple. So actors, directors, producers, as well as politicians and industrialists who knew them even remotely, made a beeline for Sia's residence. They came and met Raj, but Sia was nowhere to be seen. They all asked for her and Raj had to tell them she was in her room, mourning privately. Raj and a few others from the industry had performed the last rites. She was shattered. Without her mother, Sia felt lost. She was totally a Sulochana Devi production. She was nothing without her mother. An uneducated Sia was unable to even write a single line on paper without making a spelling mistake.

With her gone now, Sia's life was over, finished. Not knowing what to do, she had earlier sat in a corner of her room, silent and overcome with grief, yet resolutely refusing sedation. But it only proved to be a case of lull before the storm. She had raged, thrown food at the maids who tried to feed her. She even attacked Raj when he tried to take her outside to pay her last respects to her mother's body.

So the doctors had to eventually sedate her. Raj dealt with the formalities and met everyone. Keeping up appearances was a full time job in this line. He stoically met everyone, answering their polite queries. Even his family had come. Simran followed by his father and mother. He didn't know how to react. But he was spared the agony as his father came up to him and said, 'Son, I am very sorry about what happened. Stay by her side like a good friend should in one's time of need. Then come back home.' Then, not waiting for Raj to mumble back, he had patted him on his back and moved on with the rest of the mourners. Simran and his mother were already sitting there. Everyone looked at him searchingly. What was he doing there? Official representative of Sia? Self-appointed? It was written on everyone's face. Raj plodded through. He didn't know better.

Now that everyone had left, and Raj decided to put his feet up, Sia was here. Screaming like a tornado. Venting her grief. Raj held her. He allowed her to rage. He wept along with her. He remembered how she looked at the cremation ground.

Raj was very awkward over there. Sia had no relatives, no one except him for emotional support. And so, it was only fitting that he—Raj Mehra—should cremate her. *What will Sulochana Devi think? She never approved of me.* The irony of it was not lost on Raj.

But more than that, what would this act of his be saying to the world at large. *It would mean that he and Sia were officially a couple.* On the other hand, if he did not cremate her, who else would? The Pandit was chanting shlokas and the time to light the funeral pyre approached.

As Raj was about to take the torch in his hands, a familiar car drove in. It was Sia's car and soon she stepped out. She was accompanied by Mahesh and looked calm and in control. A far cry from the crazed Sia he had seen in the last twelve hours. Raj froze. The Pandit froze as well. Women traditionally were not allowed inside the cremation ground. Sia went up to Raj and calmly asked for the torch. When the

Pandit started to object, Sia calmly said, 'She was my mother. If your Shastras say I will burn in hell just because I want to say goodbye to her, I don't mind it.'

Once Sia had performed the right, she quietly allowed herself to be led back to her car and driven away.

But now she was grieving and, as Raj held her down and cried with her, he realized one thing: they were together, for better or for worse.

For Simran, every day was a challenge. Two steps forward and three steps behind seemed to be the pattern. Her victory in weight loss was balanced off by internal havoc. A whole day of dieting and hours of exercising would end up in binging at night when she was wracked with rage or anxiety.

Seeing Raj behave like a member of Sia's family hurt Simran no end. Watching him greet people ... watching him in Sia's house where he obviously spent a lot of time ... watching the domestic help in Sia's home talk to Raj as if he was the 'man of the house'made Simran feel like someone had stabbed her and was twisting the knife inside her.

But what could she tell him? Broaching the subject now, especially after Sulochana's death, seemed unpleasant. It was out of the question. He didn't even bother to explain himself or come and meet the kids. Even though her in-laws seemed disturbed by Raj's absence, they had chosen to stay silent, almost supportive. Even bringing it up with them seemed insensitive right now.

Simran decided that the best course of action would be to let this pass.

Raj will come back home. He has to. Will he ...?

The place was quiet. Raj had sent the servants to their quarters—so they could be close yet not intrusive. The only sound that could be heard was of quiet sobbing. Sia, curled up by Raj's side, was crying unabated. Raj comforted her by stroking her head affectionately, but he was glad she had finally accepted the truth and was venting her feelings. Grieving was the first step towards healing oneself.

Suddenly Sia said, 'So tell me, Raj, when are you leaving?'

'Baby, I am not going to leave. I am staying right here with you.'

Sia sat up now, tears streaming down her cheeks. She looked fragile. As if she would shatter at a touch.

'Don't make promises you can't keep, Raj. You will have to go. You have a home, a family. There are people who care about you. And me? I am an orphan now.'

Raj took her in his arms and said fiercely, 'Don't you ever say that. You are not alone. You have me, we have each other, and nothing is going to change that, ever. So now, eat something, my darling. You will fall ill otherwise.'

Before Sia could say anything, Raj rose and walked to the kitchen. Sia did not know how to react. After coming to terms with her mother's absence, Sia had been mentally preparing herself for Raj to leave.

Relationships were ephemeral. What Raj had just said made her heart light. But she was too afraid to hope.

Raj returned with food. He set down a piping hot plate in front of Sia and asked her to eat rice and daal. Sia groaned, 'If I eat I'll throw up!'

Raj refused to listen to her and fed her with his hands. 'I love you, sweetheart,' he said softly. Sia only cried. Then he gathered her up and tucked her into bed.

8

Hours turned to days. Sia's pain, however, did not lessen, nor did their bouts of weird lovemaking. Sometimes Sia just wanted to stop thinking about her mother. Raj was the only one who had the power to help her do so. She and he would then get absorbed in their own world where nothing except the two of them mattered.

To Raj, being with Sia was blissful, despite her vulnerable state; the prospect of going back to the Mehra house, especially to Simran, plain agony. Sia's vulnerability was a change. It was refreshing. It made him want to protect and possess her even more. It made her appear ethereally beautiful and desirable to him. It began with him staying with her because there was a crisis; then he tried to move away, to reduce the time he was spending with her. But now, there was no need to pretend. Raj was with her for weeks together. His driver and Mahesh had stopped checking with him where they had to pick him up from, or where to report for work.

It was so unlike Raj to not care for what people said about him and Sia or about the producers who lamented their cancelled shoots. He was enjoying the giddy feeling of being recklessly in love. It gave him the felicity to lie smoothly when he told Simran that he was only bringing Sia back on track so that they could complete the films they were doing together, or to tell his children that his heart ached for them but he was helpless. To be fair, he did feel anguished after he gave his kids that answer. But then, he had figured a long time ago that he would always be guilty in his situation, one way or another.

One evening, when Sia was browsing through an album, she saw a childhood picture of her and Sulochana's. 'How will I ever live now, Raj?' Sia asked Raj as desolation swept over her. 'Mamma meant everything to me. I never really knew my father. Mamma defined my life's ambition when I was just six. I have never known a normal life. I was always working. I never had any friends, never went to school. I never had a normal childhood. But Mamma ensured that I tasted success very soon in life. She made me reach the heights of my profession. She was the best. From taking care of my needs, my home, my finances—she did it all.'

Raj smiled and said, 'Reminds me of the one person who takes just as much care of me—Mahesh.' Sia began to cry as she said, 'Sometimes, I feel I should just end it all. I need her, Raj. Wouldn't things be simpler if I ended my life?' Raj was angry now. He knew that Sia was going through depression. He had discussed her condition with the doctor and they had both decided to wait and watch before starting Sia on anti-depressants. Raj had sacrificed his family life, earned the wrath of loved ones so that this young girl would not feel that she was adrift. He had been patient with her as he had been with no one.

'Don't you ever say that again,' he almost snarled. Sia looked startled. Softening immediately, he said, 'Sia, look at me. Look into my eyes! I will never lie to you. When I say I will always be there for you, I mean it. You hear me?'

Sia clung to him and began to cry. She said, 'Please never leave me Raj. I would die if you did.'

That night, once again, Raj did not go back home.

Simran sat up in the darkness of her bedroom with Trishala's head on her lap. She stared out, her mind a tumble of countless thoughts. Trishala was unable to sleep that night. Meshed in a nightmare of her own, calling for her father in her sleep, crying no matter what Simran did to sooth her, Trishala's face was drenched in tears. Simran brought her to her room, but the crying wouldn't stop.

A helpless Simran called up Raj and gave the line to Trishala. When Raj heard his little baby girl cry, he felt awful.

He gently eased Sia off his lap. But she woke up. 'Trishala's crying. I need to go.' Sia looked like she was about to cry. 'I'll be back, baby,' he whispered. 'I promise. Please trust me.' Raj held her, crooned to her and after kissing her hair, left.

He drove fast.

He had told Simran that he was coming. Yet she seemed unprepared when he walked into the house. He purposefully strode into their room. He lifted Trishala in his arms and took her to her own room. Trishala held on to him even in her sleep. But once she was fast asleep, he prised himself away. As he stepped out of her room, he found Simran waiting for him. She looked surprised that he was all set to leave again. Her heart sank.

'Where are you going at this hour?'

Raj did not say anything. Simran persisted, 'At least give me an answer. What do I tell her when she wakes up?'

Raj looked at Simran beseechingly, 'I'll come back, Simran. Please. I need to leave.'

Simran pleaded, 'You don't *need* to leave. You don't have to leave. Please stay here with us, stay with me ... I need you. I love you Raj, don't do this to us ...!'

Raj heard her out, then turned his back on her and walked out.

Who is going to wipe my tears? Who is going to lull me to sleep? She wanted to shriek to his back.

In the car, Raj buried his face in his hands and wept. He couldn't decide who needed him more. He groaned loudly. *Why is this so goddamn difficult? Why can't someone make things easier for me?*

Over the next few days, Raj began to frequent Vardaan a little more. However, every member in the Mehra clan knew it was just to keep up appearances.

His visits, or rather, his pronounced absence, was deeply affecting Simran. She had waited and been patient with Raj all along. Perhaps, in the recesses of her mind, she had accepted that her husband was having an affair with this woman. But a lot of time had passed, and Raj was showing no signs of returning.

Now, when Raj was around, she would stare at him, willing him to look back at her. There were terse exchanges, frequent ones.

Raj's parents had aged visibly. Simran's pain was affecting everyone around her. One evening it came to boil. 'And what am I going to tell the kids?' asked Simran, eyes blazing. 'Tarun is growing up. He is not stupid. He looks at me silently. He does not ask me anything and that is as scary as Trishala asking me pointed questions. What does that whore want from you?'

'I'll explain things to my kids, I promise!' shouted Raj. 'As for you, do keep this up. Otherwise, this will be the last you see of me!' With that, he stomped off angrily.

Simran felt pure dismay. What had she done? At least he was coming. At least he was keeping up appearances. *We don't need that woman's crumbs. He owes her nothing.*

But he came again. He sneaked in at odd hours. He came when he knew the kids were around so that he could see them, spend time with them and also, because he knew this was when Simran avoided confronting him.

One day, when he entered he noticed something was wrong. Simran, it seemed was waiting for him. She seemed to have cried a lot. She came to the point without preamble. 'A paper ran the most ridiculous piece of news about you today. It said you and Sia have secretly married each other.'

Raj shrugged it off. 'I don't even need to dignify the news with any kind of response.'

'But people believe what they read, Raj. They show things like this to Tarun and Trishala. And since you are with her all the time, they feel you prefer her over them.'

Raj stared at Simran. He was filled with loathing. Why couldn't she get the message? But not wanting another fight, he said, 'She needs me right now.'

Tears spilled from Simran's eyes. 'She needs you!' she

hissed. 'She? When did her needs become more important than mine, your children's? When did she replace all of us? How did you allow this to happen?' Simran ran towards Raj, held him and wept.

Raj's heart broke. He realized that Simran looked pale and had lost weight. But there was nothing he could do about it. He was torn and tired, but he felt an allegiance to Sia. Why couldn't Simran make this easy for herself? He had given her what she wanted. She was the toast of Mumbai's social circles and hers was the word that everyone sought at home. She gave all the time—even the time she could have spent with Raj—to the kids. Now why did she grudge him this simple pleasure? What did she want from him? He had let her live the way she wanted to. Shouldn't she do the same for him? 'Please, Simran!' he said.

Had Simran not said anything, perhaps things would have moved differently. But Simran heard the tone of despair in Raj's voice. 'If that woman needs a man, why did she have to pick you? Why can't she be happy with anyone else? Why is she hell bent on destroying my home?'

Something snapped inside Raj. 'Leave me alone,' he shouted. 'Leave us alone, Simran! Why are you so goddamn suffocating all the time?'

Simran was appalled. *Leave us alone? Us? He and Sia?*

She wiped her tears angrily. 'You are not going to that woman again. Enough is enough!'

Raj walked up to her challengingly and was about to say something when his phone rang. It was Sia. He answered it. 'Raj, when are you coming?' She sounded very sad. Undeterred by Simran's show of temper, Raj muttered that he was coming.

'I'm leaving,' he said. There was a chilling finality in his voice that scared Simran.

Of all the feelings in the world, the worst is that of being left for someone else. Simran felt her heart pounding hard as she saw her husband stalk off. She stifled the scream surging inside her head. But the tears that coursed her face, the hot tears of rage and frustration, would not stop.

Simran clutched the banister and shook it. *Help me, God. How am I going to live?*

'Bhabhi!' Ashima was calling from somewhere below. Simran heard it through the cloud of pain. 'Bhabhi!' Ashima's cheerful voice brought her back to her surroundings. 'Where are you, Bhabhi!' Forcing herself to smile, she answered, 'I'm coming. Give me a sec.'

Raj drove back. He wove through the traffic as if on autopilot mode. His thoughts were scattered. He was getting tired of the showdowns with Simran. He was tired of being on call with Sia. His sleep deficit was building up and he seemed to move like a zombie through shoots.

This is getting us nowhere.

Flitting through his head were images of the weary look on his parents' face, Sia's tear-stained face, Simran's belligerence and sadness, his kids, the disgust on the face of the producer when he faltered through his lines ... Nothing was going right.

Maybe Sia is an indulgence. Maybe it is not good for anyone. Maybe I need to gently break up with her. I will, as soon as I get her back on the sets.

He made a resolve to end the relationship, and his addiction to Sia. *It'll be okay,* he told himself.

9

Raj's car entered the gate and he saw her at the window. Sia looked like she had been crying—her nose was red, her eyes and lips swollen. *How can a woman who has been crying look so sexy?* He wanted to hold her. *And to think that I just made a resolve to ease into a break-up.*

Sia watched Raj park the car from the top room. He looked preoccupied. His hair was tousled and it made him look vulnerable and younger. Her heart tugged. She groaned inwardly. *What a mess. This is the last thing either of us need.* Their relationship was barely tethering.

Sia knew that her dependence on Raj would kill everything. She knew that he was there for her and yet there were times when he was right beside her and not with her at all.

Her mood swings were unpredictable. She sometimes felt mad at her mother for letting go so quickly, for abandoning her. She often felt rage at herself. Maybe she should have left Raj and this madness that they were into. She thought of getting back to work, and would sink in dismay at the thought of putting on all that makeup. She felt too raw to face those harsh lights. There were days when she wanted to celebrate a new life with Raj and then there were days when she didn't want to wake up and face the world.

Raj walked in. He seemed distracted and guilty. She scanned his face for signs. An intense unhappiness surged up inside her.

As if he picked up the vibe, Raj asked, 'What's the matter, baby? Are you okay?'

Sia stared at him. Impassively she said, 'Raj, I am pregnant.'

Raj's first instinct was to laugh. He felt a giggle travel up his throat. *How many movies have I done this scene in? Even in them it seemed clichéd.* Yet here he was, looking at the most beautiful woman he'd known, in the stickiest situation known to man, on the verge of making the decision to pull out of it. And all he had managed was to sink into it further.

Sia wasn't sure how she had expected Raj to react. But laughter was certainly not it. Until he laughed, she had not known what she felt about being an unwed mother. But now she knew. Setting her jaw with determination, she said in a flash of anger, 'I know this is the wrong time, but it feels right. It feels like Mamma is coming back.'

One instant, everything seemed jumbled and in the next he saw a girl, lost but determined. With two long strides, he drew her into his arms. He found her taut, trembling, and he gently caressed her back, taking in the fragrance of her hair. 'This is great news, jaan. This baby will be the proof of our love. It will bring happiness to our lives. Now shoo away these dark clouds of sadness. We must bring this baby into the world with a welcoming smile.'

Sia was astounded. Then she went limp with relief. She had feared Raj would be mad at her, or would ask her to abort the baby. But here he was, saying this baby was a very good sign.

She wept with happiness. Raj looked down at the weeping child-woman. The tiny bit of bewilderment and dismay he felt burst like a bubble and disappeared. He hugged her as he said, 'Dear God, what do I do with this woman. She cries when she is sad and she cries when she is happy!' Now it was Sia's turn to giggle.

They watched the moon rise that night, sitting on the terrace, eating Sia's favourite food. Sia's cook was happy to make things. After all his precious memsaab was finally eating.

Raj's head was in a muddle. He could not break up with her. In fact, he had to now break things with Simran. He felt slightly ill. Sia sensed the shadow around him.

She toyed with her food. She knew it was not easy for him, and that he had been everything she needed for some time. But she needed more. 'Raj, as much as this baby is good news, I will not be able to hide it from the world in a few months' time. Besides, it makes me feel very vulnerable. Every time you go away, I worry about when you will come back to me; if you will come back at all.'

'Come on, Sia!' Raj exclaimed with impatience. Don't be ridiculous. If I don't come back to you, where else will I go?'

Sia said, 'What if your wife puts her foot down and forbids you from meeting me?'

'She's my wife. Not my school principal. I'm not a baby. No one makes decisions for me.'

'But it keeps me nervous, jaan. I do not deserve this.'

Raj was silenced. *I wish somebody had some clue as to how fatigued I feel. I am tired of this too.*

He remembered Simran's face and felt irritation well up inside him. He saw Sia; her eyes were filled with tears, her hands clenched. He slowly stretched his hand and opened each finger in her fist gently. He kissed her knuckles. Maybe he wouldn't get tired of her whims. *I need to take a decision.* There was no way he could have this child and continue his shifts at the Mehra house. This required a clean break. A swift one. 'Actually, I have been thinking on the same lines of late. I don't want to have to leave you every day and go home. Sia, marry me!'

It sounded unreal, even to his ears.

Back at Vardaan, Simran spent another night alone in her room. She cried and cried like there was no tomorrow. She was so restless. Her chest clenched. She felt breathless. Was she having a cardiac arrest? *I wish I could die. It is better than dying slowly. It is better than wishing for death. It is better than contemplating death every minute.*

She knew now that she could not go on like this. Raj would have to be apprehended and she would do what it took to make that happen. She decided that, come daybreak, she would have to speak to her in-laws about the matter.

As soon as Karan and Kavita left, Simran came down.

Bhupinder was talking to Ashima. Kamla was discussing lunch with the cook. Kamla immediately said, 'Simran, beta, are you okay? Eat your breakfast and tell me what we should ask the cook to make for dinner. What would the kids like?'

She noticed Simran's swollen eyes and nervously rushed through her monologue. 'I think I'll take over the house affairs for a while. You need a break.'

But Bhupinder interrupted, 'Simran, come here, beta.'

Simran broke down.

'Mamma, Papa, we all know what has been happening for the last few months,' said Simran. 'Initially, I thought I should not trouble you with this whole affair and that it will die its natural death. But now, it's gone beyond my control. Papa, I don't know what is happening between Raj and Sia, but he has begun to spend so much time with her ever since her mother passed away, that I have begun to feel like I am the other woman in his life. Papa, please try and make him understand, he is destroying me and my children. I am his wife and yet, the only time he talks to me is when he has to instruct or fight. Papa, I have given up trying to make him see reason. You are the only person he will listen to.'

Bhupinder felt sad. Mori was not like a daughter-in-law to them, she was their daughter. He had never imagined she would have to go through so much suffering. Gently he said, 'Mori, I will speak with him. I promise.' He felt a great deal of anger against his son. Imagine letting a silly affair go out of hand.

Ashima, who stood by looking stricken, added, 'Papa, this is all that the industry people are talking about. Even I am asked about it all the time, and I don't know what to say. We must do something about it now, otherwise it will be too late.'

Bhupinder and Kamla already knew how bad the scene was, but when Ashima spoke, Bhupinder couldn't help feeling annoyed. 'Marriage is a delicate thing,' he told Ashima pointedly. Ashima flushed. 'The elders will sort it out, beta,' he said more gently. 'Take your Bhabhi shopping today. She barely eats. I'm sure all her clothes are hanging on her. I'll foot the bill.'

Bhupinder wanted to bury his head in his hands. *What is happening to my family?* Kavita and Ashima were openly hostile to each other. Simran barely managed the running of the house. Where had he gone wrong? To see Mori in pain hurt him. What was worse was what Raj's indifference was doing to Tarun and Trishala. He could see how withdrawn both the children had become of late. He knew that a decision would have to be taken now, and only he could bring it up with Raj.

Under no condition will the peace of my home be compromised. Raj would have to choose between them and Sia, and he knew his son well. *He'll choose his family.* He picked up his phone and sent Raj a message, asking him to come and see him the following evening.

Raj read his father's message: 'Want to talk to you. Come home.'

This could not be good news. He could feel the resentment of his family building up in the last few days. In a way, they were justified. He was away all the time with a woman who was not his wife. To top it all, the media had insinuated all sorts of things about them. He knew the time to put the rumours to rest had come. He texted back: 'Sure. I'll be there at 4 pm.'

What had to be done, had to be done.

The next evening, Raj resisted the urge to down a peg before meeting his father. Mahesh drove him to Vardaan. He was thankful that no one was in the living room. He was in no mood to exchange pleasantries. Taking a deep breath, he knocked on his father's door.

Simran was present in the room, so was his mother. *Oh god! My father is using all his ammunition.* He had gathered all his courage for a heart-to-heart with him. Raj had always been in awe of his father.

'Raj,' exclaimed Bhupinder with a warm smile. The atmosphere seemed cordial. Raj searched Simran's face gingerly as he sat in his father's study. Simran looked back and then quickly away.

'You'll have tea, Raj?' asked Kamla gently.

After handing out cups to everyone, Bhupinder began talking about mundane issues. Raj was surprised and stayed guarded, answering politely. Then Bhupinder deftly steered the conversation to the very influential producer who had passed away just a day ago due to malaria and said, 'There is a lesson in it for all of us. We think we are mighty, but in reality we are all so vulnerable. Imagine, a tiny mosquito killed such a titan of our industry.'

Bhupinder continued, 'We are on this earth for a very short time. Let's spread happiness and try not to hurt others.'

Then suddenly, without warning, he looked at Raj and said, 'Raj, we love you. And we know you love us too. The past few months have been very painful for all of us. It is sad that Sia lost her mother. You have stayed long enough by her side. Now come back to us and to Mori. Tarun and Trishala need you.'

Raj glared at Simran and she returned his gaze unflinchingly. He realized this was a set-up, that Simran had asked her in-laws to intervene on her behalf. He was filled with loathing for her.

As much as he hated his wife right now, Raj was a good son. He disliked hurting his parents. He also knew that what he was going to say next would cause his parents pain, and, a lot of hurt to Simran.

'Papa, I am glad you brought up this subject. There is something I have been wanting to tell you. I know lately there has been a lot of heartache due to my actions. I want to put an end to it once and for all. Papa, Sia and I love each other. It is not a passing fancy or infatuation. I want to spend the rest of my life with her, make her my wife. I want a divorce from Simran. If we cannot live peacefully together; let us at least put an end to the constant fights.'

If Raj was trying to catch anyone's attention, he certainly did a good job of it. There was a collective gasp. Bhupinder looked thunderstruck. 'I'm sorry, I don't understand,' he said coldly.

Raj's heart sank. He made sure that he did not look at anyone else. He had said it. He needed to hear himself say it again. 'Papa, I want to marry Sia. Simran, I guess it is best we get divorced.'

There, it was out.

Raj looked up briefly. Bhupinder was staring at the floor, Kamla had covered her mouth with her hands as if to stifle a cry, and Simran looked like she had been delivered a physical blow.

Raj quickly looked down. Then he rose from his chair and left.

There was no going back now.

10

No one knows how the media gets a whiff of the slightest development in a celebrity's life. And this was breaking news. One of the most powerful couples of Bollywood was splitting. All the speculation had come to rest. Raj and Sia were an item! Old shots of the two were shown over and over again. Old pictures of Raj and Simran during happier times were flashed. Colleagues from the industry were interviewed. Old quotes were pulled out of context and released. The stock market fluctuated. Marriage jokes went viral. Documentaries were made on Simran the ex-star, ex-wife. Other such break-ups were analysed alongside.

In other words, the story was examined from every possible angle.

It seemed as if the best woman had won. It seemed that Simran the 'uncool', un-slim, domesticated housewife got what she deserved, and that this is what happens if you 'let yourself go'.

On the other hand, Raj and Sia, too, were dealing with the most brutal side of the media monster that celebrities themselves helped create. Cruel jokes about Raj were being tweeted. Sia was the evil sorceress who had chosen to break a happy family. Raj was the aging star, holding on to Sia for star-power. The phone rang incessantly. So much so that Raj had to put it off the hook. Sia's secretary and media manager brainstormed on how to deal with the situation. After a while, and much tweaking, they released a press note. After that, every call on their landlines, on their secretaries' phones and their own were from powerful people from television channels or magazines, asking for interviews. They were offered big money to speak upon an exclusive basis. A publishing house, too, contacted them, wanting to do a book.

Raj and Sia could not step out. They shut themselves inside Sia's house and waited for the storm to die down.

But it didn't look like that was about to happen anytime soon.

The Mehra family grieved. Kamla barely ate. Bhupinder stopped talking to anyone. The domestic help no longer knew what to cook because no one gave instructions and no one seemed to want to eat. The kids were kept out of school. The phone was kept off the hook. Friends were not to be trusted. Who knew who would quote whom.

The media had gone berserk trying to get Simran to comment whenever they spotted her. They deliberately asked her questions that would provoke her. Simran was appalled at this attempt to punch below the belt. 'So how does it feel, Simran-ji?' one grinning journalist asked, thrusting the mike in her face. Simran, with her chunky glares that covered her swollen eyes, kept her expression neutral.

How does it feel? How should I feel? But even in her head, Simran could not dare ask these questions. She knew if she probed her grief she would collapse. *Stay focused. Remember your kids.*

Everything was done to keep the wheels of each day greased. There had to be movement. Schedules had to remain the same. Yet they were not the same. Simran barely left the house. She felt like a caged animal with nowhere to go.

Divya didn't know what to watch on TV. Other than the BBC or other foreign channels, all that any Indian channel was carrying was trash about Simran, Raj and Sia.

She had just seen an interview that Simran and Raj had done years ago for a famous series 'Simply with Romi'. It showed Raj and Simran holding hands and earnestly speaking to the interviewer. Young and beautiful, the two had unflinchingly declared how they were always going to be together. When Raj had confessed how Simran made him feel all mushy and gooey inside, the interviewer—a yesteryear star herself with a penchant for wearing all-black ensembles—had cooed and expressed her approval. Simran had blushed throughout saying she was a very lucky woman indeed, and the interviewer had agreed, telling her that she was the envy of all the women in the country.

The interview was constantly being aired and the show was getting high TRPs once again. Divya felt her eyes fill up with tears.

What must Simran be going through? Poor thing. The media are a bunch of vultures. Feeding on people's grief. She called up Simran and asked her to watch the re-run on television. But Simran had already caught it.

Seeing photos of Raj and herself on TV from the past felt as if someone was turning a knife inside her. It had switched on some sweet and sour memories of Raj and made her feel like going back and begging him. *Why didn't I get on my knees and appeal? Instead of getting on a high horse, I should have not let him leave. At least for the children's sake.*

Simran was plagued by a swarm of emotions every hour of the day. From wanting to kill herself to wanting to kill Sia, and sometimes visualizing hitting Raj with a cricket bat, she swung from rage to melancholy. She no longer cared for the frills that came with being a star wife. All she wanted was her husband.

At times she would feel optimistic about her future. Maybe it was life's way of teaching her how to get back on her feet again. Yet again she would sink in the abyss of hopelessness. She began to hate stepping out, fearing that even the watchmen at Vardaan would laugh at her. And there were times when she worried about her children. She would feign cheerfulness around them, carefully observing their reactions.

And Raj. How he had walked out of her life, deserting their children. Was the man worth it? Did he not realize what he was doing to her, to them? He had made her a laughing stock, and he looked like he was enjoying it too.

She listened to the statement they had released to the media. Something about love having no rules ... She lashed out at him one morning when he returned to their home to take some of his belongings. She said, 'Oh, so you're back. What do you need this time, more clothes? You should have sent Mahesh to collect them. Why did the high and mighty Raj have to bother?'

Raj did not answer as usual. Not getting any reaction from him angered Simran further and she said, 'If you think I am going to beg you to stay with me, you are wrong. Go back to that whore. I don't need you, Raj Mehra. Remember that hell has no fury like a woman scorned. I will get back at you if it is the last thing I do. I will, I promise.'

Raj continued taking his clothes out of the cupboard. Simran was desperate for a reaction now, and she physically pulled him away from the closet, holding the collars of his shirt. She said, 'Say something, you cheat.'

But Raj refused to be provoked. Calmly, he removed her hands from his collars and said firmly, 'Simran, there was a time I loved you. We have two wonderful kids together. I never wanted to hurt you. But I fell in love with Sia and want to be with her now.'

Simran felt stung. 'Love? You? Raj, you are only capable of loving yourself. Go to her, get lost!'

Quietly, he picked up his things and left. On his way out, he met Kavita.

'How are you, Bhaisahab?' she asked.

Raj responded with a cold 'fine', and, ignoring the sarcasm in her voice, left.

The mighty Raj. How good it felt to watch him scurrying out of the house like a thief. Such a despicable man! Kavita had never expected that Raj would stand up for anyone but himself. Now his declaration of love for Sia left her feeling confused. Love! And Raj? It's more likely to be a mid-life crisis. *Thank god for steady Karan. Thank god, I don't have to live the nightmare that Simran has been living.*

Kavita had never liked the Ms Goody-Two-Shoes Simran. She could never score with her in-laws because no one could compete with someone like Simran who was genuinely nice; who was a homebody and a perfectionist at that. And that always irritated her. Now, watching Simran go through the motions of her day, crying when she thought nobody would notice, keeping up pretences with the kids, being polite with her in-laws, Kavita felt saddened. For the first time, she wished she had tried making friends with Simran, instead of feeling insecure about her. However, the practical side of her told her, 'Stay away. It's not your problem.'

Still, making a gibe at Raj felt good. She smiled grimly to herself as she left for her boutique.

11

As Raj left Simran, he felt absolutely light. Almost like a burden he had been carrying for years had been taken off his chest. He didn't have to go back to Vardaan. But between getting Mahesh to shop for him and going home to get his favourite clothes, he deliberately chose the harder way. He wanted to see if he had the courage to go there again, after having left it weeks ago without looking back.

He wanted to see his kids and see if his parents were all right. But he also, unwittingly, missed his home. But his encounter with Simran had left him shaken. More than he was ready to admit to himself. *If only Simran could see that he was out of love. And being this way would constantly make him want to cheat on her.* And Kavita. *What did Karan see in that shrew?*

Yes, he would miss his children. Raj had timed his visit to Vardaan around when the kids were certain to be home. Yet, he had not seen them, and for an instant, he felt relieved.

He knew his kids would be hurt and angry. *I should have talked to them before leaving. I should have told them that no matter what, I was there for them as their dad.* He made a silent vow to himself that soon he would mend his relations with them.

Trishala started wetting her bed. Simran found a pile of clothes in the bath, sheets and nightwear twice in a row. The girl would not meet her eye. 'I spilled water in the night so I changed,' was what she would say. But Simran knew better.

She gently hugged Trishala and said, 'It's okay, baby.'

In the fight between parents, it is the kids who get trampled. Raj and I need to speak with the kids. Tarun is like still water. I can never tell what the boy is going through. He's close to adolescence. God knows what his impressionable mind must be registering.

Simran left a message on Raj's cell. 'We need to talk to the kids. They are very upset.' Perhaps if she asked Raj, no, requested him to think about their children, maybe he would see reason.

Raj came, warily. Simran was nervous. She had somehow convinced herself that she would beg him, tell him about the kids, and everything would turn around. In her head, the scene had already played out. Her tears, Raj softening, the kids holding their hands ... their reunion, their parents beaming ... a happy ending.

But things seldom turn out the way we imagine them in our heads.

Raj came in guardedly and that made Simran grit her teeth. They started off peacefully and Simran told Raj how she found out that Tarun had punched a boy in school and how Trishala was wetting her bed in sleep.

Raj frowned and interrupted her, 'I am leaving you, not our children. They will always be mine, and I will ensure that the divorce settlement takes care of them and entitles me to spend enough time with them.'

Stung, Simran lashed out at him, 'Spend time with them, you cheat! You never spent time with them when you were here. Now that you've decided to get suicidal with your career because of that bitch, you think she'll let you near your kids!'

And all the homework she had put into being calm and holding a mature conversation evaporated.

They screamed at each other. 'You'll be finished professionally.'

'Like you?' he had screamed back at her, enjoying that it made her flinch.

In the end, she wept. 'Don't go, Raj. I'm sorry for screaming, but please see how hurt I am. Please see how you've hurt the children ... Please, Raj! How can you act in movies where you play the good family man after this? Come back and everyone, your fans too, will forgive you. We'll sort it out together with Sia.'

But at the end of her tirade, all Raj said was, 'Pull yourself together, Simran. My children will always remain mine and there is no court in the world that will change that. I'll mend things with the kids. You'll see.'

Saying this, Raj left Vardaan, once again having had the last word.

12

Shammi tried to focus for the fifth time. But it wasn't working. To begin meditation, one must start by emptying one's mind. She started again focusing on the spot between her eyebrows. But in the next instant, she started fretting about Simran again.

She was worrying about Simran and, even though she normally made it a policy to not give unsolicited advice, this time Shammi knew that she would have to talk to her daughter.

Simran had walked into Shammi's apartment in the morning and shut herself in her old room. Shammi knew she was crying. *Kiski nazar lag gayee.* How could a happy family dissolve in front of her eyes? She strongly believed in the evil eye. She had knocked on Simran's door, but when she didn't open it, Shammi left her alone. *What can I tell her?* The truth, a voice from within her answered. Shammi wanted to cry. She got up and went to the mini bar and, pouring herself a generous peg of vodka, she began to sip it. Then, summoning all her strength, she decided to talk to Simran.

She knocked sharply on Simran's door. Simran immediately answered it, as if she had been waiting for her mother. Her face was wet with tears, her hair in a disarray.

Shammi held her. 'Simran, stop crying as if your marriage has already ended.' Simran looked at her mother incredulously and said, 'Mamma, have you not heard a word of what I have been telling you? Raj has said that–' Shammi cut her short saying, 'Simran, Raj is not God. So what if he has said he wants a divorce? You are an equal partner in this marriage and the only way it can end is if both of you want it to.'

Simran was struck by her mother's words. Her mother was right! She had equal say in the marriage.

Shammi continued, 'As long as you do not give in, there is no chance that a divorce is ever going to come through. Kamla-ji and Bhupinder Bhaisaab called me a couple of days ago. They love you so much, and they are both so ashamed of what Raj has done. They apologised to me and I said there was no need. We are all in this together, and so, whether we sink or swim, we will do it together. Kamla-ji and I have decided on a course of action but it will require you to be brave.'

Simran nodded, eager to hear what her mother had to say.

Shammi knew she had managed to calm Simran down. Now all she had to do was to convince her. She said, 'Come what may, no matter how angry or depressed or hopeless you feel, do not leave Vardaan. See, beta, men are by nature never monogamous. Marriage keeps them in check but sometimes, they stray. It is a crisis every marriage faces sooner or later. But the important thing is to not walk away. Once he is fed up of sowing wild oats, he will come back to you. However, if you leave now, he will get a chance to move in with that woman. So do not leave his house. As long as you are there, it will keep reminding him that the place is rightfully and morally yours. He will eventually tire of her and return.'

To Shammi's relief, Simran nodded her head thoughtfully. 'Okay, Mamma.'

Shammi was still feeling uneasy. She decided to go and fix herself another drink.

Ashima had been watching her parents. While she knew they were terribly unhappy, she also wondered why they did not discuss their problem with anyone.

Tonight she and her mother were watching TV. After ages of avoiding it for obvious reasons, they had gone back to watching one of the daily soaps. The serial was about a dictatorial mother-in-law who constantly kept an eye on her daughter-in-law, smothering her with rules. Kamla laughed and said, 'Which mother-in-law can afford to be like that any more? What works best these days is the ability of a mother-in-law to be friends with the bahu.'

Ashima turned off the television. She had been wanting to speak to her mother about this for a while now. Grabbing the chance to open the conversation, she said, 'Yes, Mamma, you are right. A mother-in-law must be friends with her bahu. You are good to both your bahus. But you must also encourage Simran to stand on her own two feet, at least now. Look at what has happened to her. She was the perfect bahu, always doing what everyone wanted, staying at home and raising the kids. But look at Bhaiyya. He seems to have taken an aversion to this avatar and has found the one trait he did not want in his own wife attractive in another woman. He likes Sia's confidence and independence, which he killed in Simran. And Raj Bhaiyya will probably never trample on Sia the way he did with Simran. She just won't take it, and all that is because she is not just a housewife.'

Kamla silently listened to Ashima. She agreed with what her daughter had just said. It was true. Her one son had dumped his wife for a successful career woman and the other son adored his strong, financially-independent wife. Karan respected and supported Kavita in every way.

'Beta, I will not deny it. Your Papa and I have always been uncomfortable with the idea of our daughters or bahus going out and earning a living. But we have come to accept it that girls today need to have a sense of independence that can only come through the pursuit of one's ambition. Look at Kavita. She is happily pursuing her career and we are quite accepting, and I daresay, even supportive of it. But it's just that Mori has always been a bit different.'

Ashima was quiet now. It was true. Her parents had never objected to Kavita working. And yes, Simran was more a homebody. Perhaps if she had insisted on working, her parents would not have objected. But Simran had come in, happy to blend, happy to let Raj lead the way.

Ashima realized that a lot depended on the individual too. She had wanted to make a career for herself and, despite all she had to go through, here she was today with the option of being able to go ahead and make something of herself.

Ashima said, 'Mamma, maybe Simran just needs a push in the right direction.'

Kamla nodded. If there was something she could do to quell the storm that had hit Mori's life, she, along with Bhupinder, would do it.

Ashima watched her mother. She hoped she had dropped the penny. No one knew the importance of being able to make something of oneself more than Ashima. Of late, she had begun to go for auditions for roles in movies. It shocked people whenever they discovered her connections. Once she mentioned her second name, they would give her the once-over. The unasked question was—why was a Mehra girl doing looking for work? They would invariably refuse. It frustrated Ashima. Why could people not accept that she wanted to make something of her life on her own?

Ashima did not ask her father. And of course, Raj had made it clear that he would disown her if she took a step in the direction of films. Ashima did not ask Karan either, though she knew that he would have helped. But anyone who really knew Ashima would know that she was one of those people who would rather take the stairs than go up the elevator. She wanted success on her own terms. And she was prepared to work hard. Kavita watched her from the sidelines like a hawk. Ashima knew that she would gloat at her failure.

After months of moving from one production house to another to no avail, Ashima decided to drop her surname. She cut a few CDs of her work, made a new visiting card with just 'Ashima' on it, and started circulating it. She would leave home after a small breakfast and return spent but buoyant. Under the cloak of anonymity, she hoped to find a breakthrough.

She was also worried about Simran. *Go Simran go,* she would silently goad her. She hoped that her sister-in-law would soon gather her pieces and build something out of them.

Could Simran get back into films?

But even as the thought came up, she had to toss it out. Ashima had now begun to make it a point to talk to Simran about how she was constantly going from one studio to another for auditions, about how she was enjoying herself. She hoped it would give ideas to Simran. Even in front of her mother and Simran, Ashima always tried to play up the benefits of going to work. Kamla understood what Ashima was doing, so did Simran.

Both were amazed at Ashima's resilience, her zeal to keep trying despite facing rejection again and again.

But all was not well with Ashima. Between the nightmares of her marital home and the underlying stress at her parents' place, there were trying days at the studios she was visiting.

One day, Simran found Ashima out in the garden, all by herself. She noticed Ashima hurriedly wiping away her tears. 'Ashima! What's the matter?'

Ashima tried to laugh it off. 'Nothing, Bhabhi. Something got into my eye.'

'And pigs have wings!' added Simran without batting her eye.

They both laughed. 'Come on! You were crying.'

Ashima shook her head. 'I feel very demotivated. I have been trying so hard. Months have gone by and I have nothing to show for my efforts. Even Papa and Bhaiyya ... I can't expect anything from them. I sometimes feel like it is a conspiracy against me, in which everyone in the industry is involved. Do you know, other girls are asked to sleep around to get roles but no one even gives me that option! It's not like I want to, but the thing to note is that I am not even asked! I know it is Papa and Bhaiyya's names that keep them away. They know that Bhaiyya would skin them alive if they even asked his younger sister out. But it is not helping me because I am not even given a chance to prove myself. It's a vicious circle. They don't want to take on a newcomer but how will a newcomer ever become an old hand unless he is given work?' A drop of tear trickled down her face. 'I'm just tired and irritable, I guess. Sorry. Didn't mean to burden you.'

Simran understood that Ashima had the uncomfortable task of choosing between her dignity and success. She said, 'Ashima, I know it cannot be easy seeing other girls get the one part you wanted so badly, simply because they slept around for it. But believe me, in the long run, it does not help. Taking the quick route to success ensures you get an equally quick ride to failure. No matter what happens, Ashima, your ethics and talent are all you have in this world. Don't ever compromise on them to get where you want. Success will come to you eventually. Your talent will be recognized. But never ever think of taking the easier route out.'

Ashima looked relieved. She hugged Simran, saying, 'Are *you* okay?'

Simran was slowly getting used to the fact that Raj was not going to be around. People were getting on with life. The media had decided to focus on a political scandal now and the media were not pressing for scoops. She was now worried about the kids.

Tarun and Trishala weren't small any more, and their world was, at present, off-balance. In the emotional upheaval that Simran was going through, she sometimes sought her room and went to bed early.

One night, when Simran was alone in her room, her children knocked on the door and entered. On seeing them,

Simran smiled brightly. They climbed into bed with her. She began to casually ask them about school. While Trishala answered and snuggled with her, Tarun seemed uneasy. Then he blurted, 'Mamma, we have come here to ask you something. We both know something is wrong between you and Papa. He is never home and you look so sad all the time. Besides, the teasing in school has become unbearable. Mamma, if you tell us what the matter is at least we will be able to defend ourselves from those bullies.'

Simran felt her heart crumble. Raj's face flashed before her. His and Sia's. *How many lives they have ruined without a thought for anyone.*

Simran took a deep breath and said, 'I will not lie to both of you. Yes, something has happened, and it is not pleasant. You see, this friend of Papa's has been spending a lot of time with him. And even Papa feels like being with her, but in sometime, he will be back. Don't you worry. And the next time children in school tease you, tell them that you can't help the fact that your father is so famous that every little thing he does appears in the papers. Tell them to mind their own business and not pay attention to unnecessary gossip.'

I must go to school and seek help. I need the school's cooperation to help the kids.

Trishala asked, 'But Mamma, doesn't he miss us?'

'He misses you both a lot,' Simran said. 'And he did come one day to meet you, but remember you both had to go for the annual day practice? Papa didn't know that, and he sent you both his love. Friends fight sometimes, don't they? Well Papa and I are a little upset with each other right now. But we will makeup. Don't you worry.'

As she said this glibly, Simran searched their faces. She could see that was exactly what they wanted to hear. *I need to prepare them gently. Raj needs to be here for this.* Happier than they had been in days, the kids were soon asleep in her bed. Simran snuggled up to them.

But daylight never wiped her cares. Simran noticed that the kids would drag their feet when it was time to go to school. Remembering that she had promised to go to school and talk to the authorities, one day, Simran wended her way to their school. With the help of their principal, she would speak to their teachers and then pick the kids and drive back home.

As the car made the last turn into the school lane, she found media crew and their massive trailers with their giant satellites parked back-to-back in the lane. They seemed to be waiting for someone, with their lenses poised and mikes checked. They were waiting for the kids to step out. They were waiting to ask them what they thought about their father now being with another woman.

She asked the driver to stop and stepped out of the car, eyes wild with rage. Looking at her, the crew hesitated. They had never seen Simran angry. The Simran they knew was shy, always smiling, hesitant, graceful.

'How dare you!' she screamed. How could anyone stoop this low that they would wield cameras and thrust mikes in her children's faces? *What have we all become?* She wondered, tears flowing, as cameras flashed. *Even me screaming and crying is fodder for these people. And we need them. We feed them. We are grateful for all the coverage and their positive films reviews.*

As she shouted and raved, she realized that the school

had let the children off; that parents had started gathering and children were staring; teachers and the school staff had come out.

Her anger was being converted into a sort of circus. Luckily for her, good sense prevailed and the school authorities soon arranged for the security to chase away the news crew. Simran felt violated. She wanted to cry her heart out. But quietly, and with as much dignity as she could manage, she ushered her children into the car, and they drove home silently.

Of course, that evening, Simran, in her screaming avatar, was all over the news. The news flashed that she was borderline hysterical. They were analysing that, if she was hysterical and if Raj was busy tying the knot elsewhere, where would the kids go?

Simran switched off her television. To think that a chance visit to her children's school could lead to such a story ... Simran shuddered to think what would have happened if she had not got to school in time. The media would have coaxed out quotes from Trishala and Tarun and got their friends to say something, anything. And that would have been news too.

Simran sat inside her room, turning the remote in her hands. The idea of stepping out of her home made the bile rise up her throat.

'But Mamma, it's been weeks since Bhabhi left the house!'

Ashima was at the dinner table, nibbling a carrot and talking to her mother. She was trying to convince her mother that Simran needed a reason to be pushed out of the house. The scene with the media the other day had impacted Simran in such a way that she barely left home these days. Neither did she allow Tarun and Trishala out of sight. They had not been to school since the incident.

The family initially let her have her way, realizing this was not an easy time for her. But they had received a letter from school, wanting to know when the kids would return, if they would at all.

Kamla had silently taken it to Simran who saw the school letterhead and put it away. When Kamla spoke to Ashima about it, she burst out.

'The kids have to go to school, Mamma. And someone needs to tell Bhabhi that she needs ...'

'For the first time, I agree with Ashima,' came a cool voice from behind them. Kavita's. 'I myself heard someone saying that, if they did not return to school soon, they could be expelled.'

Simran walked in, and for a moment, everyone was quiet. She looked at them quizzically. Kamla said, 'Mori, it is time to let them face the world. You need to send the kids back to school.' Simran's heart skipped a beat at the idea of her kids out in that world. She said, 'Mamma, after all that happened the other day, how can you say that? What if other news channels decide to accost them?'

Biting into a papad, Kavita said coolly, 'Simran, hiding away is not an answer. You cannot keep them in the house forever. The sooner they and you face the world, the sooner people will put the silly incident behind them. Till you don't move on, how will the kids do so? Besides, do you really want them to learn that the best way to face a problem is to hide and pray that it goes away?'

Simran said, 'Kavita, Mamma, both of you are right. But how do I ...What do I tell Tarun and Trishala?' Kamla said, 'You leave that to us. Mori, we must teach our kids to be brave and fight, not hide and wait till things go back to normal.' Simran smiled sardonically and said, '*I* stood my ground and fought. Look what that got me.' Kavita replied, 'Yes, Simran, you stood your ground and fought, but in vain and at the wrong time. But that is another matter. First, we need to concentrate on the kids. Give them some semblance of normalcy.'

Simran agreed, and that night, Kavita and Kamla talked to Tarun and Trishala, asking them to get ready for school the following day. The children, who were already scared, did not show any enthusiasm until their grandma and Kaki told them that there was no point in wasting a year and looking for another school. The kids needed no encouragement after that, since both of them felt suffocated at home and missed their best friends.

Kamla and Simran went to school with the children. The school headmistress assured them that they would do their best to ensure the children were well protected. The other children would be spoken to about bullying or teasing them.

After a few days of trepidation, Tarun and Trishala seemed a little relaxed. Now that even Project Tarun-Trishala was over, Simran seemed deflated. It was godsend that Divya came looking for her.

Divya and Mouli were shocked to see Simran. Puffy and aged, they could barely recognize their once-cheerful, beautiful friend. They dragged Simran out to a cafe where the privacy of celebrities was taken care of, and over cups of mocha planned Project-Simran.

'First of all, a personal trainer will come visiting you,' said Mouli with a glint in her eye as she texted someone. 'There! It's all been arranged.

'Next, you go on a diet,' sang Divya. 'Call your mother-in-law and tell her right now that malai chicken or whatever the Mehra khandaan loves is off your plate forever. It's going to be a quarter kilo of steamed chicken twice a week. I'll chalk out the rest of your diet.

'Not to forget the daily, twenty minute walk.'

'And,' added Divya, amid fits of giggles, 'you need to think of something to do. Whether it is a business or even something like making pickles.'

13

Project Simran was fun. Simran became the focus of her own life, thanks to her two friends. She knocked off kilos. Divya hired a personal shopper who threw out all of Simran's dreary 'tents' and picked up clothes that were quiet yet spelt attitude. Mouli got Simran's hair trimmed and Simran suddenly looked and felt younger.

Weeks later, Simran saw her reflection as she passed a mirror. She had been getting compliments and they thrilled her. *I look good.* She peered closer. The weight loss and her new hair style made her look girlish, more like Simran the filmstar of yesteryears. But she also noticed the dark circles under her eyes. *I look older, more tired. Or am I imagining it?*

Raj had sent a divorce notice. She had held the papers in her hand for long. Her heart sank. Weight loss became easier. Food made Simran feel like throwing up. For Simran it was ironic that, when Raj was around, losing weight was a battle that she fought and lost. And here she was, minus a husband, losing weight like no one's business, earning compliments, getting noticed but feeling bereft.

One part of her wanted Raj to see and notice her, while another part chided her. *He's sent you divorce papers. It's over. Pull yourself together! Stop hoping.* She remembered the letter he wrote to her: Let's part like the friends we have always been. You can decide how much alimony you want, pick the property you want. I will not object ... I'm ready to pay anything to close this peacefully.

Simran still couldn't think of it without getting her eyes fogged up. *What a waste of energy.*

She stared at her slim silhouette. *It's time to do something. I can't hang around waiting for some miracle to happen.*

Bhupinder and Kamla were mortified by Raj's act. Simran felt bitter that while they sympathized with her, they did nothing to chastise their son. *Why didn't they insist on Raj coming back? Raj wouldn't dare disobey his father!* The voice in her head raged. *What am I doing here, in a houseful of strangers?*

But Shammi's stoic support saw to it that Simran stayed put. Divya and Mouli, in the meantime, advised her not to sign the papers. Divya said, 'The ball is in your court, Simran. I say make him pay. Roast him, cut him to pieces; tear his dignity to shreds. Don't give him the one thing he wants, Simran. Don't give him that goddamn divorce. Let him suffer like hell.'

The papers were still not signed. She still tossed the issue both sides. *Let him go. Show dignity.* Simran pictured herself handing over the papers, and Raj looking at her with admiration. Then she saw Raj and Sia snicker at her. *My poor kids suffer every day. He never even thinks of calling them. I really should listen to Mamma and Mouli and Divya. He's used me all his life and he continues to work things to his convenience. I'm not going to let him off this easily.*

It was 2 am. Simran pulled out her cell and texted Raj: Meet me tomorrow.

The next day, when Raj arrived, Simran made it a point to keep him waiting for at least half an hour before she finally sat down to talk to him. *Let him sweat*, she thought to herself. She had deliberately called him at a time when no one would be around. She didn't want the task of facing his family when she was already so anxious.

Raj was playing with his phone when she descended the stairs. He was startled to see her. She looked younger, prettier. 'You look good,' he said appreciatively.

Suddenly, Simran could no longer sec what she used to see in this man. She saw his pressed suit, the way he flicked his hair from his face, the manicured nails and she was amazed that she felt nothing for him. *At one time, I would have been ready to give my life for him.* 'I wanted to see you about the divorce papers,' she said. 'You said that you want a divorce by mutual consent and I could have anything I want, right?'

Raj nodded and said, 'That is correct, Simran. I feel there is no point making a spectacle of the separation any more than it already has become.' He was quite surprised at the calmness and amiability that Simran was displaying. Without his realizing it, his wife had changed and he liked that.

But Simran was feeling anything but amiable towards Raj. Hearing his voice and the genial way in which he was discussing the destruction of her life, she felt bitterness and anger pounding her head. Raj was smiling at her and was about to say something when she interrupted.

'Raj, I have called you to tell you that, come what may, the earth can stop spinning, the sun can stop shining, but I am not going to divorce you. You can consult your fancy lawyers and do all you please, but I promise you, it will be a cold day in hell before I sign any divorce papers. So go and tell your mistress, she can rest assured that the only status she is ever going to have in your life is that of a whore and nothing else.'

Raj felt like he had been slapped. 'You know, I thought you had matured,' he spluttered in rage. 'But I was wrong. You are a selfish, cold-hearted, sadistic bitch and nothing more. You know what? If this is a challenge, I accept it. I promise that by the end of this year, I will be free of you. So get the stupid notion of invincibility out of your head. I will now see you in court.' He was practically shouting. Then he walked out, slamming the door.

Simran was shocked at his ferocity. This was not the reaction she had expected from him. Clutching the wall for support, Simran sank to the ground.

Raj walked off in a huff, his hands and legs trembling. *The gall of that woman! Calling him over, holding out a candy and then telling him he could not have it! He could throw her out of the house unceremoniously and here he was telling her, offering her whatever she wanted. The stupid cow must have thought that she could get him back! Such nerve.* He would appoint the best lawyers. He would contest visitation rights for his kids.

Tarun entered his room and kept his school bag on the rack. He went to look for something to eat. Trishala joined him. Trishala had the knack of speaking exactly what he had in mind. 'Where's Mamma?' she asked.

Ashima had found Simran curled up in the terrace. Her

hair was stuck to her face wet with tears. She seemed to have banged her head against the wall, for she was bruised and refused to speak. Ashima froze. Her first instinct was to call Raj. Then she shook her head. No. Raj won't do. Dad? Nope. Kavita? Ashima took a deep breath. The kids were hovering in the background.

'Tarun, I think Mamma fell asleep here. She must have come here to read. Go down to your room. Trishala can you help your bua?' Trishala nodded, her eyes wide. 'Go check her room. See if it has been cleaned and get her a glass of something sweet to drink.' The kids scampered down.

Ashima gently wiped the sweat and tears off Simran's face. She despaired looking at Simran. *What is this beautiful woman doing to herself? Never love a man so much that you forget to love yourself. Raj Bhaiyya is not the end of the world, Bhabhi. Please!*

'Bhabhi, Bhabhi! Wake up please!'

Simran opened her eyes. 'What are you doing here, Bhabhi?' But Simran shut her eyes again. 'Please come down. The kids will get scared.'

Ashima gently took Simran down the stairs. She sent her for a bath. When Simran came out, she looked thin and tired but clean.

'You were looking happy these days. The diet, new wardrobe ... I thought you were finally getting out of that dark place in your head, Bhabhi,' Ashima said sadly.

Tears trickled out of Simran's eyes. 'Oh god! I can't believe I still have tears,' she croaked to Ashima in an attempt to make her laugh. 'With the amount I cried last month, I was sure they would have dried up!' Ashima hugged her sister-in-law. 'Please, Bhabhi. Don't fall apart. What will the kids do if you give up? What will I do? So many of us depend on you. Have you forgotten? It's like you've set out on this path of self-destruction and nothing and no one matters any more. Come back to us. Please. I beg you, come back to us.' Simran began to cry and Ashima wept too.

'I'm such a failure, Ashima. Failed actress, failed wife, failed mother. I'm nothing. I went up to the terrace to kill myself but I couldn't even do that.'

14

Aao Romance Kare was a smashing hit and broke all box office records for the year. A clichéd action-love story set in the hilly terrain of North India that made use of many familiar Bollywood tropes. The story was about honest and incorruptible Vikram, an ex-army man, who takes on a mafia don smuggling drugs into the country, but falls in love with his sister. The movie had a sizzling item number, and the real chemistry of Raj and Sia added to the charm of the film.

Simran resisted the urge to watch the film, but reports of the its success trickled into the house. As usual, the film producers had sent the Mehra family invites to the premier. Kamla and Bhupinder went. Tarun and Trishala were reluctant to go, as was Ashima. So they stayed at home.

When no one was looking, Simran scoured through the reviews. Paid reviews gushed about the box office collections and raved about Raj and Sia's chemistry and the sizzling scenes. The off-beat reviews caustically talked about the usual mix of formulae in the film and an actor who refused to play his age.

So, one morning after the kids went to school, piqued by ambiguous reviews and sheer curiosity, Simran slipped out and watched the movie. She wanted to see the film without anyone knowing. She wanted to suffer without any audience.

Raj was aging, she noticed. The reviews were right. *If he doesn't pick character roles, he's going to slip soon.* She sat through the romance stoically telling herself, *it's okay.*

Later, when she went back home and hurled a magazine that had Raj's interview in the cover story with a tag line of Raj's quote that said, 'Sia is my lucky charm', she knew it was not okay.

One day, Simran found herself outside Sia's house. When she knocked the door and Sia opened it, she was not sure who was more surprised: she or Sia.

Sia's face paled when she saw Simran. Simran found her voice, 'May I come in?' Silently Sia stood aside and Simran walked in. They went to the terrace. Neither seemed to want to sit. Outside, the breeze was cool, making ripples in the pool. Simran felt the breeze caress her face. She felt better. Sia was watching her curiously.

'Raj is not here actually,' she said.

Simran answered, 'I know. I have come here to talk to you. Before you wonder about this, let me tell you that he does not know that I was going to come.'

Sia knew where this was leading. *Oh my god*! She squared her shoulders, bracing herself for what Simran was going to say.

Simran said in a rush, 'Sia, this thing between Raj and you. It's gone on long enough. If you don't understand that he's a married man, I don't know what to say to you.' Suddenly she felt tears prick her eyes. *What am I doing here? Begging for my husband.* 'My kids and I have paid a very heavy price for it. Now, all I ask of you is to let him return home. You are acquiring bad karma by keeping two children away from their father. Please, end this madness. Only you can do it. And you will be a better person for it.'

As Simran spoke, Sia looked at her and realized she was looking tired and thinner. A wave of insecurity washed over her. But as soon as Simran mentioned 'karma', she felt stung.

She said, 'If its karma we are talking, Simran, I quite agree. One must not keep children away from their father. So I'm sure you will agree that we should not keep Raj from his new baby.'

The two women stared at each other, one defiant and the other bewildered.

'I am pregnant with Raj's child, Simran.'

15

I can do it. One step and the next precarious one, and another and another. Simran walked out of the house. Later, she tried to remember how she manoeuvred her way out, how she got down the stairs, what Sia said as she left, how she drove back home ... she couldn't remember anything.

The only thing that seemed to touch the woozy layer that covered her was the fact that she saw Mahesh park his bike as she drove off. Their eyes met and she saw Mahesh look at her with a start. But she had driven off even before she could react to his bewilderment.

Mahesh. He is loyal to his master.

She saw through the rest of the day like a zombie. *Raj was having a baby.* Even if she had known it was over, some part of her had been unwilling to accept it. There was nothing now. Just a wall.

Later, when she brought it up, Kamla, Bhupinder, Karan and Ashima were appalled. They listened to the news of Sia's pregnancy with shame and hopelessness in their eyes. As if they were responsible for Raj's betrayal. Bhupinder and Kamla looked defeated. Bhupinder walked out silently, his lips set in a thin line.

It was Kavita who finally decided to say something. Foot-in-the-mouth disease Kavita. 'Have you thought of accepting her? You know, co-wives and all?'

Simran simply stared at his sister-in-law, her jaws clenched. *Why do you hate me?* 'Is that what you would do if Karan was having an affair with someone?' she asked in unconcealed anger.

Kavita had the grace to blush, but the words that came out of her mouth were, 'I seriously doubt Karan would let success corrupt him.'

Simran realized that something inside her had turned. She had finally come to terms with a lot of things. Later she would realize that it had to happen that way. Had it not, she would not have been able to move on.

But at that point there was only a mix of emotions. Rage. Depression. A need to prove a point to someone ... perhaps herself. She started to focus on herself. Her weight loss regime was not bent on self-destruction any more. She ate less and was careful about her nutrition. She picked up the reins of running the house, yet learnt to keep aside some 'me' time too.

And she started keeping a diary.

It was Shammi's suggestion. One day, when Simran had a fit of rage that surprised her more than it surprised her mother, Shammi spoke to her. 'Start keeping a diary.'

Simran looked puzzled.

'Start keeping a diary. It will help you vent your anger.'

Full of remorse, Simran said, 'Mamma, I don't know why but there are times I'm so angry I could kill someone.'

'That's but natural, beta,' said Shammi gently. 'You've spent a lifetime obliterating yourself. When you realize that you are not important, not only to yourself, but even to the people you've sacrificed your life for, anger is the natural reaction. You've been let down. Be kind to yourself.'

Tears coursed down her face.

After a short silence, Shammi said, 'It is okay to be angry. Please know that. But will you do something for me?'

Simran was intrigued. Her mother had never asked anything of her. She looked quizzically at her mother. 'Put your thoughts down. Write what you are feeling. Keep a dairy. It doesn't have to have any meaning. But put your day down. Put your thoughts down. They'll connect. There will be a pattern and it will—I promise you—help in the long run. I've tried my best. But your losing Raj—your grieving—has been so personal. You need to purge yourself of all the hurt.'

Simran had stopped watching TV and reading magazines for some time. Watching interviews of Raj and Sia would leave her depressed and anxious for days.

For the moment, the pair was the darling of the masses. Raj spoke of Sia at every opportune moment, and seeing Raj looking relaxed, flush with the glow of success and giving cocky repartees, only made her cry.

'It's just a portrayal,' Mouli and Divya would tell her. 'You know how it works.' She knew. Yet it hurt. *How could I have loved this man? How did I forsake everything I had for him?* She still loved him, she knew. And she felt self-loathing for this. *And here he was saying the same empty words to Sia.* Had he never loved her?

Raj had not responded to a single message after the day he had stormed out, swearing to fight in court. He had not even responded to her attempt at talking to Sia. Seeing him on TV made it hard for Simran to get out of the stupor she sometimes sank into. *He's having a baby. And I had to find out about it in that way.*

Mouli and Divya banned her from reading or watching anything that featured Raj and Sia. Without her knowledge, they also rallied support from the Mehra family to not allow any media about Raj or Sia to come into Vardaan.

The duo invited Simran and the kids for a pajama party at Mouli's place, and Simran knew it was a ruse to get her to step out.

'You should think of working,' Mouli said one day and Simran nodded. She too had been thinking about it. But she had not honed any skill other than housekeeping in the past so many years, and she definitely could not return to acting.

Sitting in the car, listening to Divya's pep talk, Simran suddenly felt a wave of nausea hit her. She and Divya made their way to Mouli's home where a party was being organized. *Almost all the people who were present at Trishala's party will be there.* They will be laughing at her, worse still, pitying her. *What am I doing? Why am I putting myself through this?*

Her chest hurt suddenly and she felt breathless. Sweat trickled down her face and back. Divya suddenly noticed.

'Are you okay?' Simran clutched her hand. 'I need to get back, Divya. I'm feeling unwell.'

'We can go back, Simran,' Divya said, holding both her hands. 'But if you are freaking out thinking of the people coming there and what they will say, please think about it again. You've done nothing wrong. The person who should be slinking in shame for abandoning his family is brazenly walking in and out of parties with Sia.'

Simran stayed silent until the car reached Mouli's house. Then Simran squared her shoulders, swallowed her fears and walked in.

The party was in full swing but Mouli hurried and drew them in with a happy grin on her face. The chatter, the light, the music suddenly seemed alien. When Mouli went to attend to another guest, Simran sought and slinked into a quiet corner.

As she sat quietly, paying more attention to her drink than to the people around her, she saw Sanya, Rupal and Megha approach her. These women were married to successful producers and film directors. As with everyone in the business, these women maintained their weight and kept themselves in mint condition. They came and sat beside Simran.

'Hi Simran, you've lost weight and look really pretty,' started Megha. Simran smiled, but before she could say something, Sanya added, 'Babe, you should be celebrating your looks now instead of sitting in a corner and feeling sorry for yourself.'

Simran, embarrassed at being spoken to so directly about her shattered marriage, said, 'It's not like that. I was just ...'

Megha said, 'Look Simran, men will be men. They will stray. That is a fact as sure as the fact that the sun rises in the east. We just cannot change it. What you can change is your reaction to it.'

'So you mean I should just get used to it?'

Rupal, who had been quiet all along, said, 'No, Simran. What we mean is, divert yourself. Look elsewhere.'

Simran looked at the women. Were they trying to say something to her? Sanya said, 'Simran, we know what you are going through. We all went through it—maybe not as badly as you did. But after a point, we found our own defence mechanism. What we are trying to tell you is, find your own distractions. Look at us, we have all faced infidelity, and now we turn to each other for comfort ... and pleasure.'

Simran felt her blood rush to her face. *What were they suggesting?* Megha nodded her head, but the others knew she did not understand. Looking pointedly at her, Megha said, 'Really, Simran. A woman will never break your heart like a man. Trust me.' Simran blankly looked at the smiles. Then tilting her head, she excused herself, 'I need a drink.' As she walked out, she heard the women tittering at her.

That night, on her way home from the party, Simran barely heard the gossip Divya was doling out. *I myself must have been gossip item number one,* she thought wryly. In her mind, she revisited the conversation she had had with the women who had propositioned her. Her skin crawled. *Did I do something to make them think they could approach me?*

Divya dropped Simran home. 'Are you okay?' she asked her with a searching look. 'Yup,' said Simran with a smile. She went back and stood under a hot shower for what seemed like an age. The hot tears that coursed down her face mingled with the water from the shower.

I have to get my life back. But I have to first give Raj the divorce.

Making that decision, Simran went to bed. After a long time, she had a restful night.

16

Kavita stood outside Simran's door with two cups of coffee. She knocked again. Simran opened the door. 'Coffee with Kavita?' said Kavita with a grin. Simran could not hide the surprise on her face. 'Come, Simran. Let's go to the terrace. The weather is brilliant.'

Behind the casualness, Kavita was nervous. Simran's hesitation was not lost on her. She understood where that came from. *I've been quite nasty.* But she hadn't been able to help it. Simran's sweetness, her need to serve, her devotion to her in-laws ... Kavita had been wary of them from the start. She would have loved a friend. Someone to laugh with, someone to bitch to, someone with whom to exchange glances with, someone ... well someone of her own kind. To Kavita, Simran came from another planet. She had never understood Simran's need to please everyone around her or Simran's instinct to place her needs after everyone else's ... If Kavita were to be honest about it, she was terribly suspicious of Simran at first, and later, she was simply incredulous of her simplicity.

Adversities usually throw off masks. Simran's battle with her grief was evident. Yet Kavita had noticed that at no point did Simran ever break her rules of grace.

She had watched with grudging admiration. *It's called good upbringing.*

Then after a few days, Simran did something that stunned everyone. It had stunned Kavita more than she would ever admit.

'Ma and Papa, I need to say something.' The kids had left for school. Karan and Kavita had come down to have a hurried breakfast and everyone was in their own world when Simran spoke. Kavita looked up. It seemed like Simran had spent one more night without sleep. Yet there was something arresting about the expression on her face.

'I've decided to sign the divorce papers,' Simran declared. There was a collective gasp. 'Beta ...,' started Bhupinder.

'No, Papa. Please don't say anything. This is hard enough for me. But I have decided ...'

Kavita looked from face to face, surreptitiously. Ashima had squeezed her eyes shut and her hands were clenched. Karan looked on impassively and her mother-in-law seemed to be crying.

'Mori, don't do it,' Bhupinder said. Then he swallowed as if it was getting hard for him to speak.

'Papa, I thought ...'

Then Kamla spoke, 'Mori, we support you. But we don't think you need to make it legal and binding.'

Bhupinder agreed, 'Beta, we are with you. This is your house. One day, Raj will come back. He will, I know it. We just have to be patient.'

Simran felt sad hearing them speak, 'Papa, I have been patient beyond my own limits. You are my parents. But, Papa, this hatred, it's consuming me. I feel it is destroying who I am, every day, bit by bit. I cannot go on like this. I feel like

I am stuck in a limbo, not knowing what to do. Raj and Sia are welcome to be with each other. I want no part of them any more.'

Kamla began to sob. Something twitched in Kavita's heart. She blinked furiously to hide the tears that threatened to spill when Simran spoke with a sense of defeat yet with so much dignity.

She had felt angry with her in-laws. *How could anyone be so blind?* She had been infuriated by the way Simran had initially dealt with it. *Pleading with a man who was screwing around! He should have been grovelling. Somebody should have caught him by the collar and shaken him. How dare he put them all out there with his indiscretions? On top of that, his double standards and his attitude!*

That night, when Kavita had slipped in after a late night, she had found Simran asleep in the study. She seemed to have signed the papers, wept over it, and fallen asleep right there. In the half light, Kavita stood wrangling with a peculiar feeling: a need to stretch her hand and touch Simran's hair.

The coffee was good. Simran and Kavita strolled on the terrace at sunset, without exchanging any words. Kavita had come prepared to speak. But Simran—after her initial surprise—seemed comfortable in the silence.

You've grown more beautiful, thought Kavita, glancing at Simran.

Bhupinder had agreed to let her sign the divorce papers on one condition—that Simran would never leave Vardaan. Simran was hesitant, but she did not really have any long-term plans in place; besides, she did care for Raj's family. 'I shouldn't be telling you this ... but perhaps I should,' Bhupinder had told her, his head bowed. Simran noticed that he had greyed a bit more. 'I did try to stop Raj from leaving. I told him to end his affair with Sia. But he walked out on me.'

His eyes shone with unshed tears. Simran felt something lighten inside her. Consciously or unconsciously, she had felt hurt about her in-laws not taking a stand. *At least they tried. Thank you.*

'Bhupinder, the semi-successful film producer, could not impose anything on his super-successful actor son. I'm sorry, Mori.' Simran was taken aback. She held her father-in-law and tried to comfort him, tears coursing down her face. *There is only so much we all could have done. I'm sorry I didn't trust you.*

Tarun and Trishala did not trust anyone any more. Not even their mother. They had to be told, so Simran went to their room one day, with a tub of their favourite ice cream.

When she nervously knocked on their door, it didn't help to be met with hostility. Trishala was reading and continued to read even when Simran asked her how her day went. Tarun saw her and pretended to be busy with his homework. He turned his back on her. She stood there feeling wretched for a minute. Then she said with false cheerfulness, 'You can ignore me, but do we dare ignore Alps—the Swiss favourite ice cream? Huh?'

'Stop it, Mamma!' screamed Tarun. Simran was so taken aback that she dropped the ice cream. 'You may be a dimwit but we are not!'

So they knew everything and had perhaps heard unsavoury things they were not supposed to hear.

'Stop pretending!' he screamed on. 'You've always lived in a fake world. I hate you! You told us all this while that nothing was wrong. You told us and we trusted you. You lied to us, Mamma. You lied to both of us again and again. I told myself nothing was wrong. When my friends laughed at me, I still believed you. I still said, Mamma knows best.'

He was sobbing now. Simran tried to hold him, but he was livid. 'Don't touch me. The whole world knew the shit my mother and father were in, but us. I can't meet anyone's eye and it is your fault. You and your fake world! Favourite ice cream! My ass!'

Simran was stunned. Trishala was sobbing now. Simran stood back, confused. She tried to move towards Trishala but she ran to Tarun and the two stood hugging each other.

'I want Papa back, Bhaiyya!' blabbered Trishala. 'I want him back with Mamma, even if Mamma is not that pretty! Why is this movie not ending, Bhaiyya? Why?'

Simran stood trembling. She leaned against the wall and sat down on the floor.

'Answer her, Mamma!' Tarun screamed again. 'Tell us what you have told us before. That Papa will never leave us. That he will come back. That he and Sia are friends. Tell na, Mamma. Why can't you make him come back? Mamma, you lied to us.'

Simran wrote and wrote. It was as if a magician had touched her fingers and words flowed. They unravelled. They carved poetry, they chiselled thoughts; they sang out her sadness. They helped her find words for her bewilderment, rationalize her pain, smooth out the grief of her children. Through her diary, Simran found words, and words found her.

'Have you thought of alimony?'

Simran found herself sucking her breath in and grinding her teeth. This was a question she found hard to answer. *Do you mind if I don't feel like discussing it with you.* Simran sighed. She had been telling herself that they were asking only because they cared.

Shammi asked again, 'Have you thought of alimony?'

'Mamma!'

Shammi was most disapproving and vocal about Simran's decision to consent to the divorce. And now that it was too late to lament it, she—like a handful of others—had been asking her to demand a stiff alimony.

Simran knew how her mother felt, but money was the last thing on her mind at this point. She was still in a very fragile state, picking up the broken pieces of her life. *I need to become financially independent. What am I doing with my life?*

17

Ashima's fingers were clammy. *It's okay. It's okay.* But it was not. She swallowed hard and smoothed her hair for the nth time. If *Aao Balam* failed, she would be finished.

Eight months ago, after pitching for days for the part, Ashima actually signed a film. She had been over the moon. Delighted, she hugged the secret to herself. She could not have told anyone, but the family guessed it. Everyone—at least most of them—had kept their fingers crossed for Ashima's sake.

She took this break seriously and worked very hard.

Everyone reacted to Ashima's performance and her film differently. Karan watched with hope; Raj with undisguised disdain. For Simran, it was a delight to see Ashima buoyed by her first film, worrying about the smallest detail of her role and appearance. Bhupinder watched the process with much trepidation. He knew what this line of work had to offer and his protective instinct as a father wrestled against that of a producer. Kamla watched with hope and nervousness. She wanted Ashima to succeed. Kavita, with all her spiel about gender equality and financial independence, seemed resentful of Ashima's career.

The film bombed. Ashima sat in the theatre watching the final cut and felt her heart sink. The promos for the film, the post-production work, all had gone well. Yet, as she watched the movie, Ashima thought: *This is not working*. Her fingers felt cold and she felt a wave of nausea overcome her. *It's nerves.*

She went home. But the next day, the reviews were exactly what she had feared they would be. They wrote the film off. A week later, the verdict was out: *Aao Balam* was a disaster.

Ashima was devastated. She wept for hours. The only silver lining was the fact that a well known reviewer of a major daily had mentioned that the only thing worth noticing in the otherwise forgettable film was Ashima!

It is an unwritten rule in the Hindi film industry that when a newcomer's film tanks at the box office, he or she is instantly branded 'unlucky'. It is a miracle if the actor is given a second chance after that.

A week after the film was out, Raj made an appearance at Vardaan. The family sat together, and for a while, the only sound at the table was that of cutlery. Then Raj said, 'So I hope you've come back to your senses, Ashima.'

'What do you mean, Bhaiyya?' asked Ashima, a spark of anger in her eyes.

Raj waved his hand casually and said, 'Don't pretend. Enough is enough. You asked for a chance and we gave it to you. The film released and I don't see you achieving success of the earth-shattering kind.' Then arrogantly ignoring Ashima, he turned to his father and said, 'Papa, we need to do the right thing now and start looking for a suitable boy for her.'

Ashima bristled, 'Bhaiyya, I am surprised you are talking about ...'

But she was cut off by Karan who said, 'Ashima, wait. Papa, it was just one film. At least, let her try once again.

You read the review she was given by the *Hindustan Express,* right?

Raj looked at Karan with irritation. But before he could snap back, Bhupinder said, 'Ashima, beta you wanted a chance. You got it. I know you got one positive review. But you cannot throw away a life on the basis of that one review. I believe this film's failure was a sign from God. We must accept what He wants and move ahead. Instead of waiting for two years, we must try to settle you down soon. After all you are not getting any younger.'

Simran sat through the conversation at the table with varying emotions. She had hoped the family would stand as one and support Ashima and the film. It was disappointing to see that, despite not making a single attempt to help Ashima in her determination to make a career in films, they were quick to pull her down in failure. *Such double standards; one set of rules for the sons and different ones for the daughter.* Simran watched Ashima leave her food unfinished and walk off, blinking back her tears.

She glanced at Raj. He seemed to be satisfied that he had got his message across to his sister. She felt a wave of revulsion wash over her. *To think that I loved this insecure bastard.* Simran loathed Raj's negativity and posturing. He was an established star and one word from him could have actually ensured that Ashima would not have to slug it out from one studio to another any more. But he was not only unwilling to help his sister, he was also downright discouraging.

The next day, Simran found a chance to tell Ashima what was on her mind. 'I know that no one is keen that you continue in films. But search your heart. See what you want to do and then, if this is your dream, then please give it two more years. Don't let a one film-verdict break you. If you give up before that, you will do great disservice to yourself. Faith is a very powerful thing, Ashima; it can move mountains. Have faith in yourself. Don't give up while there's time.'

'Thank you, Bhabhi. Just needed to hear that. You are right. I really need to get out there and do what it takes to find success.'

'It's Father's Day, Mamma,' Tarun said to her. Simran felt her heart miss a beat. She looked up. After his outburst, Simran felt as if there was a gulf between her and the kids. She never brought the subject up. But someone must have spoken to the kids and, though there was no exchange of words, there was a general feeling of remorse on Tarun and Trishala's side.

It was after ages that Tarun had come to her.

'Would you like to meet Papa?'

Tarun looked at her searchingly, then gave a short nod.

After all, he is their father. One part of Simran felt angry that the children missed a man who seemed to have given them up so easily. The other part knew that he was their father and that, if fairness was to prevail, she would have to allow them the visit.

When the kids left for school, Simran phoned Mahesh and conveyed the children's wishes. Mahesh assured he would get back to her on priority. Then, as Simran was about to hang up, Mahesh said, 'Bhabhi, please take care of yourself.'

Despite herself, Simran smiled. 'I will.'

In less than thirty minutes, Raj called. He was delighted that the children wanted to see him and asked her to send them over as soon as they returned from school. 'I'll take good care of them,' he said. Simran could nearly hear him grin.

When she told the kids they were going to see their father, they literally whooped. Simran moved away after helping them pick their clothes. She blinked back her tears. First, Raj behaving like he had been given an unexpected birthday gift and now, the kids ... Simran sighed. He's their father. *I should be glad both parties are looking forward to seeing each other.*

But she wasn't glad. She felt betrayed.

Tarun and Trishala were full of silent enthusiasm as they reached Sia's house. Mahesh ruffled their hair and then escorted them to the door where Raj stood beaming.

The kids burrowed inside his arms and Raj felt a lump in his throat. 'Missed you,' he said gruffly. Unable to speak, the kids nodded. Trishala handed him cards that Tarun and she had made for him on Father's Day. Raj blinked back his tears and said, 'Okay, so are we ready to make this day the funnest day ever?' The kids jumped for joy.

Sia walked in. Tarun and Trishala immediately quietened. Raj said, 'Children, we kick-start our day by going out for lunch.' Tarun darted a furtive glance at Sia and then blurted, 'Is ... is she also coming?' Sia blushed. Raj looked anxiously at his kids. 'Yes, beta. Sia aunty would like to come with us. You see, she wants to make friends with you. So what do you say? Shall we ask her to come along?'

Trishala said all too quickly, 'But, Papa, today is Father's Day. So you should spend time only with us.' Raj was uncomfortable now but he said, 'Yes, so let's all go out as a family. Come on!'

Tarun and Trishala exchanged glances, dismayed.

Simran had deliberately kept herself busy. She was writing in her diary when she heard the car in the drive way. She felt her heart clench. *Raj's car.* She walked over to the window.

The car stopped and out came Raj, then the kids. By the time Simran reached the car, Raj was unloading the gifts. *He still needs to buy them things.*

She said, 'So had a nice day?'

Tarun said, 'Yes.'

Trishala held on to her dad and looked up at him, 'Come in na, Papa!' Simran felt a pinch of jealousy seeing her daughter cling to him. But Raj merely hugged them hard and left abruptly.

When Simran tucked the children in and went to her room, she found Ashima sitting on her bed and reading something. With a jolt, she realized what it was. 'Ashima! Put that down,' she said sharply, suddenly blushing with embarrassment. 'Hasn't anyone told you it's rude to read someone's diary.'

'It was lying on the bed,' said Ashima, staring at Simran with a strange expression on her face. Simran remembered what she was writing when she heard Raj's car bring in the kids.

She shrugged. As she left, Ashima said, 'Have you thought of a career in writing, Bhabhi?'

'Yes, I have. But I'm scared, Ashima. I've put down my thoughts. I have written stories, and what is coming through is a story of beauty and complexity. But I'm scared. What if I'm overestimating myself? What if people laugh at me? I've just about learnt to stand without wobbling. Do I need to expose myself further? Will I be able to withstand mockery and derision again?'

18

'I am leaving.'

Simran said it as gently as she could. Yet her words resounded at the breakfast table.

The divorce had come through. Raj had been decent by every standard. He provided for a huge alimony but all Simran could think was bitter thoughts. *Had he given me nothing, had he made me fight in court for the kids, I would have been angry. Now that he's given me enough so that I never have to worry about my daily expenses and the children's future, here I am, feeling resentful that he seems happy to be getting rid of us. Is it never a win-win situation?*

Simran felt odd in Vardaan. It wasn't anything that anyone said or did. Yet she knew that she must not stay there any longer. She got in touch with a few brokers and quietly started looking for a two-bedroom flat close to the children's school. Every day she saw a couple of places.

Going with brokers and seeing small, pokey places with peeling paint made her squirm, but she plodded on.

'Why?' Kavita was the first to voice objection. 'Why are you leaving?'

Of all the people in the world, who would have thought that Kavita would be the one stopping her?

'I need to,' Simran replied quietly. *I feel small and uncomfortable now. Raj would eventually want his access to Vardaan back ... And I don't think I will learn to spread my wings unless I step out of here. I will never be able to move on with the past staring me in the face.*

Simran, Tarun and Trishala left Vardaan for a small flat in Santacruz. Even though Bhupinder and Karan wanted to help her move, it was Shammi who organized the movers and packers. She helped read and sign the lease documents.

Shammi had been unhappy to the point of panicking when Simran agreed to the divorce. She kept thinking that if Simran stayed on, Raj would somehow weave his way back. But when Simran signed the papers without discussing it with her, Shammi was shocked.

It felt as if a line that she could depend on had been cut off abruptly. The little voice in her head told her that Simran needed to do this alone. But Shammi had steered her daughter through every twist and turn in her life. *I am responsible for the situation Simran has landed in. I forced her to give up her career. I taught her to serve and be compliant. Every time that man strayed, I assured her that it was all right. It was not.*

Shammi was distraught with guilt. The what-ifs bothered her to distraction. *The karmic circle has made its round. I once walked out on my husband. Today, my daughter has been served the same.* Shammi, at some point, even toyed with the idea of meeting Raj and talking it out with him.

When she saw the apartment that Simran had decided to move into, her heart sank. But Simran was looking for approval. So she smiled and said as honestly as she could, 'It's not too bad.'

Simran laughed and they hugged. They would be okay.

Everything was different—from waking up in the morning in a different space, to the size of things and the fact that there was no domestic help at their beck and call ... Everything seemed smaller, harder. It took all of Simran's willpower to not cry. She knew the kids were fragile. She could not break down.

It was a massive fall from grace. The invites for parties and functions vanished; people who swore they thought of her every day suddenly developed amnesia, and the media chased the story as much as it could.

Hold on. When it felt easier to wallow in self pity, Simran reminded herself: *You chose this. You can't give up now.*

Now that Simran was on her own, Shammi did what she did best. She stood like a pillar of support, goading Simran into becoming independent and searching for work, and distracting her whenever she saw her daughter blue.

In retrospect, Simran would understand that it is only in strife that true friends reveal themselves. Ashima came to see her and she was grateful that Ashima made it look so natural. Mouli and Divya were around, either insisting on her coming over or going to Simran's new house with grocery or things that the kids loved.

One day, Karan came along to see Simran. Tarun seemed to be very happy to see him and hugged his uncle. It made Simran feel very grateful to see him. 'Do you need anything?'

asked Karan. *Thank you for coming*. Simran shook her head, overcome by the way Tarun seemed to cling to a male role model. 'Kavita wanted to come too,' said Karan. 'She said she'll come soon.' Simran nodded.

When Karan left, Simran asked Tarun, 'Missing Papa, Vardaan or both?'

Tarun shook his head and walked out of the room. Simran was saddened. Trishala came to her and said, 'Mamma, we tried to get Papa and you back together. Tarun Bhaiyya was sure if we tried, it would work out.' And that's when Simran heard what the kids did on their visit to Sia's house.

In their heads, the children had imagined a time solely with their dad. They would meet him like old times, hug, chat, catch up with school stories and their dad would regale them with his on-the-sets stories. They had made cards and thought that they both would hold their dad and tell him that they would not eat until he returned with them to Vardaan for good. They would appeal to him to return to their mother and home. But the visit went wrong from the word go.

They did not find Raj alone. Sia came with them everywhere, and Raj did not take any hints to drop Sia off. Raj and Sia made cheerful conversation while the kids looked at each other in disappointment. 'We didn't get a chance to say what we had planned to,' cried Trishala.

Simran hugged Trishala. 'Poor babies. My poor, poor babies.'

There was a discernible shift in the relationship between Simran and the children. But the change in their circumstances took a toll on Tarun and Trishala's health. Tarun would complain of constant headaches. Trishala would have frequent asthma attacks. When Trishala's attacks grew more frequent, Simran was forced to call Mahesh for the number of Trishala's doctor. Mahesh used to be the one making appointments and picking the medicines back in the days when Raj was with them.

The very next day, Mahesh delivered the medicine. A bit later, Raj called up to ask after the kids. Ridden with guilt, because he knew that Trishala's asthma attack meant only one thing—the girl was under stress—Raj asked Simran if she needed any help.

The specialist's medicines could help the body, but Trishala's mind was another matter. Simran knew both her kids were depressed, but Trishala's medical condition worsened. It seemed she had lost the will to fight her condition. One night, a violent cough racked her body and that was followed by a horrible asthma attack. Simran immediately called the ambulance.

Trishala was admitted to the intensive care unit in a tizzy. Simran made a call to her father-in-law informing him. The entire Mehra clan reached the hospital. The doctor's managed to pump out the congestion from Trishala's lungs and she felt better. Reluctantly, Karan informed Raj of what had happened.

Raj dashed to the hospital. Sia wanted to join him, but Raj dissuaded her. It was when he saw his little girl strapped to big machines that the enormity of what was going on in their lives truly hit home. He gently touched her face. She opened her eyes and smiled at him. 'Papa, you came to see me?'

Raj broke down. He held Trishala tight in his arms, wishing this had not happened. Then Simran stepped in and Raj restrained himself. He knew he would have to do more to settle his kids down and decided to help as much as he could. Once they stepped out, he asked Simran for five minutes with her and they walked into a small, private room.

'Simran, I know this is not an easy time. But I want you to know I am there for you.' Simran replied bitterly, in spite of herself, 'I know, Raj. But so are Ma, Papa, Karan, Ashima, Mamma, Mouli and Divya.' Stung by her response, Raj said, 'Simran, let the kids come and see me regularly for a few days. I can help them try and fit the pieces of their lives.'

Simran smirked and said, 'Wow, funny how things change, Raj! Earlier, your children asked for some of your time. Now the great superstar Raj is asking his ex-wife to let him spend time with his children. What difference will it make, Raj? Will they be able to live in the same house as you? Will they be able to see you whenever they want? They want to know how they wronged you, why you decided to leave them. They blame me and themselves. Why do you want to torment their little souls with more questions, Raj?'

Raj was upset now. He said, 'Torment? Can a father ever torture his children? Actually, if they see me more often, they will come to terms with their situation.' Simran shook her head and said, 'They went to see you. Did you know that, without telling me, they planned to beg you back into their lives and mine? Could they even speak to you? Even then, Sia was thrust into their faces. Again it is my fault. I should have checked your itinerary. I should have known that you would not have the foresight or the sensitivity to understand their needs. It's after the visit that things went downhill for them. I've not told you, but Tarun has been suffering from migraine and my little baby is in the hospital because of you, Raj. She cannot deal with the pain. You have done this to her.'

Her words found their mark. Raj shouted, 'Stop your lies, Simran. Shut up. I am trying to find a way here.'

Simran sobered up, looked him in the eye, and said, 'Did you find it then? The only way I see you have found so far is to this hospital.'

Raj looked at Simran with anger. *She is so blind in her own pain. She refuses to see anything else but her rejection!* Softly but firmly, he said, 'Both of us know that if we get into the blame game, even you had a lot of faults.'

Simran said, 'And what were they? Was I an awful wife? Possibly, I never gave you a moment's happiness. But what did our children do to deserve this? And if, to be in your presence, they have to be with the person who took you away from them, I'd rather not put them through the grinder. They are better off missing you for a bit. You had a fleeting presence in their life in any case. They are secure in the knowledge that at least for their one parent, they will always come first on the priority list.'

Raj looked at Simran, lost for words. He felt ashamed but he could not show it. Suddenly, he wanted to leave. The place was stifling him. He said, 'I'll talk to you when you are ready to listen.' Then without another word, he walked away.

Mahesh turned up a day later when Trishala was discharged. Simran was not surprised to learn that Raj had covered all the hospital expenses. She would have liked to pay. It hurt her pride to accept money from Raj. When realities of life hit home, pride was a luxury Simran could not afford. *One day, I will earn so much that I will never give Raj the satisfaction of assuaging his guilt with money.*

Once her anger died down a bit, Simran began to realize that what Raj said made sense. If he spoke to the children, spent enough time with them, they would be able to cope better. But Simran had also to contend with her possessiveness for Tarun and Trishala. How could she give away her babies to the very man who had pushed them to the brink of destruction? She did not want another fight and she sure as hell did not want to send Tarun and Trishala to Raj's house with Sia. After spending days arguing back and forth in her head and playing devil's advocate, Simran finally asked Raj for some time to think it over.

19

Sia found herself dressing carefully once again. She chose a pastel kurta with smocking on it that looked fresh and summery and covered her bump well. There was lightness in her step. *Would they be excited too? Would they be sprucing themselves up like me?* She giggled to herself. *They will,* she told herself.

Ever since Raj told her they would be moving to Vardaan, Sia had dreamt up the scene a hundred times. Her entry. The welcome she would receive from her in-laws who would stop her from touching her feet, how she would be led up the stairs to Raj's room ... Her room now.

Raj had informed his family that he would be moving back in with Sia.

'After all, Vardaan is his home,' Bhupinder had softly said to Kamla. 'And now that Mori has left ...'

The Mehra family was uncomfortable with the thought.

'But it's not like anyone is giving us a choice,' Kavita had said to Karan.

Raj started out by renovating Vardaan. 'It's been a while since we did anything, forget painting the house,' he explained to his dad. I'll ask Rozina's interior designer—the one everyone's talking about—to redecorate the house.

Suddenly, there were people in and around the house measuring things, taking estimates, getting swatches and pulling prints out.

'It seems so disloyal,' Ashima muttered one day and Kavita looked up in surprise. That was exactly how she saw it too. Almost as if someone was dead and before the mourning period was over, there was someone celebrating.

It was evident that there was less renovation and more of let's-get-all-traces-of-Simran-out-of-this-place going on.

The colours of the house—both interior and exterior—changed. The theme in the hall was ivory and purple. The staircase—Simran's choice in design—was pulled down and a marvellous crystal stairwell was installed, along with an elevator service. 'I want mom and dad to be comfortable without having to climb the stairs,' said Raj, when most at Vardaan thought that he didn't want Sia slipping on the crystal staircase in her condition.

No one was happy. Yet no one chose to voice it.

When Sia and Raj arrived at Vardaan, not everyone was there to welcome them. Kamla stood at the door with a pooja thali, haldi kumkum and the other paraphernalia. Kavita had excused herself and so had Ashima. If Raj was piqued, he didn't show it. After Kamla took the thali and circled it before the couple to ward off the evil eye, she fed them sweetmeats and hugged them, saying, 'Welcome home, Sia.'

Raj picked up Sia and started on the stairs. Then laughing, he headed for the elevator. 'Welcome home, sweetheart,' he said to Sia and kissed her.

At dinner, Karan was civil towards Sia. They had done a film together and so they knew each other. Kavita was distant, speaking to Sia only as much as was necessary. Ashima said her hello and then politely left, saying she was watching her weight.

Kavita's kids had homework and school the next morning. In the end, it was only the senior Mehras left at the table. Kamla made conversation and Bhupinder nodded politely. Sia was disappointed, but she shrugged it off. Raj kept looking at her and smiling reassuringly.

'Eat,' he cajoled her. But Sia could barely eat.

'Is the food not to your liking, Sia? Bhupinder asked.

Sia shook her head. She didn't want to look up and let the others notice her tears. *Why couldn't they have tried? What did I do?* Then she felt a giggle coming up. To think she had expected them to wait on her! *Stop getting hysterical. It's okay. I should have expected nothing more. At least his parents are kind. Raj is with me. The rest does not matter.*

When they went back to their room, Raj held her close. 'I love you. Do you know that?'

Sia nodded, looking up, and showing Raj that she was hurt.

'I'm sorry about my family. They should have behaved better ...'

'Hush!' said Sia. 'Give them time, Raj. This is not a film where people's feelings change from one shot to the next. Simran was a part of this family for all these years. They need time to forget her and only then will they be able to accept me. I don't mind waiting.'

I hope you are right, Sia. Raj was not sure.

Bhupinder and Kamla were never really rude to Sia. They spoke to her when required, but Sia always felt it was more like they would behave with a visiting guest. They interacted with her out of courtesy. Ashima moved around like Sia did not exist. Kavita slyly watched Sia's moves, but avoided conversation as much as possible.

One morning, when Sia was alone, feeling listless, she decided to do something. She went to the kitchen and checked the refrigerator, talked to the cook and discussed possible menus. She straightened the storeroom and the cutlery cupboard. She ordered furniture for the hall, replaced the cushions and got her flooring redone.

'Why don't you relax,' Raj told her. She was looking pale when he got home. *It's either pushing on or getting into depression, Raj. I don't know what I am doing here and yet, I will not go away.*

'I'm relaxed,' she said, with a tight smile. 'I was thinking it is time we held a party in this house.'

'Have you talked to Mummy?' asked Raj, casually.

'I will.'

No matter what Sia did, she ran into the wall called Simran. Kamla would often call her Mori by mistake. Sia was also aware that, while Ashima was always busy with something or the other, she seemed to have time to visit Simran. Kavita was a puzzle, yet Sia knew that her neutrality was not exactly bordering on friendship.

Sia found, during her monthly checkups with the gynaec, that her blood pressure was high. *She's not around and yet this woman is wreaking her revenge. Simran. Simran. Simran! That is all I hear. Here I am trying my best to get everyone to see who I am. But it's like they are simply staring in the wrong direction.*

She was not used to being the second fiddle in life. She felt lonely. *I wish Mamma was here.*

Things came to a head one evening. Sia had given the evening's menu to the cook and instructed him to make Raj's favourite vegetable, bhindi, sautéed. The cook dared to tell her that saab liked his bhindi fried. *The insolence. I saw the sneer on his face, like he was questioning me.*

Sia gave him a dressing down. Kamla came out of her room and looked at her questioningly. The cook left and Sia covered her face with her hands.

At dinner that night, bhindi was served, but it was the fried kind. *It's like they can't hear or see me.* 'How did you know I like my bhindi this way? Raj asked, with a smile. Sia's eyes darted to her mother-in-law. Was she looking sneeringly at her? Was she jubilant? But Kamla was silently eating her food.

I must find out what Raj likes.

But Raj had been so compliant. At her place, he would eat whatever she offered. In Vardaan, everything revolved around Raj. *All because of that stupid cow.*

Sia was in a dilemma. Should she continue with the avatar that Simran has created of Raj and everyone here, or should she show everyone how Raj was cool with everything she decided? *Would he have eaten the sautéed bhindi in his house?*

'You okay? Penny for your thoughts.'

'I am the one who is putting her heart and soul into this house, running around the entire day trying to get everyone to like me. But it is always, "Simran used to do it this way. Simran, I need to go shopping, come with me, Simran I am not well, let's go to the doctor", Simran this and Simran that.'

How on earth am I supposed to banish the thoughts of that woman from their minds?'

The minute the words were out, Sia regretted it. She didn't want Raj to think she was already whining about his family, considering it was she who had relentlessly pitched for moving to Vardaan.

Raj held her tight and said, 'Easy my darling, just have patience. Just like you needed time to get used to the idea that you are a part of this family, they need time too. To the whole world, you are Mrs Raj Mehra now. The family will come around too. Just be patient.'

She said, 'I know, I know. Didn't mean to sound like I am complaining, but I want to feel loved and be pampered. I am pregnant and your mother does not bother about what I eat or should be eating. She doesn't care. If Mamma was alive right now, she wouldn't have let me lift a finger. She would have ensured the world was at my feet, doing my bidding.' Raj said, 'They will love you too. Wait until this baby arrives. Just be strong until then, Sia. Please. You had promised me before we came here that you will.'

I will be patient. I will get them to like me. Mamma used to say everything comes to the one who is patient.

20

As the National Anthem ended, Ashima crossed her clammy fingers. Here she was again—waiting to see her next film. It was a small budget, high-risk film for her. The story was off-beat, but she had a good feeling about it. Ashima knew that if this film bombed, she could bid adieu to her film career.

Love Shaadi Etc was about a couple negotiating the teething problems in a marriage. The film ended and Ashima looked around to check how the audience reacted.

The dark horse of a film that had been predicted to sink without a trace became the year's biggest grosser.

Critics heaped praise on Ashima, going as far as to say that a star had been born. There were calls every day for interviews. Suddenly, everyone remembered Ashima or what they had done to help her or encourage her. Ashima was accosted for autographs. *This was what she was hankering after. Or was it something else?*

When she was asked about her biggest strength, Ashima would say, 'My Bhabhi.' Then, after a deliberate, pregnant pause, she would clarify, 'Simran believed in me, stood by me and taught me to believe in myself when no one else was willing to give me a second chance.'

Raj seethed about it. Suddenly, his kid sister, who no one thought could do much, who he had wagered would be cowed down by defeat, was being called an actress in the league of the stars. He felt jealous. *It's just beginner's luck ... a flash in the pan.* Worse still, he could not afford to show his insecurity. He congratulated her civilly. He simply hated that she made a big deal of her performance and her need to purposely talk of Simran.

What was the need to be dramatic? What was the need to give an Oscar-award-winning speech when it should be obvious to everyone that Ashima's success was a one-off thing? Anyone could have a single hit. That doesn't make them a star. The trick was to be able to sustain the stardom. What Raj didn't tell anyone was that Ashima's interview irritated Sia the most. She had not taken on any new projects since her pregnancy and was worried about Ashima usurping her place as the industry's most in-demand heroine.

'Ignore her,' Raj advised. 'Her's is a one-film success. You know Bollywood. It's going to forget her in half a tick.'

The power equations, especially between the women at Vardaan, were in a state of flux. Simran's absence had mellowed Kavita. In fact, this was a confusing time for her. She had always felt superior to Simran because of her own career. But now, with Sia in their lives and Ashima too stealing the thunder, Kavita was no longer sure.

She had already eased up with Simran after Raj left the house. But with Sia around, Kavita realized how much she missed her unassuming sister-in-law. The Mehras did not treat Sia any differently because of her celebrity status. In fact, they seemed to lean more towards Kavita because she had lived with them longer.

Sia had the absolute backing of Raj, and together the two of them were a formidable team. So Kavita decided to lie low and watch.

Not one to get carried away by the sudden though hard-earned fame, Ashima stayed grounded and made the most of her breakthrough. The good part of the victory was that film scripts and offers started pouring in. The media dug out her past, dissected her marriage and subsequent divorce. They had to. Ashima worried if they would distort the truth for a sensational story.

Karan—on the other hand—exulted in Ashima's success. He promoted her, recommending her wherever he could. Bhupinder too conceded—after seeing the film—that Ashima was good. 'You have that extra,' he said to her gravely, 'what industry pundits call 'the X factor'—that will make people want to see more of you.'

'So?' asked Ashima, her eyes sparkling with unshed tears.

Bhupinder didn't say anything but he knew what she was asking. Yes, there was no turning back for her now. It was a path that he had never imagined a daughter of the Mehra khandaan would walk. He and Kamla comforted each other when panic set in. Kamla reminded Bhupinder of the need to stay in tune with the times.

Ashima went to her room to cry in private for the battles she had fought from the time she got married and left Vardaan. Then she felt liberated. Her father acknowledged there was no turning back for Ashima now.

She was soon on a roll. One hit was followed by two more in a row. She had her pick of the meatiest roles, the most exclusive endorsements, and the best directors and producers lined up at Vardaan to sign her on.

This can't be happening, seethed Raj.

For anyone else exposed to so much success, it would have been a one-way ticket to self-destruction. But Ashima had seen so many people in her family reach the heights of success and plummet that she was always able to stay grounded.

She soon gained the reputation of being punctual, unfussy, disciplined and friendly. She was every director-producer's dream come true.

While Raj was confounded by Ashima's success, he tried not to give it importance. He had predicted she would fail, but here she was, charging ahead on her own steam. Besides, he had too much on his plate to pay that much attention to it. He often felt a bit trapped lately, but he resolved to concentrate on his work. If Ashima's success story had taught him anything, it was that the audience today was always on the lookout for variety. *If I don't shape up, I'll be shipped out.* Mahesh's work suddenly doubled. Raj wanted analysis reports and expected him to strategize, along with setting up appointments with new and powerful producers. Mahesh had to meet and convince them that Raj was always ready for new projects and roles.

It had always been Raj's policy to give his producers a discount if they signed on a young heroine opposite him, because that meant he could still project himself as young hero material. Now, with Ashima's success, he could not star as her romantic interest ever. It rankled that he could never act opposite the actress who was being touted as the next big thing. Mahesh became the butt of Raj's frustration.

Then the baby was born. Raj and Sia named their little girl Manvi. A baby in the house after a gap of over ten years brought back life to Vardaan. Kamla and Bhupinder welcomed her with genuine love. Ashima, Kavita, Karan and the kids milled around, admiring the tiny parcel.

The media went all out, reporting the details of when Sia was driven to the hospital, who her gynaecologist was and how she had a virtually painless c-section.

Who did Manvi look like? A bit of both her parents. Raj forgot his recent apprehensions looking at the child. If there was no work, he told himself it was because he chose not to work. He told anyone who was listening that he did not want to make the mistakes he made with Tarun and Trishala. He wanted to be around his new bundle of joy.

Tarun and Trishala felt miserable. 'Hey, you have a baby sister,' said someone in school and that was how Tarun came to know about Manvi's arrival. At first, he shrugged it off, not registering and not paying attention to it. Trishala too heard someone in her class talk about her 'half-sister'.

So their Papa had had a baby from the other woman. Tarun asked Simran about it and saw his mother cringe. She explained the meaning of half-sister to them both and spoke about it as objectively as possible.

But Trishala was terribly unhappy. From the press features and magazine interviews, it seemed as if Raj Mehra had just one child and that was Manvi. What happened to the rest of them? It was as if someone had pressed delete on their memories. Simran felt miserable. She had to absorb the misery of her kids. 'Don't think too much about it,' she urged Tarun and Trishala anxiously, hugging them. *The fickle world we live in. It is as if we do not exist.*

But that was easier said than done.

'I hate him,' said Tarun one day. Simran was startled.

'That's no way to speak of your father.'

'Whose father? You mean Manvi's?' he spat out the name Manvi like a cuss word. 'He never once cared for us. He never will. I wish I had seen that.'

No matter what Simran told him, she knew that he was raging at his dad. Tarun's grades, that had been stable so far, suddenly began to drop.

Trishala, on the other hand, took to grieving. One day, Simran found a whole bunch of her clothes that she used to wear as a child tied up in a plastic bag and kept outside the door.

'Mamma, please have another baby, no?'

'Why Trishala?'

'I want someone to play with. Tarun Bhaiyya is so boring!'

'Play with your dolls. You are Mamma's doll. We don't need another baby.'

'No, Mamma! Please! I've kept all my baby clothes for my baby sister ... Please have another baby, no.'

'Achcha, so my doll wants me to have another doll so that she can doll her up.' And they would both burst into fits of giggles.

Despite all the changes they had gone through, Trishala had secretly kept her baby clothes and had brought them along. Simran's heart sank when she saw the clothes outside their main door. With Manvi's coming, Trishala had finally given up hope.

Simran wasn't sure how she felt about the baby. She was practical enough to admit that she did not have anything against the little child. Yet it was the most glaring symbol of the death of her marriage. That baby was the reason Raj had stuck by Sia's side, so she did not have any intention of going to see Manvi.

Shammi watched the three and worried for all of them.

There were days when Simran wished she had never met Raj. And there were days when she told herself that this too would pass. She would catch her mother looking at her whenever she slipped into a broody silence. *Does she somehow blame herself for the problems I am facing? Doesn't she know she did the best she knew?*

One day Shammi said, 'Beta, you have been very brave. You never once made me feel bad about what was going on in your life when the truth is that I am squarely to blame. I never let you fly. I tied you down to marriage.'

Simran held her mother's hand and said, 'Mamma, you did what you thought best for me. How can I ever blame you? Your intention was pure.'

I always thought that marriage was the most important goal in life. I believed that, if one was a good human being and did good to others, no harm would come to oneself. The truth is different. All her life, I've seen Simran working hard to please her family—her husband, in-laws and her children. What good did it come to?

Shammi nodded. 'But it will be different for Trishala. We must see to it that her future is different. She must build her own identity. She must carve her own space.'

Simran concurred silently.

21

Simran hung up. It was Raj's call and she had not been prepared for what he asked her. He sounded absurdly happy.

'Will you send Trishala and Tarun to Vardaan? I want them to meet Manvi. I think Trishala will love her. I know she loves babies.'

After mumbling an 'okay, let's see', she had hung up. A whole lot of delayed anger surged. She wanted to scream. Why had she mumbled 'let's see'? What was there to see? *Is he dumb? To think I was madly in love with this jackass! I should have yelled at him.*

Simran cried with rage. With trembling hands, she first dialled Mahesh. Then she hung up. *Coward, call the creep himself!* She dialled Raj. 'I think the children will need time,' she said in as calm a voice as she could manage. 'They are already going through a phase of rejection and seeing the new baby will make them miss what they had even more.'

Stung, Raj retorted, 'What the hell is wrong with you, Simran? I mean, we all know how much of a control freak you are. But this is the limit! You can't control our children's lives as if you own them.'

'Oh, it's "our" now, is it? Since when, may I ask? Since you started sleeping with that woman or after that? If I remember correctly, even when we were married you barely had time for the kids, Raj. And, of your own will, you've given them up, remember?'

Raj was hysterical now and said, 'Remember? You never let me fucking forget it, Simran. You remind me all the time that I walked out on you. But try and look at yourself for a change. You never tried to keep me tied to your apron strings. You never ever—'

Simran had had enough and for the first time in her life, she did not want to listen any more. She cut off Raj saying, 'Enough, Raj. I have had enough! You would tell me earlier that you didn't feel like talking when I really needed assurance. Well, I am telling you today that I don't want to talk to you any more.' And, without waiting for his response, Simran hung up.

Simran's heart was beating hard. Suddenly, someone hugged her from behind. 'Good for you,' came Shammi's calm voice. 'That's another milestone for my daughter. I'm glad you realize that there is no need for you to ever be scared of that man.'

'He's the limit, Mamma!' sobbed Simran. 'Does he have no clue as to what his kids are going through?'

'You've done the right thing,' murmured Shammi soothingly. 'Tarun and Trishala don't need a Manvi right now. It's not right. Raj is really thoughtless.'

He's a selfish, self-absorbed, nincompoop who needs to be strangled. I'm so sorry that I allowed you to marry him. I'm sorrier that, when he was cheating on you, I still advised you to stick on. I'm sorry I never taught you self-respect. I'm sorry I never equipped you for life. I'm sorry you have to learn all this the hard way.

Shammi found herself crying with Simran.

Manvi had just been fed and Kamla had her on her shoulder and was walking up and down to burp the baby. Kamla remembered the birth of Tarun and then Trishala very clearly. Tarun, the first child and a boy, was cherished and celebrated. Trishala, a dainty, beautiful doll came next and was perfect. She had loved those children from the start. They never seemed like her grandchildren but her own children. Kamla jointly raised them with Simran.

She could not bear to stay away from them, nursing them through sickness and health. Kamla remembered the first time Tarun had high fever because of tonsillitis. She remembered how Trishala had hurt herself and bled after she fell off her cycle.

For Manvi, Kamla had mixed feelings. She instinctively loved the baby. She was so beautiful. Yet Sia never gave her complete control of the baby the way Simran had. Sia had hired a live-in maid for herself and the infant. While Sia always seemed happy to have Kamla around, she hardly asked her mother-in-law for advice and seemed to consult her gynaecologist or paediatrician for anything she was confused about. She was independent and organized.

When Kamla held the baby, she was riddled with mixed feelings. Every time she cuddled the baby or kissed it or rocked the child when it had colic, she felt as if she was somehow letting Simran and her kids down. Manvi irrevocably represented the breaking of ties the family had with Simran and her kids. Kamla felt disloyal to Simran,

Tarun and Trishala. She knew Manvi was innocent, but she could not bring herself to rush to her every time she cried. She was emotionally exhausted. And she knew that Bhupinder, who was quiet on this matter, also felt the same, because he generally made himself scarce when Sia or Manvi were around.

Karan was out of the house most of the time and when he was around, he did interact affectionately with Manvi. Kavita, however, was having a tough time. While she grew closer to her in-laws and found herself spending more time with Kamla and taking on a bit of what she knew Simran would do, had she been around, she was unsure of her position in the house. Sia seemed to make sure no one forgot her star status.

Kavita found herself avoiding Sia and the baby as much as possible, which was easy as Sia and her staff had taken camp and cordoned off one part of Vardaan. Sia made it a point to be down for breakfast—the only time Raj sat with his family—to have breakfast with them. Kavita could see that Sia, despite her C-section, was all set to regain her figure and set off to work. *She has to,* thought Kavita, *considering all Raj Bhaisahab does is go to his office and sleep.*

Kavita thought it was karmic how worked stopped coming Raj's way as soon as his divorce with Simran came through. But what incensed her was the fact that Sia was playing superstar at home and Karan was toeing the line.

Kavita knew that compared to Karan, Sia was far more successful. In fact, the way things were going, Sia would soon supersede Raj. But she hated to see Karan playing second fiddle to Sia at home. Karan was a gentleman. But Kavita did not, and would not, play into this invisible hierarchy that was slowly building in Vardaan. She hated everything connected to her. Kavita would not be affectionate to Manvi.

For the nth time, Kavita found herself thinking of Simran.

An hour later, she was at Simran's door, ringing the bell. She realized that Simran's present living condition was a far cry from her Vardaan days. But all her doubts at her warmth being any less were dispelled when Simran answered the door. Smiling, she enveloped Kavita in a hug and Kavita had tears in her eyes, though she did her best to blink them back. They chatted over tea, bonding for the first time.

Kavita told her about Kamla and Bhupinder, about how Vardaan had changed completely, her current work scenario, about her kids and how they would kill her if they knew she had come alone to meet Simran chachi. Every time she said Raj's name or mentioned Sia, she looked for signs of resentment or hurt on Simran's face. But throughout, Simran heard her without flinching.

'I'm glad you're taking care of Ma and Papa,' Simran said at the end. 'They are really good people.'

'I know,' said Kavita, not adding that 'Mori' often came out of their mouth, and how she thought that they missed her sorely. She didn't speak of a hundred instances where they all unknowingly muttered 'Wish Simran was here', or the times *she* ached to have Simran around because she saw how Sia treated her husband.

Kavita didn't say any of this. She did not want to make it harder for Simran.

22

Raj was breathing hard. He was back to his strenuous fitness training. There were two back-to-back releases to look forward to, and he was convinced Manvi would bring him good luck.

Things will turn for the better. I've got to lose weight and change my look. His new trainer designed a rigorous, new regime for him. Raj was going to consult an image consultant too—without letting Mahesh know, of course—and see what was required to polish the rough edges.

The first film flopped. Raj was mad but not down and out. However, when the same happened to the second film, it came as a huge blow. He had been waiting for the verdict, praying, making promises to different gods. This was not meant to happen to him—destiny's favourite child. He had managed to not take the critics comments seriously when the first film bombed. But when the second film came a cropper at the box office, Raj was not able to ignore the media's barbs.

The reviews were scathing and relentless. The press mocked him for saying that Sia was his lucky charm. As one TV journalist snickered, 'I guess the lucky charm was lucky only before marriage.' Slowly yet insidiously, after the box office bombing of these two films, the media that had been crazy about everything Raj did previously, wrote him off unceremoniously.

Reporters, who once waited for hours to get a single bite from Raj, did not even respond when Mahesh called them up, expressing Raj's desire to be interviewed and have a photo shoot with them.

Raj spent a few days sitting in his office amid all the reviews, covering his face with his palms. His head was blank. He could not understand what was happening. *I never thought this would happen so soon.* He went to the full-length mirror in his changing room and looked at himself. *I still look good. Why did this happen? I'll make a comeback. It is not the end of the world. If I react to this like a failure, the world will only trample me.*

He went to an astrologer who told him Saturn and Mars were in the seventh house, and it could be righted after he wore a blue sapphire in the middle finger of his left hand. With a massive sapphire ring made by a well known gemologist, Raj felt he was armed to face the world again.

Sia was back at work. Manvi was three months old. A belly tuck right after the C-section, a strict diet and a vigorous two-hour workout every day, and Sia looked as good as new. Slim, svelte and youthful.

She was the beautiful and gorgeous current Mrs Mehra, and she would always stay that way. As soon as she got to work, the press began to gush about her looks. Sia basked in the attention she got.

'How nice to see you back so soon.' said one fashion designer, 'All your measurements are just the same!'

'I love my independence and my supportive in-laws make it so easy,' said Sia, knowing that the designer was a snitch. 'They dote on Manvi so much that I don't think my baby is even aware that I've returned to work.'

But the truth was that Sia didn't have an alternative. Not only was no one encouraging her to stay back home, Raj's dismal condition didn't leave any room for choices. Sia had worked all her life and would have loved to enjoy her baby for a little while before resuming work. Yet she knew that she was still sought after in Bollywood, and with Raj down, it seemed prudent to start work as soon as possible.

Of course, Sia still commanded the highest rate in Bollywood and yes, she paid a price, because she could not breastfeed her baby. But, as Raj put it, perhaps her absence would help the members of Vardaan bond better with the baby.

Sia was heartbroken. She did not want Manvi to have to go through what she had suffered. But Raj had categorically told her not to give up her career. His line, 'You are different because of your ambition and your skill and beauty. Please don't do a Simran on me!' put much in perspective.

But she couldn't tell that to the world. Her words to the fashion designer were well rehearsed. She wasn't Bollywood's best-paid actress for nothing. It made good PR copy and was printed in film magazines many times over.

Acquiring his sapphire ring, Raj decided to form a company of his own. It would give gifted newcomers a chance. And once the company took off, he would, eventually, cast himself in a few films. Sunil Dodiya, his fan and financer had promised to back him. Nothing could stop Raj now.

Raj and Sunil began by hiring wonder CEO Sandeep Guha, who had changed the fortunes of many MNC's, at a phenomenal salary and with huge publicity around his joining.

Raj was aware of his reputation and did not want to be caught promoting anyone average or run-of-the-mill. He spent money like water in his attempt at a comeback. He knew it was worth the look on the faces of all his detractors once he was back in the game. And so, without holding back, he kept up the blistering pace of hiring the best people around, whatever the cost.

Sia was a little worried about this extravagance and she said as much to him. 'Sia, I have been here for a really long time,' Raj snapped back. 'I know what I am doing.'

Sia was taken aback by the anger in Raj's voice. She held her tongue because it was Raj who was now managing her contracts.

Raj named his new film production company Manvi Productions and launched it with much fanfare. He and his team went from city to city, looking for fresh faces with a flair for acting. They found talent aplenty.

Raj had informed the family, just before he took a formal decision, that he was going to produce a movie. All eyes turned to Bhupinder who remained silent. Ashima was the only one to express her thoughts. 'Are you sure, Bhaiyya? I hope you are not taking a hasty decision.'

'Why don't you concentrate on bagging more B-grade films?' He shocked everyone into silence.

'I'm sorry,' muttered Raj. 'I'm just tired of everyone advising or dissuading me instead of supporting me.'

'We are always with you. You should know that by now. All the best, Bhaiyya.'

Without wasting any more time, Raj and Sunil announced their first film. The lead actors were introduced to the media in a press meet, and Raj declared that his stint as a producer was the beginning of the next phase in his life.

The story was as old as the hills—a love triangle between one guy and two girls. Raj preferred to get into a venture with a successful formula. Old story, new technology, new look was what was being mixed here. Raj went on a recce for a month and decided to shoot the entire film abroad.

'It will be expensive,' Mahesh warned.

'Tell me something I don't know,' Raj snapped back.

It is going to be an expensive deal, but at the end of it, if Brand Raj stands out, it will be worth it.

The outdoor schedule of the film was entirely in London. Raj moved there with his crew and cast for two months.

When the news broke, it was one of the most beautiful mornings that Raj had woken up to. Most of the outdoor scenes had been shot and on schedule. Raj had only three days to go before they packed up.

Raj took the call from an unknown number thinking it was the sound engineer from India. But the breaking news that day in September was that Sunil Dodiya had been declared financially bankrupt in India. He would now be facing an avalanche of court cases and legal tangles.

The ground beneath Raj shook.

He returned to India, with seventy per cent of his first production and no takers to see it to completion. He didn't call home; he didn't talk to anyone. It was almost as if he couldn't believe his ears. Dodiya would not come on the line and Raj had to dip into his personal finances to wrap up whatever he could. He was deep in debt.

After two bombed films and a failed attempt at production, Raj ran out of steam. In the industry, he became untouchable. No one wanted to launch a film with him as the lead, at least none of the best banners. He compromised and began to work in smaller films. It hurt him like hell that while his wife was being signed on by the biggest A-grade projects around, he was not even doing B-grade ones. The irony of it was that he had made these banners what they were today.

23

Raj found a new astrologer who made unbelievably accurate predictions about him. His new gemologist made him wear two pendants, and his numerologist made him change his name to 'Raaj'.

Sia witnessed Raj's frustration with growing sadness. She wanted to tell him that it did not matter, that they would ride this out together. But she knew how gigantic his ego was. If she so much as tried to console him, he would insult her and she would end up in tears. 'Raaj' was the industry's biggest joke. Sia could see that the numerologist was not a solution. She tried to make Raj see that neither she nor Ashima were following any numerologist but were still was doing fine. But every time she tried, Raj would stomp off in a huff.

Sia often tried to play down her new assignments in front of him, but it was hard when he managed all her contracts. He noticed, with bitterness, how the best banners were still lined up at the doors of Vardaan, but now they either asked for Sia or Ashima.

Ashima was actually doing better than Raj, a fact that hurt not only him but Sia as well. This was not the way things were meant to be. There was only one superstar in this house and it had to be him. Raj took it badly and began to distance himself from the family including Sia and Manvi. If Sia ignored him, he blamed her for being insensitive and if she went to him and tried to talk things through, he thought her patronizing.

He took to drinking, and Sia took to going out to social functions minus him. Raj accused her of being ashamed of him. As Sia's informal manager, he had a complete record of his as well as her earnings. He knew that he had absolutely no earnings to speak of, and it didn't help to know that Sia was the breadwinner. Even the alcohol he was drinking was paid for by Sia. He started resenting everyone.

'Imagine this fucking industry ... The reigning stars are a divorcee and a married woman. Bollywood has totally lost it.'

It was a no-win situation for Sia. Worse still, she had to keep up appearances all the time.

Muted fights turned into shouting matches. If Bhupinder or Kamla tried to intervene, they were blasted with 'What are you both doing here? Go run to Simran! She is the only one worthy of your love.'

Sia sank into sheer despair. *It'll be okay. The storm will pass.* But whenever she was sad, the first face that came to her mind was Simran's. *Is this her curse? Is karma paying me back?* The media was having a field day, writing about how Karma was a bitch and Raj was being punished for deserting his wife and kids for Sia the seductress.

It is difficult to watch someone you love stumble and fall. It was harder for the undemonstrative Karan to convey his helplessness and his desire to extend his support. Karan would try to talk to Raj, but Raj shrugged him off. By himself,

Karan was a content individual, happy with his two-films-a-year routine. It was not that he was not ambitious enough or that he was lazy. Karan would have loved to step up his career by a notch or two if he could. He secretly nursed the ambition of becoming a producer like his father. He would never admit it, but he did want to make many films and get wildly famous like his older brother.

The only difference however was that Karan was a bit more practical. Knowing how fickle returns in the industry were, he was loathe to put his hard-earned money at risk. Even the hard-nosed, ever realistic Kavita discouraged him from doing so. She played it safe, hoping for a break or a miracle, whichever came sooner.

Around this time, Karan received an offer to dance at a controversial yet influential businessman's son's wedding in Dubai. His first reaction was to turn it down. After all, if rumours were anything to go by, the man had links with the underworld. But the money on offer was too tempting. He succumbed. He travelled to Dubai and performed at the event that turned out to be a super success. The businessman couldn't stop raving about Karan's performance. A few weeks later, Karan couldn't believe his eyes: in front of him lay a contract to sign for a film as the lead. It was a slapstick comedy, but nothing changed the fact that Karan was being offered the lead role in a big budget film.

'Don't take it,' many told him. Apparently, the businessman had strong connections with the underworld. But Karan and Kavita felt that the source of the money was irrelevant. The break was big. 'And I'm doing my job; I'm not joining the underworld,' he said to Kavita who nodded. If he refused the offer, would an opportunity like this ever come again? There was so much talk about the offer that Karan didn't even want to consult his father or brother.

It was a rustic film which involved Karan dancing around with village belles to songs that bordered on the obscene. He dressed tackily, spoke cheaply and pandered to all the typical male machismo stereotypes that the masses loved. He played the kind of guy who would crack jokes about the anatomy of women and treat the female lead as furniture and little else. In short, it was a crass, loud and tartish comedy, the kind that would appeal to the front benchers. Not something you would take your family to see.

The film was an instant hit. It provoked a lot of whistles and catcalls. Karan was flooded with offers from other directors. All of them were similar roles. But Karan had had fun doing his hit film, and the money was like nothing he had seen before. So he went ahead and signed all of them.

'Are you sure?' Ashima had asked him. 'I mean, do you really want to play the village buffoon over and over again?'

'Love it!' said Karan, with a twinkle in his eye.

One man, who had long been too silent a witness to the events in his family, was Bhupinder. He wondered what the fate of this first film family that he helmed was going to be. Raj was fast plummeting down the popularity charts. Sia was ruling the roost, no small feat by any standards in the male-dominated industry. Ironically, the reason she was not the number-one actress was the arrival of Ashima who was doing so well for herself that, slowly but surely, she would have the pick of the best assignments and endorsements. At long last, the understated Karan was also getting his due. He had become a star in his own right.

The only cloud on Bhupinder's horizon was Karan's involvement with the businessman who was financing these films as rumours of the identity of the man behind the front man now began to be discussed in the media. Karan had recently been signed on for two more movies backed by the same man. Bhupinder knew that one wrong move with these people could mean crossing the fine line between life and death.

He watched Kavita enjoy Karan's success. Karan was one of the few actors who had crossed the hundred crore-mark in box office collections in a solo lead. No matter what critics said about it being a populist movie, the fact was that it was a successful film. Karan was a very busy man now, wanted everywhere from at the openings of shops to major award functions. Kavita couldn't stop smiling.

Bhupinder sighed. The filmy microcosm was a fickle one. One day up did not mean you could occupy the privileged seat forever. Worse, there were no formulae that guaranteed access to the top or ways to stay there. Raj was languishing on the fringes of stardom yet again, so fickle was this business. *Raj is such a bad sport. He does not know how to take defeat gracefully.*

With the underdog finally rising up, Kavita decided it was time she too acquired the status that suited a star wife. She decided to start something else of her own, apart from the fashion designing studio. She eventually zeroed in on a spa. This would be no ordinary spa. She decided to open a high-end, state-of-the-art spa fit for the stars. When Karan asked her, 'But you already have the fashion business. Why do you want to get into other things?' Kavita replied smugly, 'I am your wife. Like people know you, people should soon know me too as a public figure. This is the first step in that direction.'

While Sia did express her delight over Karan's good run, she was guarded in doing so. She was suffering for Raj's failures. Life was so ironic. She was at the top, she had the pick of the choicest films and everyone wanted to work with her. Yet it was embarrassing because everyone was busy writing Raj off. Every day she went to work knowing Raj was going to spend the day watching television and doing little else while she would be working with yet another heartthrob. Such was her life that, in order to promote a film, the makers were never above spreading salacious gossip, especially if it involved the lead actors. Sia's name was currently being linked to her co-star Bakhtawar. There was no truth to it, but Raj would look uncomfortable if his name cropped up.

At the home front, too, it was not easy. Sia had given her best in trying to get the family to love her. But the Mehras still missed Simran and things went on pretty much the way Simran had streamlined them. And with Kavita always so wary around her, how was she supposed to bond with anyone?

One evening, after dinner, Sia and Raj were strolling near the guarded beach outside their home when she decided to talk things through. She said, 'Raj, I don't know what problem Kavita and Ashima have with me. Kavita always keeps her distance from me, like she is waiting for me to make the first move.'

Raj said, 'Then why don't you? I am sure she would like it.'

Sia said, 'I have tried, but somehow I never get the response I expect. She is cold and nullifies any effort I make towards friendliness. Oh Raj, this was not what I had expected when I moved into this family! I had wanted everyone to love me, but nobody does, not even Ashima. She is one of the most famous actresses now. But she is still so wary of me. I agree that professionally we are rivals, but that does not mean we cannot be friends at home.'

Sia was talking, but she knew Raj was too preoccupied with his own life to bother about anyone else. Irritated, she said, 'Raj, are you listening or am I just talking to the wind?'

Raj was stung by her tone. *How dare she speak to him like this? Just because she now earned more than him, it did not give her the right to treat him as if he was her servant.* He pursed his lips. If she wanted him to speak, he would give her the opposite: silence. Sia stopped walking and shouted at him, 'Raj? Did you hear me? I am talking to you!'

Raj lost his cool and shouted back, 'What!? What do you want me to say? That it will be okay? It won't. Nothing will be okay any more. You should have listened to me when I said moving here was a bad idea. They can never love you, Sia. They love Simran too much for that. Don't waste your time trying to bond with them.' He stomped off to their bedroom, leaving a stunned Sia alone.

Things were tough, but if there was one thing Sia had learnt from her and her mother's life, it was this: nothing in life worth fighting for ever came easy. She knew things were depressing, but she would eventually triumph. Things would go the way Sia wanted, eventually. They would have to. Her mother was her angel, looking out for her. She would give Sia the strength she needed to overcome all obstacles.

She sat down on the cool sand. The night breeze felt good against her face. She stared out at the endless sea and knew she would prevail in the end. All she needed was patience.

24

All those months of writing had finally paid off, thought Simran as she looked at a bunch of papers bound together. She was staring at her screenplay. She had been so full of doubts, so uncertain to begin with. If it had reached completion, the credit went largely to Kabir. He had been a true friend, philosopher and guide to her these past few months. Every time she felt the script was not worth the effort, he was there to ensure she soldiered on. He had been so good to her, so supportive of her even though he had no reason to be so.

Simran was glad to be in her current frame of mind. She did not have famous or terribly important people in her life any more. But the ones she did have were worth more to her than the entire world. There was Kabir, to begin with. And then, last night, Divya had insisted on a party to celebrate the completion of her script. So the three of them had gone out together, teasing and joking all the while.

In the course of writing the script, Simran had realized how much she enjoyed writing and how much she had been missing out on all these years. She knew now that this was what she was born to do, irrespective of the outcome. She knew she could happily grow old writing. *I need to now pitch this to producers. Stop building castles in the air, Simran.*

The doorbell rang. Simran opened the door to see Raj standing there. *Oh shoot! He was supposed to take the kids out this evening.* She smiled a little and said, 'Come in, Raj. The kids are ready. I'll just call them.'

Simran was about to walk away when Raj spotted her screenplay on the table, and asked, 'Is that your script? The one you were writing?' *How did he know that? The kids must have told him.* She nodded a bit self-consciously.

Raj walked in and seated himself in the living room, saying, 'Simran, before you choose to approach producers with it, please think hard. Don't make a fool of yourself ... and me too. You don't know a thing about writing; you've never taken a formal course or anything. If you really want to do something with your life, try something else; something that is not so entrenched in the film industry.'

Piqued, Simran asked Raj, 'Really? Like what?'

Raj calmly said, 'You could open a boutique, you know. It'll give you something to pass the time and save you the effort of going from office to office trying to convince people ...'

Simran felt shaken. Nodding vaguely to Raj, she called out to Tarun and Trishala.

Soon, after Raj left with the kids, Simran was assailed by self-doubt again. She did not feel so sure of herself any more, and said as much to Kabir over coffee later in the evening.

'Simran, how can anybody else decide what you ought to do?' said Kabir. 'The least that you can do is decide what you want to spend the rest of your life doing. Why are you scared of showing your work around? Show it, and if it is not good enough, make it better. If it still does not work, only then must you take a call on what to do next. But please do not do this to yourself before you have even taken the first step.'

Simran sighed. 'Thanks, Kabir. I don't know what I would have done without you.'

'Don't thank me. You can return the favour by giving me a role in your film later; the hero's if possible,' he said with a poker face and she began to laugh. Kabir was right. She really did not have anything to lose. On the other hand, if something did come out of her writing, it would give a direction to her aimless life. She would finally have an identity as someone more than just a famous actor's ex-wife. Her resolve strengthened yet again.

Simran had not expected an easy entry into the world of films just because she had been an intrinsic part of the line for so long, but she also did not expect what she got. Even after appointments had been fixed, producers, who had earlier fallen on their knees to impress her when she was Mrs Raj Mehra, would now mysteriously disappear as soon as she turned up at their offices. They would either be 'out of town', or 'in a meeting,' or simply unavailable. Simran would wait with her file in hand for hours and then be turned out.

But she plodded on. She kept visiting offices and kept getting a 'we aren't really looking out for anything' wherever she went. No one even had the time to listen to her story. Surprisingly, the more Simran heard a no, the more she became determined to ensure her script saw the light of day. She reminded herself of Ashima every time she felt dejected.

Things were not quite hunky-dory at Vardaan these days. Karan's fortunes were poised for another turnaround, though this time veering towards a dead end. Pictures of him dancing at the don's wedding many months ago came back to haunt him as they were flashed across the media, accompanied by rumours and accusations that flew fast and thick. Overnight, he was out of work. No one wanted him on board their assignments now because of the baggage he came with. Bhupinder and Kamla were silently devastated.

Since Ashima was the star at Vardaan these days, she knew the press would soon be hounding her. Sure enough, as soon as the media saw Ashima, they went into a frenzy. 'Is it true, Karan is involved with the underworld?', 'What is the extent of his assets?', 'Is Karan Mehra a traitor to his country?', 'Is he ashamed of his actions?' But Ashima kept her head low and mouth shut. All she wanted to do was to help Karan get over this mess.

It broke Raj's heart to see what his younger brother was being subjected to, and for a minute, he was glad he had never reached such a phase in life where he was linked with the underworld.

As tough as Karan's sentence was on him, it was tougher on Kavita. She wept for days, refusing food or any kind of consolation. She blamed herself for not stopping Karan at the right time. Karan was paying a heavy price for Kavita's unbridled ambition.

The one person who made a big effort to pull her out of her misery was Simran. She began to visit Kavita and tried to coax her out of her shell. She told her that none of this was her fault. They could not have foreseen how all of this would end. Moreover, she assured Kavita that this too would pass. 'You can't sit around moping. Think of Soham and Aanya.'

Even Ashima reached out to Kavita. The meaning and importance of family became clear to Kavita then. The people she had never valued were the ones who stood by her in hard times.

In the midst of all of this, Simran was busy trying to meet producers. On one such trip, she bumped into Subhash Bhai. She was surprised but Subhash Bhai was positively embarrassed about meeting her this way. He remembered the time when Simran was the wife of Raj Mehra, the queen of her castle. Now, here she was, going from office to office like an ordinary scriptwriter. He felt bad for her as he asked, 'Simran bhabhi, what are you doing here?'

Simran replied, 'Subhash Bhai, I am here trying to show the producer my script. I ... have written something.' Instantly, Subhash Bhai remembered Simran's script intervention once and how he had been impressed by it.

'Why don't you give me the script? I can read it and let you know if I can be of any help.' Simran gladly handed him her story. She was nervous, but she knew Subhash Bhai meant well.

Once she had given away her story, panic set in. She could imagine him laughing at her. She could imagine him calling someone over the phone and reading out parts and mocking her.

After a month-long, agonizing wait, Simran decided she had been foolish to expect anything from Subhash Bhai. *Should I give up on a dream because I find no believers*? It was better not to wait for his call and to start going to producers' offices yet again. Someday, luck would smile on her.

The next day, just as she was setting out, she received Subhash Bhai's call. 'Will you come to my office? Right now?' Before she could ask him more, he had hung up. Simran was a bundle of nerves as she waited in his office. She was mentally preparing to defend her effort if he decided to berate it. Soon Subhash Bhai entered, beaming. He sat down and apologized saying, 'Simran Bhabhi, I am sorry about not being able to get in touch earlier. I was really, well ... busy.' He smiled sheepishly and Simran relaxed.

He said, 'So I know the question topmost in your mind right now: what do I think of it? I will be honest with you ...' Simran braced herself for the worst, as he continued, perhaps deliberately building up the suspense ... 'I liked it. In fact, I liked it a lot. Your script has a lot of promise, Bhabhi. But you will need to work on a second draft to iron out some issues that I have marked. But it's really very good for a first effort.' Simran could not believe what she had just heard.

Subhash Bhai saw the look of disbelief on Simran's face and the tears in her eyes. He knew she had been through a lot and he was happy for her. He did not know what to do, whether to step up and pat her shoulder, or clasp her hand, or merely stay put. In his mind, flashed images of her in the fifteen years he had known her and Raj; from the time she was an actor to when she became the lovely wife of a superstar, to a hands-on mother, and now, to a humble, struggling writer. He got up, patted her shoulder and gave her his spanking-white handkerchief. Then he walked across to the wide bay windows of his office to offer Simran some privacy to compose herself.

'I'm sorry,' said Simran, regaining her voice. 'I'm really sorry, but I don't know how to handle happiness after so much sadness.' Subhash Bhai felt sad to hear this. 'I understand, Simran Bhabhi. But put the past behind you and look ahead to a new career. I am going to speak with Nikhil Patel to produce this film. I assume you are okay with the idea.'

Simran gasped. 'Okay? Subhash Bhai, how can I ever thank you for this?'

'Write more such stories. Really, you do have the talent. Don't doubt yourself, not one bit. You are very good, just keep at it.'

Simran stepped out of the office into bright sunshine. On the way home, she stopped to pick up macaroons from Tarun and Trishala's favourite bakery. She bought lots of them, in all flavours. She felt so happy, she could have bought the store as well.

She surprised Shammi and the kids with her news and, while they were very happy for her, Simran was a bit cautious about her achievement. She was scared of being too happy. They all practically lunched just on macaroons. 'Shall we go out for dinner tonight?' she asked. 'I have one more thing to do,' Simran said.

She had to tell Kabir. Not over the phone but in person. She had called him up and asked him to meet her at a restaurant. Today's meal would be on her. And now, as she saw him enter the restaurant, a feeling that had been rearing its head these days assailed her yet again. She loved seeing Kabir, but today, she had noticed a look of discomfort on Tarun's face when she said she was going to see him, and especially since she had taken pains to dress, unlike most days before this. But children were like that, possessive about their parents, friends and teachers at this age. *Maybe I am just imagining all this.*

Kabir's baritone voice, which had always told her not to doubt herself, was like a lifeline when she felt she was drowning in a sea of desperation. She loved the way he handled everything. He treated her like she was special. He had all the time in the world to listen to her problems and he never made her feel small. This was a new feeling, and she knew she was getting far more attached to him than she should.

'What are you so busy thinking about?' asked Kabir and, immediately snapped Simran out of her reverie. She smiled and said, 'I am so happy to see you! Sit down, I want to tell you something.' Kabir sat down and said, 'Well, if you want to tell me you want to marry me, I'll consider the offer!' Simran laughed out loud. 'Just what I was thinking! Dream on, Kabir! No, I wanted to tell you something else. Guess what? Subhash Bhai called me to his office today and told me he loved my script!'

Simran looked at him with anticipation and Kabir did not disappoint. He sat at the edge of his chair as he asked, 'And ...?' Simran continued, 'And he has passed it on to Nikhil Patel. He wants him to produce it!' Kabir punched his fist in the air and said, 'Yes! Simran, I knew this would happen. Your story is really good and you definitely have the talent to pull it off. Not just that, once it is released, it will set the box office on fire. You wait and see.' They ordered champagne to celebrate and Kabir raised a toast, saying, 'To Simran, the screenwriter, who is about to take Bollywood by storm.'

Simran grinned and took a sip of her champagne. She had not felt this happy and excited in a long time. Things were indeed beginning to turn around. Her children were settling down to a routine, accepting their surroundings. Shammi, her mother, who was unhappy with her decision also seemed to realize it was for the best, and could not hide her joy. Things were indeed looking up for Simran and she had only one man to thank for it all. That man was looking at her affectionately now and she realized how much he meant to her. If she did not see him for a few days, she would begin to feel helpless.

Simran loved meeting Kabir, but she dared not admit it to herself. Now, as she sat in front of him and he looked into her eyes, no words were necessary. Simran felt strangely vulnerable, and she tried to get a grip on the situation by saying, 'Kabir, this lunch is to say thank you. I would not have been here if it weren't for you. I can never thank you enough. I will remember this all my life.'

Kabir now put his finger on his lips and said, 'Shhhh. You don't need to thank me, Simran. Everything I said to you, ever, was born out of the belief that you really do have the talent to do something big with your life. So, if there is anyone you should thank, it's yourself.'

He knew he would have to say the one thing that had been tormenting him for a while now. He had to tell her how he felt about her or else it would be too late.

Kabir delicately held Simran's hand in his. Simran was surprised, but Kabir continued to look unflinchingly at her and said, 'I don't know what you will think of me after I say this. But believe me, Simran, it has to be said. I have fallen in love with you. And I really fear that if I do not tell you this right now, some other idiot will. And where will that leave me?'

Simran gently pulled her hand away. How could he be saying this? She had felt it herself too, but now hearing it from him ... She had been enjoying his company, looked forward to meeting him, had felt young and happy again after a long time ... Yet something didn't feel right, and the minute Kabir said it, she felt uneasy. Kabir was so young. Undaunted by her silence, Kabir looked at her and continued, 'I know it's too soon. But, marry me, Simran. I can't live without you.'

His words were like magic. They sounded so beautiful. But ... There was always a 'but'. Simran had to think not just about herself but her family. *No one is going to be happy with this. He is a mere boy. Tarun, Trishala, Mamma ... I have so many to think of before I encourage this.* She looked at Kabir and lied, 'Kabir, thank you so much for saying what you did ... for making me feel so special. You've been a wonderful friend to me.'

Kabir looked stricken as she continued. 'Kabir, I have been through so much, that now, I really have nothing left of myself to give to a relationship. For me, my children always have and always will come first and, besides, look at you. You're so young. You deserve someone your age, someone much better than me.'

Kabir gripped her hand and said, 'But I don't want anyone else.'

Simran shook her head and said, 'That is what you think now. But believe me, you will feel differently in a few years. What can you get from a life with me? Lots of emotional baggage, and two stepchildren who are half your age. No, Kabir, it is not a good idea.'

Simran was torn by conflict, but she knew she was doing the right thing. She loved him, but by being with him, she would only harm him.

Kabir was deeply affected. He said, 'You alone do not get to decide what's wrong and what is right. I love you, Simran. And if you feel you are not ready, I will wait. Simran, I promise I will wait till the end of time. I know you will feel differently one day.'

'Please don't do this, Kabir,' said Simran coldly. 'Please don't make this more difficult than it already is. I will not feel differently.' Kabir's face crumpled. He gathered himself and slowly got up from his chair.

He walked out, leaving Simran alone. She felt crushed. How had things become so complicated so suddenly? Here they were, toasting to happiness just a few moments ago. Little had Simran known that Kabir felt the same way about her as she did for him. *Why could life not be easy? I wish you could have held me, Kabir. I wish I could live a lifetime with you. I know you will be gentle and considerate with me. I know I will be happy. Why did happiness and sadness always have to go hand in hand?*

But this was how she had felt with Raj when she decided to marry him. She had been absolutely sure. She had known he would be gentle and considerate. She had had her precious children with him. And how things had turned. Could she trust another man—a much younger one this time—again? Tears began to flow from Simran's eyes. Her heart wanted Kabir but her head pulled in the reins. *You've done the right thing.*

Simran rose from the table and picked up her keys. *He'll be all right.* She already missed him. One part of her wanted to call him back and apologize.

25

While Simran was busy finding her foothold in the industry, Raj was losing *his* fast. The downside of drawing one's entire sense of self-worth from one's profession and performance at work is that, if one's work life suffers, one's personal life does too. Raj was no exception. With his market worth going downhill, he took to drinking excessively and often turned up at shoots in an inebriated state.

He would bicker on the sets, making life miserable for anyone who had the misfortune of being around him. Mahesh saw his boss slide from number one to a has-been. It was still not too late to pick the threads and figure out the pattern of the maze. Mahesh only wished his boss would clean up his act soon.

But Raj refused to listen to anyone. He had begun to have constant fights with Sia too. He blamed her for everything that was going wrong in his life. Sia earned for them both to spend as they liked. Despite that, she had to listen to him rant. Raj had run into debts and she dared not bring it up, fearing it would destroy his fragile ego.

Eventually, all offers dried up. Raj, being Raj, would not touch roles that had been rejected by others. The few stray offers that did come his way were so insignificant that he declared one day to Mahesh, 'Mahesh, stop wasting my time with this trash. It's beneath me to even entertain the idea of taking up these roles.'

'Sir, listen to the roles, they are interesting. Sometimes, a smaller part carries more impact than even lead roles.'

'Mahesh, who's the star here, you or me?' yelled Raj. 'Don't try to teach me. Do as I say. Throw these crappy offers back at the people who sent them to you. I don't do such shit.' Raj Mehra felt no regret in refusing these roles.

In his decades-long career with Raj, Mahesh had never felt as infuriated with him as he did lately. The man was on a downward spiral and did not even want to cut his ego to size in an effort to stop it. At times, he felt like leaving his job and putting an end to his silent suffering. But then, life was not simple. He had a family to take care of and, so far, the pay had been good.

Simran was a bunch of nerves as she dressed for the meeting of a lifetime. In just two hours, she was going to meet Nikhil Patel, the man who could launch her. She dressed carefully, choosing a crisp, cotton Fab India churidar kurta. She smiled as she put on a hint of kajal and remembered, for the nth time in these last few months, the time when she had been married to Raj. How different that life had been!

Back then, the most important activity of her day was getting dressed, with a host of designer labels to choose from. It seemed like a lifetime ago. She sprayed on her favourite Chanel, the one physical reminder of her past she was still happily attached to.

If things had been fine between her and Kabir, she would have been on the phone constantly with him, talking about the various aspects of her story, finding loopholes and plugging them. But she had not spoken to Kabir since that lunch. And she did not think she should either. A clean break was the best bet for him. Trishala had asked her a few days ago why she was not meeting Kabir lately. 'My work is over,' Simran explained to her, 'I no longer need to meet him.' If Simran had raised her eyes and looked at Trishala, she would have found her daughter looking visibly relieved.

Nikhil's office was done up in an elegant way, unlike many of the film company offices she had earlier seen. It was designed to make people feel comfortable rather than impose the importance of its occupants. Simran was not made to wait too long. She was surprised to see Nikhil Patel in person. He looked thinner in real life than he looked on screen at various award shows, and younger as well. *Only a couple of years older than me, at the most.*

'Come in, Simran,' said Nikhil, waving her in. 'Finally we meet. Subhash Bhai gave me your script, which I have gone through.' Simran looked at him smiling nervously. 'And ...?' she asked.

'Let's make it.' Simran let out a sigh of relief. These were the sweetest words she had ever heard. It was a defining moment in her life. Smiling, she said, 'Thank you, Mr Patel. You have no idea what this ...' He interrupted her saying, 'Please, call me Nikhil.' She nodded. 'Nikhil, you have no clue how much this means to me.'

Nikhil looked serious as he said, 'Simran, you have been in this industry for so long. You should know that no one does anyone a favour. Ideas and talent are all that matter. I have not done you a favour by signing you on. You really have a good script and it deserves to reach out to people. But you will work on a revised script with the director and, if we are satisfied—and there is no reason why we should not be—we are in business.'

Simran took in the praise and, emboldened by it, she said, 'Nikhil, there is something else I wanted to mention. I know I have no experience in this line. But experience comes only with ...' 'Experience?' Nikhil interjected. Simran nodded eagerly in agreement and said, 'Exactly. Nikhil, if you are okay with the idea, I would like to assist in directing the film, too. That way, I will learn a lot and improve my writing in future.'

This was totally unexpected. Nikhil wondered if it would be a wise idea to trust a first-time writer with direction. It wasn't a big film anyway, in terms of budget, and would fit in nicely as a small scale project for their subsidiary company. Nikhil believed in his creative hunches and he would be damned if he let ambivalence get in the way of it now. Looking at the beautiful, talented woman in front of him, he decided to go with his instinct. 'Okay,' he said cautiously. 'We will think about it.'

'You will not regret it,' she grinned, unable to conceal her joy. They shook hands and Simran left Nikhil's office with the mantle of Assistant Director and a signing amount in hand.

When Simran went home, she didn't tell anything to anyone. Shammi anxiously looked at her, not wanting to ask because Simran seemed to be fighting something inside her.

After a while, clutching an envelope, she said, 'Mamma ... I got it.'

Shammi wept and then laughed loudly. Simran stood there, blinking and smiling.

Later, when it sank in, Simran called Ashima. She wanted to call Kabir and tell him. She knew he would be supremely happy. But she didn't want to open that door, for his sake. Then she waited to tell the kids.

Ashima was ecstatic. 'I discovered you first, Bhabhi! When you get famous, remember to tell that to everyone!'

Simran's story was a romantic comedy about a village that was starving and how a spunky young girl from the village turned its fortunes around by faking the discovery of a few antique artefacts there, and in the process, turned around her own life too. Ashima had always liked the story, but a hesitant Simran hadn't dared to share its screenplay with her, until it had been validated by someone in the know of such matters.

Today, Simran confidently read it out to her, scene after scene, peppering it with all the expressions and passion that she had heard scriptwriters put into their narration with Raj through the years.

After the girlie hysterics died down, Ashima had something else to say to Simran. She said, 'Bhabhi, the reason I came today is because I wanted to tell you something. I want to act in your debut film. Will you recommend me?' Simran laughed. Ashima was a major actress in the industry now, and it was a huge risk for her to do this small film, so Simran hadn't dared consider it. She was moved that Ashima herself wanted to do it. She said, 'Ashima, you are a sweetheart, but please understand that you don't have to do this for me, unless it's right for you.'

Ashima held her hands and said, 'Even you did not have to stand up for me every time you did. Bhabhi, I am doing this because I want to. And about a film being right for an actor, no one can say that for sure anyway. I love you, so let me do this for you.'

Ashima was signed on for the lead female role in Simran's debut film. To Nikhil, it was just another confirmation to always follow his gut feeling. He had wanted to work with Ashima for a long time, and now she had practically attached herself to the project. By now he felt completely okay with Simran at the virtual helm of the movie. She had written it and he knew she could faithfully help the director, Diwakar Pandey, recreate her vision on the camera.

After months, Simran began to sleep well. She was amazed by how little she thought of Raj. To think the man had written off her work so recently. While flipping channels, she had seen that Raj and Sia were sliding off the popularity chart. But she felt no sense of vindication. She missed Kabir very often. She missed swapping notes with him. She missed calling him up for trivial things and her long conversations with him. But most of the time, she had no time for anything except taking care of the kids and going to work.

26

Everything seemed unfamiliar to Raj. *I'm looking at people who can't see me any more.* He didn't realize that a large part of why producers and other professionals from the industry avoided him was his own doing. If you go to public places in an inebriated state and tell people what you think of them, there aren't many who will look forward to meeting you.

At home, he snarled at his parents and nothing Sia did for him was seen minus suspicion. 'Just because you bring in the money, don't think you've bought me over!' He would scream.

But Raj didn't really see it that way. The media had written him off. Film offers had dried up. Sia was soaring professionally. Everyone's life at Vardaan was the same as the money that came in through Sia was flowing. It was only he who was suffering. He and his massive ego kept him from getting himself out of the financial mess he had slipped into because that would involve going out and asking for work. As Raj Mehra, the superstar, it was beneath him to do that.

Then came in the news that Simran was scripting a film, and was also going to be assistant director to one of Nikhil

Patel's films. *Was it possible?* Raj decided to ignore it. *Simran? No way!*

Considering how awful his life was, Raj was most surprised one day when he bumped into Shubham at a paan shop he had stopped by to get cigarettes very late in the night. Raj thought it was ironical that the Shubham he had always ridiculed and cast aside, the friend he had considered no threat to him was, today, a name to reckon with.

Shubham, a slightly rotund guy, not considered good-looking by conventional Bollywood standards, had learnt to swim with the flow, and with the coming of the current wave of new generation cinema, he was a much wanted man.

On seeing him, Shubham affably got into Raj's car, telling his own driver to follow. He looked at Raj and said, 'What are you doing to yourself?' Raj laughed sarcastically and said, 'For full details of what I have been up to, you can consult any tabloid. It will tell you how I am on a downward spiral, waiting to be finished and—'

Shubham cut him off saying, 'Stop feeling sorry for yourself. You still have a lot going for you, Raj.'

Raj looked at him and asked, 'Really? Like what? A failed marriage? A super-successful wife? A flop career?'

Shubham then said, 'Raj, you never believed me then, but I will still say it again. The reason I managed to survive for so long was that I changed and adapted to the times. I began my drama school, I kept myself involved with theatre, and I also took quality roles over quantity. Today, if I have reached somewhere in life, it's because I adapted. You can do it too.'

Raj leered at him. 'So you are telling me that you want me to go from being the lead to doing smaller parts? Are you telling me to make way for someone else?'

Shubham nodded saying, 'If you don't make way, you will be forced to leave. Raj, do roles that require real emoting, not the ones where you play a college boy. You will pull it off. Believe me. And you will be better at it than I can ever hope to be.'

Raj shook his head saying, 'It's okay for you to do what you are doing. But I was a superstar. For me to take small parts will be a telling act. Big words my friend, but really tough to follow through.'

Shubham insisted, 'The Raj I know can do it. The question is: are you that man, or have you let this world get to you?'

Raj petulantly ignored him the rest of the way. Shubham left squeezing Raj's shoulder.

But something Shubham said struck a chord and he mulled over it all the way back home.

Raj and Sia had not been speaking to each other for a week. She had, yet again, insisted that he go out and ask producers for some roles and he had, yet again, told her that he would not do it. Things had turned bitter and she had accused him of putting her through so much stress with his failure and financial mismanagement that she had to get back to work just to bring in the funds to maintain the appearances they had to keep up in society.

It had hurt Raj to be told what he had known all along. He had walked out on her that night and spent the hours drinking. Sia, for her part, felt bad about having said what she had to Raj, but she had to shake him out of his complacency. She knew that he had it in him to make a fantastic comeback, but he did not want to do the work required for it. So, she had kept up with her blistering pace of work. She genuinely wanted to take things a bit easy, but the huge debts they were in, and the need to show a solid front in society, ensured she had no respite.

Sia had begun to believe this was all the result of her bad karma. She was getting as good as she had given. Hadn't she forced Simran out of her marriage and house? Hadn't her desperation to have Raj all to herself forced his children to get used to a life without their father? She had begun to experience bouts of overpowering guilt, and, try as she might, she could not shake off the feeling.

Simran's first film was a tough one to make. It was set in a village and so, while a set was created for the indoor scenes, major portions of the film had to be shot in a village. Ashima had been unstinting in her support for Simran, and once she had signed on for the film, it was not difficult to get more talented people on board her dream project. The unit went to a dusty village on the outskirts of Nasik and began shooting.

Simran had always been an eager learner and she did not hesitate to admit any mistake on her part. The director, a young man who had made two films before, liked Simran's work ethic. He praised her to his crew, saying that, if at Simran's age she could learn new skills, why couldn't the rest of them? The unit was friendly and everyone worked as one big family, supporting and standing up for each other, sometimes fighting and arguing like family members would. It was an exciting time for Simran. With Shammi taking care of the kids in her absence, there was nothing to worry about. On the sets, Simran's maturity often helped her iron out many a squabble between unit hands. She was nicknamed 'agony aunt' by Ashima who herself was quite the prankster.

Simran also proved her worth, giving deeper insights to the actors about their characters and why they did what they did. She learnt a lot on the shoot, and went out of her way to put everyone at ease as she sprung around the sets, serving cups of tea around, or helping put rollers on Ashima's hair when the assistant hairdresser played truant. It made her feel young and sprightly as she had never felt before, never mind that it took the others some time getting used to seeing and accepting the ex-Mrs Raj Mehra in her new avatar.

Nikhil dropped in on the sets a couple of times too. Even Divya and Mouli made a day trip to see her with pastries and cupcakes for everyone on the set.

Once the film was shot and pack-up announced, Nikhil took a look at the first rushes. He was impressed by what he saw. Simran, he realized, was a rare combination of beauty and brains. He had not expected the film to look this good and was glad he had taken her on.

The release of Simran's film coincided with Sia's, but that did not bother her. She had learnt long ago that hard work never went to waste. She had faith in her own work. The media made a big deal of the two films going head to head, almost like this were a war between Raj's wives—ex and current. Simran, who had risen above all the pettiness, wished the media wouldn't play up on the wrong things. She remained silent.

The film was a much bigger hit than Sia's latest. Since the subject was so woman-centric and yet, a commercial one, the critics were impressed. Simran suddenly found herself being analysed by the media as well as news weeklies as the chosen one—the one writer and assistant female director who would overcome gender stereotypes that limited women in this field.

Simran had been in the film world for too long to take anything that the media said seriously. She decided that she was not going to let today's reviews go to her head.

I'm going to try different things. As she told Nikhil when he teased her about what was being said, 'I'm going to work on stories—it does not matter if what I have to say has a female-centric angle or a male-centric theme.' But she realized that Nikhil was only pulling her leg, and laughed. *I want to make quality films. I want to tell powerful stories. I don't want to get carried away by titles or tags.*

One day, while sitting by herself, Simran realized how far she had come. *When it happened, it just happened. There was no struggle. I met Kabir by chance. We worked on the story for a bit and then, the appointment with Nikhil Patel happened. What is meant to be just happens. It flows. There is no struggle. One struggles when one resists the inevitable. I resisted the break-up of my marriage. It was a struggle simply because I did not accept that it was for my best. I would have been brain dead in that marriage.*

Simran also marvelled at how women in general had come a long way in this profession. Here was Simran, the wife of a superstar with no identity whatsoever of her own. But thanks to the people in her life, she had found her feet in this world of stories. Then there was Ashima who had walked out of her marriage and the industry had tested her tenacity by giving her a flop to start with. But talent alone made her reach the highest position today. People now respected Ashima and fell at her feet with offers.

Simran could see the change in the attitude of press towards her. They were always championing her cause, her words. The same people who chased her, calling her fat, now celebrated her stories, marvelled at the irony behind her humour. The film industry was a forgiving place, a trusting place, a kind place, a place where one entered in whichever way one liked, but could never leave. Showbiz did have a soul, it had a heart. It was just. It rewarded the worthy and punished the ones who deserved worse. But most of all, it was home. And to Simran, it was her happily ever after—the knowledge that she would always be accepted here. Simran was exactly where she wanted to be.

27

I can die now. Shammi was thrilled for her daughter. Simran was being hailed. She was the toast of the town. Life had tested her and she came through victorious. For a long time, she tried to steer Simran's life and had made wrong decisions for her. Now, she knew Simran would be all right. The kids too were growing up. The stigma they had faced with a high profile divorce had disappeared and now they were basking in the glory of their mother's success.

But Shammi knew that even if things turned—and life had a way with turning things—they would be okay. They had grown up in a storm. They would appreciate good weather and would know how to tide over bad ones too.

I can die now. I know they will be okay. Shammi was feeling tired. She wrote it off as fatigue. *I'm getting old.* I've been on high alert for too long now. Tarun and Trishala ... Need to go down and pick them up from the gate. Wearily, Shammi shuffled into her slippers.

Both kids returned home with their nani, chattering and telling her about school. Shammi listened and smiled. With them around, she always felt more energized. Trishala was holding her hand and Tarun was taller than her. Both the kids had voluntarily begun to maintain a distance from their father. If Manvi's birth had created cracks in their relationship, Raj's decision to give up custody of his children had cemented their dislike for him. It had hurt so much that their father did not want them.

Tarun would have loved to have a male role model to look up to. But when Simran began meeting that young man, Kabir, Shammi sensed the children's intuitive hostility towards another man. She sighed. Life would take its own course. Whoever looked after everyone would look after these two uncut diamonds too.

Raj had brought upon this burden upon himself. When Simran got her huge break in the form of her first film, Raj continued to show the world what a bad sport he was. Instead of congratulating her, he went around telling anyone who would listen that Simran was a dimwit and must have received a lot of help from Nikhil and Subhash Bhai.

When he accidentally bumped into Simran at one of the rare parties she went to, he grudgingly acknowledged her success. 'I'm surprised,' he said. 'Beginner's luck, huh?'

Success had made Simran realize the necessity to stay close to ground level—like the importance of earthing to electricity, as her electrician had once philosophized. She smiled and said, 'Thank you, Raj.'

One look at his tried, puffy face told her he had enough problems of his own. With that, she walked past, leaving behind a confused Raj.

This was the first time she had walked out on him in the middle of a conversation. All those years, it was always he who had decided when to end an exchange.

The one thing that Simran had to accept, whether she liked it or not, was the fact that the media would stay in their lives.

The newspaper made a story of Raj's comment that Simran's success was pure luck. *Cosmopolitan, Savvy* and *Femina* wanted Simran on the cover of their magazines. She would make great copy and good pictures. Everyone wanted to know her journey from divorce to discourse as one journalist put it. They wanted to know how she coped with the kids, with divorce, with unhappiness and rejection. The media now wanted to become her best friend.

But Simran refused to speak about that time. 'Can you please focus on my work rather than my personal life?' she had asked one persistent journalist.

Unfortunately, one magazine did some research and ran a half-baked story about Simran and Kabir. *Anything for a scandal,* thought Simran as she flung the tabloid in disgust. The magazine insinuated that Simran and Kabir had had a sizzling relationship. Ignore it, Simran thought stoically, wondering if Kabir was okay.

Little did Simran know that the story would cause a furore in her house.

When Trishala came to Simran with the story, she was crying and said, 'Mamma, I never thought you would do this ...' She looked accusingly at Simran. Simran was stunned. *How on earth did the kids get a whiff of this?* Simran knew she had to deal with this issue head on, or else, it would fester into something much worse.

'Trish, baby, just sit down and stop crying. I will tell you, if you listen to me.

'You really think Mamma is involved with this man? Do you think what the papers say is true?'

Trishala nodded.

'Trish! How could you!'

'Oh Mamma, whenever Kabir uncle called you would blush ... Bhaiyya and me noticed it!'

Simran was startled. She held Trishala and looked her in the eye. 'Yes, I was, I am and I will be fond of Kabir,' she said, willing Trishala to meet her eye. 'Look at me, Trish! He was a friend to me when I needed one. He helped me, encouraged me to begin writing. If I am here today, it is because of him. Aren't you happy when your friends meet you, or talk to you?'

Trishala nodded.

'But, darling, I would never ever do anything wrong,' Simran said softly. Trishala looked at her.

'Trish, he is so much younger than me. I realized that and bid him goodbye. If you still think that I had an unhealthy relationship with him, then I am sorry ...'

Trishala took in Simran's words. Maybe her mother was telling the truth. Yet she had to be sure. 'Isn't this the way you told us that Papa would be with us forever? And that Sia aunty was a just a friend?'

'Oh, baby! I'm sorry. At that time, I too hoped and believed it. I had not lied, Trishala. It was just that I had read the situation incorrectly. But with this, I'm sure. And, like always, I am not lying to you.'

'Oh, Mamma! Thank you! I guess I got a bit carried away. I always felt a bit envious of you. I did not realize that even you needed a friend. I am sorry, Mamma, I should not have believed in such lies.' Simran felt a burden lifting off her chest.

Nikhil was a happy man these days and he had Subhash Bhai to thank for it. If not for him, he would not have met Simran. He immediately checked himself. If it had not been for Subhash Bhai, he would never have got such a big hit. Then he wondered about Simran yet again. She was such an enigmatic woman. Wife to a superstar, but dumped so cruelly. Yet, somehow, this woman had found it in her to rise above a situation, get back into the game, and win.

What was more, Nikhil liked her. He liked the way she carried herself, he admired her grace. She was unaware of her beauty. She worked hard, never checking to see what she was wearing. He liked her ability to see the funny side to any situation. Everyone from his team came back with reports of how she put everyone on the sets at ease with her warmth and wit. She had no airs.

Good lord, I think I'm falling for her. Nikhil thought of his wife Aarti. They had been childhood sweethearts. He had married her when they were both twenty-one. He had become a widower at the age of twenty-five when he lost her in a car accident. He had never remarried.

He had had flings. But at no time did he consider them long-term or promise anyone anything.

Yet, here was Simran. Nikhil checked his thoughts immediately. He had no clue how she felt about him. He was sure of one thing: he wanted to work with her on another project. Maybe she could direct the film this time.

A few days ago, Nikhil had finalized two themes—one was male-oriented and the other, female-oriented. He was quite sure Simran would pick the female-oriented movie about a woman scorned by her family, who had gone on to become one of the biggest druglords in the country. It was a sensitive subject and was written by an established writer known for his fondness for women-centric themes. The other was by a first-time writer and was quite male-oriented. Nikhil couldn't wait to discuss them with Simran.

'You want me to direct a film?' Simran repeated, incredulously.

Nikhil repeated it again.

'Oh, I could dance!'

Simran went to Nikhil's office and picked up both the scripts. She read them both and liked them equally.

'Which one?' Nikhil asked her over the phone.

'May I take the one by the debut author?'

There was silence on the line and then came Nikhil's loud laughter. 'You never cease to surprise me! Go ahead.'

It was the story of a teacher in a sleepy town of Kashmir who discovers an extraordinary gift in one of his most ridiculed pupils. How he convinces the child to get over his fears and shine in the world formed the crux of the story. Simran loved it. It was sensitively written and yet, it had its light moments.

The author had worked hard on the characterization. Simran wanted to show the author how she visualized the characters. The character of the teacher, for instance, was of a man with his own demons.

Once she agreed to do the film, Simran and Nikhil were in touch regularly again. One day, at Nikhil's office, as they were going through the list of locations for a recce, Simran said something that surprised Nikhil. She said, 'Nikhil, I have someone in mind for the lead. Someone who will do justice to the character of the teacher; someone who will be able to portray his torment and confusion.'

Nikhil looked at her expectantly. They could afford to sign a big star for the film, and he wondered whom she had in mind. 'Raj,' said Simran, unflinchingly.

Nikhil was stunned. 'What? Raj?'

'I think he will be able to do it well.'

Nikhil simply stared at her. *Why on earth would you want to work with a man who behaved with you like a jerk? How can you forgive someone like that? Besides, Raj is done with, finished.*

'Your call,' he said, shortly. If Simran felt he could deliver the goods, it was not his place to interfere.

On her part, Simran was expecting some sort of objection from Nikhil, but when he calmly agreed, she liked him for it. This man looked at her with faith. She did not want to let him down. It felt good to be trusted. Whenever she was around Nikhil, she felt strangely protected. But she turned herself away from the idea and began to talk about the film.

Since this was a film about emotions, Simran wanted the songs to convey their depth. She decided she would go in search of a poet instead of a songwriter. Songwriters wrote catchy numbers, while poets brought in lyrics. Simran wanted to do her bit for the poet who has long languished in anonymity despite having real depth and meaning in his compositions. The songwriter, meanwhile, could get away with superficial lyrics about a woman's body and still bag popular awards. Simran promised herself that in her movie things would be different.

But considering Raj for a part was one thing, getting him to accept the offer, another. When Simran called Mahesh to fix up a meeting with Raj, she was surprised by his answer. Mahesh told her she could see him anytime; he was not doing anything lately.

'Sir, Simran-ji wants to meet you.'

Raj grunted.

'When shall I say you will meet her?

'Oh, come on, Mahesh. What is this Simran-ji, Simran-ji and meeting-sheeting? I'll meet her at her place, today or tomorrow.'

'Er ... I don't think it is personal, Sir. I think you have to meet her at her office.'

Raj stared at Mahesh.

'I think Simran-ji is calling about a story narration. For work,' Mahesh faltered.

Raj continued staring at Mahesh. Then he sneered. 'I see,' he said softly. 'So now she wants to order me around on the sets, is it Mahesh? Whatever you do to banish your ex-wife, she always seems to crawl out of the woodwork!' Raj laughed at his own joke, but Mahesh didn't join in. *Simran will have the last laugh*, Mahesh thought.

On the appointed day, Raj and Simran met in her office. Mahesh came first, telling Simran apologetically that Raj would be coming in half an hour. *Star tantrums. He still loves to throw his weight around.* Mahesh told Simran he really liked her maiden film, and knew she would make many wonderful films in future. Simran smiled at him. She had always liked him, his calm nature, his competence and his loyalty to Raj.

When Raj came, he smirked on seeing Simran's office. It was a small place, and he made it evident. Simran ignored his airs and said, 'Raj, I called you here to offer you a film—the lead role, as a matter of fact.'

'Wow! You want me to fall on the floor and touch your feet, Madame? Thanks but no thanks, Simran. If you think I want to take orders from you on the set—'

'I think no such thing, Raj,' Simran cut in. 'I have a role I feel will bring you back into the game. The reason you have had such dismal outings at the box office lately were the roles that let you down. By marrying a younger woman, you thought you could continue playing younger roles. The result: you were rejected by the audience. What I am proposing to you is a strong, author-backed role, something that will allow you to play your age.'

Simran could see Mahesh nodding discreetly at the back. But Raj exploded. 'My age? You talk as if I'm ancient!'

'No, Raj, all I mean is that it is a role in which people can judge you by the range of emotions you display,' Simran interrupted scathingly. 'Not by your paunch or your botoxed face.'

Raj felt slighted. He got up needing to escape. 'I'll look at the script,' he said gruffly. 'Mahesh will revert.' And with that, he left.

Simran was exasperated. *Every time I meet him, I am reminded why I am better off without him.* Raj could be stubborn, and she was already tired with this encounter. She believed Raj would be good for her film, yet she would be okay if he rejected it.

But within a day, Raj agreed to do the role. To Simran, it meant that he was going through a really tough time.

When Raj told Sia that Simran had offered him a role in a small movie, she was taken aback. *What is that woman up to?* But Sia knew that any movie was good for Raj, as long as he got out of the house and set off to work. She also knew that being offered a role by a director who had just had a smashing hit to her credit was a big deal. It was she who convinced him to take the film.

The tabloids had a field day. They analysed and cross-analysed the development. Their intervention only helped Nikhil, Raj and Sia. An interested public often meant box office success.

Raj read his part and started researching his role. He looked forward to going to work. But he couldn't help playing mischief.

One day, unknown to Mahesh, he called up Nikhil and asked to see him at a restaurant. When they met, Raj quickly came to the point. He said, 'I am going to do the role, but Nikhil, why not take the standards up a notch? I have spoken with Pravin Bhai whose last two films crossed the hundred-crore mark. He is ready to work on this film with us. Why not sign him to direct our film?'

Nikhil pursed his lips in anger. *Who do you think you are? You are in this film only because of Simran. To think Simran wanted to help this rat.* 'Raj, I will not change my mind. If the film is made, it will be with Simran. You, however, are free to walk out.' Saying so, he got up and left.

Raj felt like he had been slapped. He had thought that Nikhil and he would bond over a drink or two and they would do the film with bigger names. But it seemed like he had no choice now.

The next day, he had Mahesh call up Nikhil and inform him that Raj would sign on the dotted line. He hoped Nikhil would not tell on him to Simran. He liked the role and did not want to lose out on the project.

Raj need not have feared that, for the thought of telling Simran that Raj wanted her out of the film did not even cross Nikhil's mind. Simran and he were making a film together, and it had to be a huge success; these were the only thoughts that occupied Nikhil's waking hours.

Appreciation was always welcome to Simran, but what made her day was a surprise visit from Bhupinder, Kamla, Ashima and Kavita. As Simran was about to leave for work, they dropped in. She welcomed them with so much happiness and there was not a dry eye in that flat.

As tea was served, Bhupinder said, 'What you have done and achieved is no small feat. Congratulations, beta. We are all very proud of you.'

Kamla agreed and said, 'Simran, I am proud of you. You did not let a crisis break you. That is real character. I am so glad I have two such lovely and talented bahus,' she said as she glanced at Kavita and Simran.

Ashima pouted and said, 'You forget your daughter—still discriminating against your daughter, aren't you?'

Everyone laughed as Kamla hugged Ashima and said, 'Yes, of course. How could I forget our little princess.'

Then Bhupinder said, 'Simran, your wanting to work with Raj, your wish to do good for him ... When we learnt you had signed him on for your next project, we were speechless. I speak for everyone when I say that we never forgave him for what he did to you. When he came back, we were courteous towards Sia, but that was it. But when I heard that you decided to give Raj a big role in your next venture, I realized that our daughter, the pride of our house, who was so unceremoniously asked to leave, really has forgiven Raj. Simran, you have taught us to move on even though we can never do so without you. Thank you, beta.'

So that was why they were here; to express gratitude for helping their son. While Simran was aware that they never extended their love to Sia as they had done to her, she also knew that they could not openly watch her movie or praise her, especially since Vardaan largely ran on the money Sia brought in. *Poor things.* Her in-laws had aged. *We've all aged.*

'Papa, I am not a saint. But time and life have taught me a lot. After my first film's success, I realized that life is too short and precious to waste time on hatred. Raj was in a mess and, whether I like it or not, I really loved this man for half my life. Seeing him in pain bothered me. I guess this role I offered him was my way of telling him that, if he changes his roles, he still has a lot going for him.'

Ashima said, 'Simran, it is true that it takes a lot more courage to forgive. You have really set an example.'

Kavita, who had been quiet all the while, spoke now: 'Simran, it makes sense. You have proved that it is better to slowly work one's way up rather than look for a quick formula to success ... Karan and I ... we learnt it the hard way.'

Simran was glad. She had not relished the tough times, but she now realized how important they were in shaping her as a human.

After a few initial hitches, Simran's second film—her first as director—went on the floor. They shot the initial part in Mumbai and, soon after, left for Kashmir.

As Simran had expected, working with Raj was awkward. He didn't try to make it easier either. He did not like being asked for retakes and made his displeasure evident at such times. Simran ignored his anger and went ahead with her job. Sia began to make regular visits to the sets. She did not like the idea of Simran's presence around Raj for such a long time during the day, and her jealousy was evident. Simran did not pay heed to that either.

One day, Raj took the liberty of turning up drunk on the set. He had an altercation with the costume man about his clothes. He refused to wear what he was given. Meanwhile, Simran was ready for the shot, but the leading man was missing. Soon, a stricken costume man came running to tell her that Raj had cancelled the shoot for the day. When Simran found out what had transpired, she decided to confront Raj herself.

Raj was angry when she walked into his van. He looked at her, sneered and said, 'There is no way I am wearing that kurta. Get me a dressy one designed by Mohit Pal.' Simran asked in an even tone, 'And why is this one not good enough?'

Raj looked at her and said, 'Simran, you know who I am. I refuse to wear rubbish from a flea market. All I am asking for is a costume that befits my status.'

Simran said, 'Yes, Raj. I do know what you are saying. But a Mohit Pal kurta is going to cost time and money, two luxuries we cannot afford. I have noticed your attitude towards retakes and suggestions. You don't realize your old ways have failed. It is time to begin afresh. By not shooting today, we lose out on a lot of money and matters might take a turn for the worse if that happens. Raj, I am done with your tantrums. You want to stop shooting, we will, but I am done with you after today.'

She looked at Raj unflinchingly. Raj was wild with rage, but Simran's words had shaken him. He needed her more than she needed him. Yet he did not think she would actually do it. Just then, Simran whipped out her phone and dialled Nikhil. 'Nikhil, I give up. We will have to call the Producers Guild.'

Raj immediately interrupted her. 'Wait.' Simran saw his face and decided to hang up saying she would call Nikhil back. Raj then said, 'I realize I have been difficult. I guess ... I don't understand why you are being so good to me. I mean, I caused you so much harm.'

'I have moved on, Raj. If you had not left me, I would have not found myself. This movie ... it's my way of thanking you. Take it or leave it. If I were you, I wouldn't throw away this chance.'

Tears pricked the corner of Raj's eyes, but he could not allow himself to cry.

'Give me ten minutes and I will be ready for the shot.'

After that, Raj became more receptive. Even Sia dropped her guard and tried to interact more with Simran. At Vardaan, she attempted to emulate Simran in all she did. It was evident to the entire family. Ironically, she began to dress too a bit like Simran. She made more efforts to connect with Ashima and Kavita and, this time, she encountered less resistance. Even Karan noticed her attempts at trying to be like Simran. He had been trying to cope with life after his fall from grace, and was pleasantly surprised to receive yet another offer. He was told later that he was highly recommended by Sia. All in all, the unpleasantness at Vardaan was slowly, but surely, dissolving bit by bit.

Ashima was now surer than ever that Simran was their lucky charm. When Simran was comfortable, only then was the Mehra family all right. When Simran went down, the whole family did too. Today, when she was finally out of the darkness and had made a place for herself in the sun, the Mehras were peaceful.

The biggest turnaround overcame Raj. A chastened man, he developed faith in his ex-wife's dream. There were times on the sets when her way of handling crises, big and small, reminded him of why he fell in love with her and why his family was still devoted to her.

On the sets, Raj, who used to be like the sun—with everything at home and work revolving around him—learnt to get used to not being fussed over. He learnt to be happy with the fact that people still listened to him when he spoke.

One day, Ashima dropped by on the sets. During a break she sat with Simran, Nikhil and Raj, looking at the shots that were canned.

'I wish I could have been a part of this film, Bhabhi!' Ashima groaned.

'You couldn't have,' Raj said. 'There is no scope for it.'

She sat up straight and, ignoring what Raj said, exclaimed, 'You know what, Bhabhi! I can still be in the film. This film is too serious, all work and no play. Why don't we throw in an item number?'

Simran, Raj and even Nikhil looked at her blankly.

Ashima said, 'Don't look at me like that. We can have a nice item number, a kind of change of pace in the film.' Simran said, 'But, Ashima, I don't know if we can put one in.'

Raj broke into the conversation saying, 'How can you even think of doing an item number?'

Ashima cut him off saying, 'Why not, Bhaiyya? Times have changed. Nowadays, no top notch actress can be considered an all-rounder until she has an item number under her belt. Bhabhi, let's do it. We can choreograph it tastefully. I won't do anything raunchy.'

Simran was unsure and Raj was definitely not for it, but Nikhil liked the idea. Eventually, even Simran came around, but Raj still did not like the idea one bit. But he was out-voted.

He was also beginning to notice Nikhil and Simran's friendship. Nikhil made it a point to visit the sets on and off. There was nothing he said or did, but there was a different shine in his eyes when he spoke to Simran, and Simran seemed more cheerful with him around. They shared an easy camaraderie. They thought alike, had the same sense of right and wrong, and never took undue advantage of anyone. What surprised Raj was Nikhil and Simran's rapport with every crew member. They even addressed the spot boys by name! Raj had never even bothered to learn the names of his hair and makeup men.

Soon it was time to shift location to Kashmir. Nikhil accompanied the crew to set everything up and Raj was to reach a few days later. He was surprised at himself as he faced his feelings when he saw Simran and Nikhil leave for the airport together. *Am I really jealous?* Sia was his wife now and he had a daughter with her. *Is this how Simran must have felt?*

Then he shook off the thoughts. He had a movie to make and his place in the industry to reclaim.

On resuming the shoot in Kashmir, Simran was a thorough professional as usual. She shot the movie in record time. After the last shot had been canned, and Simran triumphantly announced a wrap, the cast and crew went sightseeing.

Simran was too tired to go. She was unwinding at the poolside when she saw Raj walking towards her. She was surprised and asked him, 'You didn't go with everyone?' He answered, 'No, been here many times before.' She nodded as Raj sat down beside her. She resumed reading her book and Raj got busy with his iPad.

Looking for a distraction, she asked a waiter for a glass of lemonade. Raj grinned and said, 'Still on the soft stuff, I see.'

Simran said, 'Never really liked the hard stuff.'

'How are Tarun and Trishala doing? I miss them.'

'Do you now?' she asked, sarcasm lacing her words. 'They are fine; busy with school.'

'They must be proud of you, of what you have done.'

Simran nodded.

All of a sudden, she did not want to be around Raj. She did not want to rehash the past, while, strangely, he seemed rather intent on it. For her, her marriage was a lifetime ago. She got up saying, 'I think I'll get some sleep.'

Raj protested saying, 'So soon? I just got here. Let's have lunch together, shall we?'

Simran declined, feigning fatigue. While she was leaving, Raj said, 'If it's okay, I'd like to take the kids out once we get back.'

'All right. We'll see.'

28

Agreeing to let the kids go out with Raj and actually letting them go with him were two different things

Simran had seen the change in her kids. It was a slow, gradual process; from hero-worshipping their dad to looking at him disdainfully and not trusting him at all, they had come a long way.

They did not make their anger towards their father evident, but Simran saw it every time Raj showed up on TV; they changed the channel. Lately, when asked about their parents, they spoke rather gushingly about Simran. A couple of times, when Simran had suggested they go see him, they had used schoolwork as an excuse. Simran did not press the matter, but she was not fooled either. *Raj asked for this.* And Simran didn't want to intervene.

Raj persisted in his request, and Simran was forced to bring it up with Tarun and Trishala after returning.

'Mamma, we need to go to the mall tomorrow. There are things I need to pick up,' Tarun said. They looked at Simran expectantly, but Simran remembered that she and Raj had decided the kids would spend the Sunday with him. She said, 'That will not be possible tomorrow because there is something much more fun-filled lined up for you. Papa will come by and pick you both up. You are spending the day with him.'

Simran had expected loud protests. But both the kids were silent.

'Kids? I just said something.'

Tarun then said in barely concealed anger, 'Mamma, we don't want to see that man.' Simran swallowed, taken aback.

'That man is your Papa and you will call him that,' she said firmly. 'Why don't you want to see him?'

Trishala said, 'Isn't it obvious? We do not want to be with someone who did not want us, never bothered about us and walked out on us when we needed him the most. Mamma, he never even bothered to find out how we coped when he left us.'

Simran tried to placate them. 'Now, now, calm down. You both know that is not entirely true. Your father has tried to reach out to both of you.'

Tarun said, 'Maybe, but Mamma, it is a little too late. I don't want to fight with you, but we are not going tomorrow.'

The determined look on their faces told Simran that they would not change their mind. She did not drag the issue. But she had to admit that she secretly felt pleased to see how her kids felt, without feeling in any way that she had something to do with the indoctrination.

Raj sounded sorely disappointed to know that the kids would not be able to make it. Simran willed herself not to melt with compassion for him. *Every dog has its day. It is my time to savour the security of career and family. I think it's going to be okay. I think I've finally crossed the bridge.*

But Simran was wrong. Shammi, who had been feeling tired and had been complaining of severe headaches, had a blackout a few days ago. 'I'm just tired,' she told Simran. But Shammi looked awful and Simran took her to their doctor who recommended a few tests. The lab called the same evening for retests. Shammi was diagnosed with Neurocytoma, a rare type of cancer that originates in the fluid cavities of the brain.

Once again, Simran's world was torn. *Neuro what?* She called Nikhil and he recommended a brain specialist. The reports were taken. A few more tests were done. Another specialist was consulted. The verdict and the diagnosis remained the same. The only silver lining was—if you could call it that—it could be cured through surgery and radiotherapy, provided not a moment was lost.

Dr Badrinath suggested that the best place for treatment was a hospital in Seattle that used cutting-edge technology. 'Don't waste any more time,' he urged Simran.

Simran packed up. Shammi tried arguing with her about going alone, but Simran was not in a mood to listen. This was a very crucial time for her, as far as editing and marketing her directorial debut were concerned. Within two days, their tickets and visa were done and, more importantly, the hospital and their specialist were alerted to keep a room ready for Shammi.

There was very little time to tie up the loose ends. Simran called Nikhil to inform him that she would not be there for the post-production of the film and the marketing campaign.

She could not take the kids along to Seattle. Could she keep them in Vardaan? Was it possible to make boarding arrangements with someone else? Simran called Mouli and Divya. Both told her that she could leave Tarun and Trishala under their care.

Life is so unpredictable, thought Simran. *Just when I thought I was out of the woods ...* Simran glanced at her mother. Shammi was extremely calm. Simran swung from anxiety to sadness. She would have to talk to the kids. Shammi reached out and held Simran's hand. This was not the time to be weak. *I will get my mother's strength back on track.*

Shammi said, 'Simran, I am so sorry to put you through all this when things have already been so rough for you.'

'Oh Mamma, how can you think like that? Let's get on the next plane to Seattle.'

Simran carefully took her mother back home. In the quiet of her room, Shammi broke done. She couldn't tell Simran, but she was scared.

Ashima called. Simran told her, crying into the phone. 'I'm coming there, Bhabhi!'

'No, no Ashima. Don't bother. I have too much at this end to take care of. I'll talk to you later.'

But Ashima must have called Vardaan and, in a bit, Bhupinder called. 'Leave the kids with me and Kamla, beta,' was the first thing he said. 'If you consider us your own, you will honour us with your trust.'

Simran broke down again. 'Papa, please don't talk like this. I will have to talk to the kids first. It's not that simple any more. You know how I feel ... about Sia and ... I will feel uncomfortable about Tarun and Trishala being in the same space. They have gone through enough hurt for one lifetime.'

Bhupinder understood. He said, 'Beta, I know. I realize that was a very tough time for them. If you feel it would be better if they stayed at Divya's, I have no problem with that. In fact, Kamla and I will keep looking them up from time to time. You take care of Shammi-ji because that is most important right now.'

That afternoon, over lunch, Bhupinder and Kamla were talking about Simran leaving the kids with Divya and Sia happened to overhear them. Immediately she informed Raj about it. Raj was surprised by Simran's decision to leave the kids with Divya.

When he called on Simran's phone, it was switched off, so he called on the landline instead. Shammi answered the phone and heard Raj's voice on the other end. She said, 'Raj, Simran is not at home right now.'

Raj then said, 'Mamma ... how are you? I heard about ...'

He broke off. Shammi knew Raj had never been good with words. She said, 'Simran insists on coming with me to Seattle. We will leave tomorrow.'

Raj said, 'Mamma, I heard Simran is leaving the kids with Divya. I called up to ask her to let the kids come and stay with me instead.'

Shammi knew it was not a good idea, but she did not want to be the one telling Raj that; this was Simran's prerogative. So she simply said, 'Raj, I'll ask Simran to call you. You can discuss it with her.'

Surprisingly, she felt sad for Raj. Simran had moved on, so had the kids. But she knew that Raj was still trying to come to terms with the new order of things.

When Simran heard about Raj's call, she stiffened. She did not call back. She had a hundred things to sort out before leaving—the last thing on her mind was having an argument with Raj about where the kids should stay in her absence. She was still busy sorting out the new logistics at dinner time when the doorbell rang. Raj stood at the door. Tarun and Trishala met him, said a cursory 'hello', and went into their rooms. Shammi settled Raj down, gave him a cup of tea, and made herself scarce. Simran was left to deal with him, and she groaned inwardly as she sat down across from him.

Raj said, 'You have been avoiding me the entire day.'

'Raj, I have had too much to deal with. You know about Mamma, right?'

He nodded. 'I am so sorry to hear about it. If there is any help you need, even in America—'

Simran cut him off saying, 'Don't worry about that. Dr Nath has arranged everything. We just have to show up there.'

'And the children? Simran, they have a family here, a father, and you insist on leaving them with friends?'

'Raj, they are no longer comfortable with you.'

'Are you telling me that they are no longer comfortable at the house they were born and brought up in?'

Simran answered calmly, 'Raj, the house they grew up in does not exist any more. And the people? Well, there have been changes, you know.'

Raj looked at Simran. 'Simran, leave them with me. Please. They will be fine, you know that.'

'Raj, I don't think so. Do you realize they don't want to meet you, even for a few hours? How can I force them to be with you for so long? I don't think they will be comfortable at all.'

'What makes you so sure? They are my kids too, Simran. I love them.'

'But things have not remained the same for them. You have had another child. They feel the love you had for them has been given to Manvi. Raj, it is a bad idea. You can go meet them at Divya's whenever you like.'

'Simran, they are mine. I want to be with them. Tarun, Trishala, please come here.' As he called out to them, both the children came out of their rooms. They seemed uncomfortable. Raj walked up to both of them and asked, 'Kids, you will come with me, right? For as long as Mamma is away. Papa can be there, right?'

Simran protested now saying, 'Raj, don't bring the kids into this.' She asked the children to go back to their rooms. They left blankly.

Raj took off the minute they left, 'Yes, Manvi is a part of my life. The sooner they accept it, the better it will be for them.' Simran said, 'They have accepted it, Raj. They didn't have a choice. They just need space to be able to move on. Try and understand, it is better if they stay elsewhere. Even Papa agreed to it.'

Raj felt hurt hearing that even his father supported Simran on the issue. But he was not surprised. He said, 'If you are trying to tell me that staying away from their father is good for them, I refuse to believe you. Yes, I made mistakes, I was never around, but if I am not given a chance, how can I rectify things?' Saying so, he left the house.

Simran felt bad, but she had much else to worry about. After a quick dinner, she packed everyone's bags.

Sia felt bad for him. Things had improved between the two of them after Raj found work. 'Go to sleep, Jaanu,' she said. 'Who knows. Maybe Simran will change her mind.'

'I know her, Sia,' Raj said wearily. 'Simran can be very stubborn.

Sia caressed his forehead and said, 'We'll see. You try and get some sleep now.' Despite all his angst, soon Raj was snoring, but Sia was wide awake.

Raj's longing for his kids had surprised her. It had been a while now and Simran was considered perfect, not just by the entire Mehra family, but by Raj too. The film she had signed him on had only served to point out how Simran was much superior to her. If now she could somehow get Simran to send the children here, it would not only make the family happy but also earn Sia some much-needed brownie points with Raj.

She decided to go see Simran first thing in the morning and ensure the kids came to Vardaan. Once Sia made up her mind about something, failure was not an option.

The next morning, when Sia made her way to Simran's house, it was like déjà vu. She remembered the time Simran had once come to her, begging her to leave Raj.

This is not going to be easy. A twinge of guilt pricked her conscience remembering how she had turned Simran away back then. If Simran refused to hand over charge of her kids to Sia today, she could not blame her. For a mother, her children's welfare always came first.

When Simran opened the door, Sia decided to abandon all games and speak from the heart. If Simran was surprised to see her, she did not show it. As they sat down, Simran ensured Sia was served tea, and then there was silence. Both women wondered what to say. Sia said, 'I heard about Shammi aunty. I am sure she will get better soon.'

Simran nodded. She wondered why Sia was here. There were too many things to be done and she was not in the mood to put up a mask of politeness.

Sia spoke again. 'Simran, I know you are wondering why I am here. Raj asked you to send Tarun and Trishala home. And he has been feeling awful ever since you refused.'

Oh God, Sia! My life no longer revolves around how Raj feels.

Simran felt a surge of irritation towards Raj. 'Don't tell me he's sent you, Sia, to plead his case. Why didn't he remember he had kids a few months ago, when it would have made all the difference to them?'

After Raj had left last night, Simran had again spoken to her kids and they had refused outright to go and stay with their father. Tarun had even gone to the extent of saying that he was not ready for any more drama and he did not want to revisit that ugly phase of his life.

She said, 'I know he has sent you as his emissary but please go back–' Sia cut her off now and said, 'Raj did not send me here. He had accepted, although sadly, that the kids would not be coming to him. I came on my own. I wanted to do this for him.'

Simran was surprised now. The fact that Raj had accepted Simran's decision was surprising, but what astonished her even more was that Sia had voluntarily come to ask her to send her children there. She said, 'Sia, you are a mother now. You know how it feels, the desire to always protect one's children. They are not comfortable with the idea of living there. So why force them?'

'I realize that, Simran. I know they are not comfortable. I also know the reason: Manvi and I. But Simran, if only you gave them a chance, if only you give me one chance to set things right. They may be very angry with Raj. They may hate seeing him. But he is their father. All the anger they have for him is coming from a sense of hurt. They are hurting, Simran. If Raj can be around, spend some time with both of them, barriers will break.'

Though surprised at Sia's words, Simran understood what she meant, and said, 'Sia, there are some wrongs that can never be set right. We are adults, we move on, but children—'

Sia interrupted saying, 'Children are even more forgiving, Simran. They are incapable of holding grudges. Once they see for themselves how much Raj really loves them, once they know his reasons for doing what he did, they will not hold it against him.'

Simran looked at Sia. She somehow looked different. While motherhood had served to enhance her beauty, there was a certain maturity about her lately. It was evident in the way she spoke too—a genuineness.

Would it actually be good for the kids to erase the bitterness they had for their father?

Taking Simran's silence as a 'no', Sia said, 'I know you think I will be a bad influence on them. But Simran, when I look at the Mehra family, at you, I realize I never had all this. I was never taught the importance of family. I never had a childhood. I was raised on film sets. I had to begin working too soon in life to support my family. Where was the time to learn values? I know you will never forgive me for what I did to you, but please, give me a chance to show I can do better too. Besides, don't alienate the kids from their father.'

Simran was confused now. What Sia was saying did have its merits. She was quiet. Sia stared at her, willing her to say the words that would make Raj happy. She did not realize, but it was the one way she could finally be at peace, even with herself.

Simran finally realized that it would be a better idea for the children to deal with their baggage and resentment against their father now, rather than let it fester and hamper their own development in the future. She was worried because she did not have the luxury of time. She looked at Sia and said, 'Fine. I will bring the kids over. Tell Raj that. But Sia, please do this much for me. If they don't like it there, don't force them. Let them immediately go to Divya's.'

Sia nodded, with a lump in her throat. Getting over her emotions, she said, 'Thank you, Simran. This means a lot to us. I assure you, I will never let such a situation arise.'

She was so grateful, she felt like hugging Simran. Touching her on the shoulder, she left.

The kids exploded. Tarun said, 'You guys are too much. One day we are shunted out of one place and then, another day, we are packed off right back there. Are we furniture? Don't we have feelings?'

Trishala said, 'How could you, Mamma? When you know how much we hate—'

Simran cut her off saying, 'Hate? Hate is a very strong word, baby. And Tarun, what do you mean "you guys". Are you talking of people who brought you into this world? Please show some respect. What happened was unfortunate. Neither me nor your Papa would have allowed it to happen if we could have helped it. You've got to trust me on that. I know it does not reduce the pain. But I think everyone makes mistakes. I think your Papa has realized his. Why not let him try and make it up to you?'

Tarun asked, 'By giving us expensive things and buying us out?'

Simran shrugged and said, 'It worked earlier, didn't it? Anyway, now we are all wiser, aren't we? And, I promise you, if you are uncomfortable, no one will keep you from going to Divya aunty's place. Nani is very unwell. If I do not rush her to the hospital soon, she could be in real danger.'

The children realized this was not the time to trouble their mother. They nodded their heads quietly, not liking the idea one bit.

Tarun said, 'Mamma, it's fine. We will go, but only because we care about you. Don't worry about us; just make sure Nani comes back to us soon and healthy.'

Simran began to cry and tightly hugged both her children. Just then, she heard an SMS alert on her phone. It was Raj. He had texted: 'Thank you.'

With clarity on one decision, everything fell into place. Mahesh arrived at Simran's house to get everything in order, and to settle Simran's domestic affairs while she would be away. She was crying when it was time for the children to leave. She could not bear to see them go this way, but this was not the time to be weak. If Simran's resolve wavered, she knew Shammi and the children's resolve would topple like a house of cards. She was to go back to Vardaan, settle the kids there, and meet Shammi at the airport.

The roads that led to Vardaan somehow looked different. She felt like she was going back to a life she neither remembered nor could relate to any more. Mahesh noticed the change in her. Over the years, he had seen Simran change so completely that she was almost unrecognizable now. He was very happy for her, and believed she deserved all the accolades that came her way. He had stayed loyal to Raj's wife and could never forgive his boss for leaving his family for another woman.

Of course, the way he felt mattered little to his boss. But Simran had always been a very generous woman, and Mahesh felt attached to the family. God always set right the wrongs humans did, and so, today, Simran was where she was because of her karma. Mahesh hoped that she would go from strength to strength.

When the car pulled up into the driveway of Vardaan, if Simran was expecting any pangs of nostalgia to hit her, she was in for a big surprise. Everything about her erstwhile home was different to such a point that it was almost unrecognizable. Everything, right down to the doors, was different. Every trace of her life there was gone. *Raj really deleted me from this house in every possible way.*

Sadly, she could not have known how much she was missed every single day by the inhabitants of this house. As she walked in, Kavita rushed to give her a big hug, saying, 'Simran ... welcome.' Her words were enough to send Simran down memory lane. She still loved this house. Only on returning today did she realize how much she had missed being here. Then Sia stepped out. On seeing her, Simran stiffened unconsciously. She then realized that this was the woman she had chosen to trust now. She would have to get over her bias.

Soon Ashima, Bhupinder, Kamla, Raj and Karan came out of their rooms to greet Simran. Some of the old staffers too came to her. It was a very emotional moment, with Kamla crying as she met Simran.

Bhupinder looked on like a proud father and, when Simran bent down to touch his feet, he hugged her, saying, 'Take care of Shammi-ji. You have made us so proud, Mori. You have done what a son of this house should have done.'

At his comment, Raj and Karan looked suitably chastised, but Bhupinder held no bitterness. He was genuinely happy to see Simran. It struck her that she had heard the word 'Mori' after ages.

When Ashima walked up to Simran, she said, 'Simran hold on to all that strength and bring Aunty back with you soon. We are waiting. Don't worry about your kids. They are safe and at home.'

Simran felt at ease. It was true that everyone would take great care of the children. She was just anxious about how they would deal with the new circumstances.

Raj looked delighted to have them over. He said, 'Simran, thank you for trusting us enough for this. I promise we will not let you down. You take good care of Mamma and if there is anything you need ...' *Thank you, Simran. I know this must be difficult for you. You are bigger, braver than I ever cared to admit. Do give me a chance to make it up to you some day.*

When Simran looked at Raj, she knew he wanted to tell her she could rely on him. They had been married for a long time and could fill each other's silences. A lock of Raj's hair was out of place and she longed to touch it and tuck it back. She was surprised. Raj and she were done. There could never be anything more than social niceties between the two of them now.

Simran suddenly felt the urge to leave soon. She could not bear being back in her ex-husband's house. To make things even more obvious, he had gone ahead and removed every trace of her ever having lived there, and now, he was looking at her as if she was the most important person in the whole world.

She got up and said, 'I am running late. I am meeting Mamma at the airport, so I must leave.' No one protested.

She began to walk out after touching the elders' feet. She called Tarun and Trishala, hugged them, and left before either of them began to cry. She did not let her own tears spill either. She had to be strong.

Sia went to see her off till the car. 'Simran, thank you. You have given me a chance to be a better person. I will never forget this trust, and I promise, I will never let you down.' Simran smiled through her glistening eyes.

Sia stood there all alone, watching the car drive off with Simran. She smiled. Raj had been delighted with her and that had made her very happy. She was beginning to realize that it was all very well to keep taking in any relationship. True happiness, however, came only when one gave. The look on Raj's face early that morning, when she told him about the kids coming over, had proved that. Simran had honoured her word.

It was Sia's turn now.

By the time Simran reached the airport, she was emotionally drained. She had cried her eyes out in the car. She cried for the home she had left, for all the sadness she had taken from it, and for the long journey that refused to end.

But there was more to come. At the airport, she found Shammi comfortably seated in Nikhil's BMW.

Simran said, 'Oh my God, you? Here?'

Nikhil grinned as he said, 'Could not let my star director leave without fanfare. So ...' He signalled to a boy standing at a distance and he came ahead carrying two bouquets. Nikhil presented them with a flourish, saying, 'For two of the most beautiful and wonderful women I know.'

Shammi happily accepted the flowers, and Simran blushed as she protested, 'But, Nikhil, we won't even be allowed to carry them inside.'

Nikhil said, 'So what? You'll carry this moment with you. Come on, take them.'

Simran took them. 'My producer indulges us, Mamma.'

Shammi smiled. She was seeing something wonderful happen to Simran once again.

While Simran was talking to Nikhil, a reporter happened to run into her. Not wanting to waste the opportunity, he thrust a microphone in Simran's direction and asked, 'Madam, after one successful film, you are about to launch another film soon. It is being touted as the next best thing. How do you feel right now?'

Simran looked at her mother and Nikhil. She did not want to let this moment pass without acknowledging how much her family and friends meant to her.

She said, 'I feel God is watching over me. He has sent such wonderful people into my life. My mother, my children, my family, my closest friends and Nikhil—I am sure, with such lovely people around, I cannot go wrong. However, as a writer, I have often experienced that, when a film does well, the credit goes to the director or producer, but what about the writer? He is the one because of whom the film comes about and, often, he is left on the sidelines. Which is why, if my second film does well, I plan to send credit where it is rightly due, and that is with my writer Anand Patel who has given me such a powerful story to work on. If it were not for him, I would not have this gem of a film'.

Nikhil, who stood quietly until now, said, 'I second that opinion. Let's give credit where it is due. The writer of a film is the real star, and we would like to acknowledge that. Now, young man, please leave us alone.'

The reporter left with a grin. He had got something quote-worthy.

The KLM-NorthWest flight they were leaving on was announced. Nikhil looked at Shammi and said, 'I am going to see you soon.' Shammi smiled and firmly held his hand. Nikhil looked at Simran and instinctively hugged her.

29

Raj, the star, had never needed to be a particularly sensitive man. He never had to consider someone else's feelings. For a very long time, he and everyone—his parents, his siblings, his wife, producer, director, crew, other contemporaries—thought about and for Raj.

Naturally, he had no clue how to break ice with his children. Had he shown some consideration towards Tarun and Trishala earlier, things would have been different. He did not know how to vend his way through the sticky terrain.

Tarun and Trishala had come to stay at Vardaan, but from their point of view, they could have been living on the other side of the world as far as Raj was concerned. With post production work on the film that he shot with Simran over, Raj had time on his hands. So he pottered around, looking for excuses to make conversation with the kids.

But Tarun and Trishala barely responded. When Raj looked into their eyes, he saw hurt, and something he was afraid to recognize—hatred.

The children kept their distance from him, Sia and even Manvi. All of Raj's attempts at getting them to play with her were met with stiff resistance. Raj did not know what to do. How could he confess, to anyone, that he did not know how to connect with his own children? So he kept quiet about it as he tried and failed.

Mahesh knew Raj inside out and felt sad for him. If he could, he would have told Raj to be honest. His children would respond to honesty.

Even Kamla noticed what was going on, so did Kavita and Ashima.

Sia was also watching and aching. She felt hurt every time Tarun or Trishala stepped away from Manvi, who was just a baby. She felt it was unfair. *But they are children. They were very young when their father walked away.*

But things could not go on like that too long, she realized. She found Raj one evening in his room with the lights out.

She switched on the lights and stood caressing Raj's hair wordlessly. 'Today I got Tarun and Trishala's favourite macaroons for them. Earlier, when I used to get it, they used to jump at them, not letting go until they had finished off the last one. Today, they did not even touch it.' Sia tried to soothe him saying, 'They must be full or maybe they have outgrown their fondness for them over time.'

Raj shook his head. 'No, Sia. They were talking about macaroons just yesterday with Soham. I overheard them. They haven't outgrown the macaroons, they have outgrown me.'

Sia cajoled him into sleeping it over, assuring him things would change for the better soon enough.

But she couldn't get any sleep. She looked at her sleeping husband. He had softened a lot since his shoot with Simran. Sia was woman enough to realize, even though she did not like to admit it, that Raj was drawn to Simran again.

It was the little things he did when he was around her that clearly reflected his feelings for her. But, strangely, she did not feel envious. She just realized that she could not afford to lose him. If the past was not corrected, if she did not right the wrong she had done, her entire life would fall apart. Sia decided that she would begin by admitting a few truths to herself as well as others.

What she had told Simran was true. She had never known what it was to be a part of a family, what it meant to stand by one another. As long as she could remember, she had been at work. Her mother had never taught her anything else. She was asked by her own mother to sleep with other men, just so she could get ahead in her game. From whom could she have learnt compassion and love? She decided to take the onus of undoing the damage that she had caused to Raj's children's lives on herself.

One evening, the entire family was going out to have dinner at a friend's place. Tarun had decided to stay back as he had an assignment to complete, and Trishala had to prepare a school project. Raj tried to convince them to come, but they did not want to. Seeing this, Sia too declared that her head was hurting and that she wanted to stay back. This was the perfect chance for her to confront the children. Eventually, everyone left and Tarun and Trishala retired to their room.

Sia knocked on the door. Trishala asked her to come in. Sia was never fond of children. *How does one talk to kids?* She went and sat on their bed. The kids continued to do their work.

To break the silence, Sia said, 'Can I hang around with you guys for a bit?' Tarun looked distinctly uncomfortable and Trishala blurted, 'You should go and rest. I mean, don't you have a headache?'

Sia smiled. She was caught in her own lie. She immediately said, 'I feel better now.'

They turned their backs on her and worked in silence.

'I actually came to talk to you both,' Sia said quietly.

They still didn't look up.

'Children, your father has been trying really hard to connect with both of you. He tries to get the things you like to eat, tries to do what you want and yet, you both thwart all his attempts. You are his children. Please do not do this to him. He really loves you.'

Now she had Tarun and Trishala's complete attention. They both looked at her passively, but their eyes betrayed pain.

Somewhat encouraged, she continued, 'He really does love you. When you decided to come here, he felt like his children were coming back to where they belonged.'

Tarun spoke: 'Correction! We did not want to come, we were forced to.'

Sia nodded and said, 'I know that. You did not wish to come back to the house that has given you such painful memories. We've all made mistakes. But I know we can rectify the wrong. We can, if you let us.'

Trishala was angry now: 'Really? Sia aunty, if we mattered so much, how come Papa never once came to see us during the divorce? How come he never tried to keep us with him afterwards? He just wanted to get rid of us to begin a new family with ...' she broke off.

Sia said, 'With me. You are right about the part that he should have tried harder. But ... he just did what he thought was best then.'

Tarun retorted, 'Mamma would have corrected Papa if he was going wrong somewhere. Why did you never correct him when you knew he had wronged us? Is it right for a father to abandon his children?'

Tarun's words pained Sia. She had been struck where it hurt the most. Yet, it was a relief to hear the words spoken aloud. It meant that she could now address the issues and give her side of the story. She said, 'I want to be honest with you. It is very difficult for me to admit it, but I am the one you really need to blame. If your father had fought for your custody, the divorce would have been long drawn and bitterly contested as your mother, quite rightly, would not have given you up. I wanted it to end soon and without a fight, so I begged Raj to let go of you both; I wanted to marry him soon. So I am responsible for your father leaving you, not him.

'Your mother could correct Raj because she had known better, she had been taught better. Her mother made sure she had a childhood. I, on the other hand, have been working without pause since the age of five. My mother never taught me to differentiate the right from the wrong. I am not saying she was bad. I loved her dearly. She just did what she thought was right for me. She had lost everything when she was young. So she taught me to only take care of myself. She wanted me to do well in my career and did everything conceivable towards that aim. That is the way I was raised, to get what I want by taking it away from someone else.'

Tarun and Trishala were listening attentively. A tear made its way down the side of Sia's cheek.

Trishala said, 'That does not mean you can take away someone's husband, someone's father because you feel like it.'

Sia said, 'I wish I had not done it. I have a child of my own now, and I realize that, if what I did to you happened to her, it would destroy me. But your mother ...' Sia swallowed hard, then continued, 'Your mother is a very courageous woman. She made a life for herself when everyone dear to her deserted her. I could not have done it. In her place, I would have been a complete wreck. She is a wonderful person. And you two ...' Sia choked on her tears.

She looked at Tarun, then at Trishala, and continued, 'You two take after her. You did not let problems break you. Even Raj and I face problems, and we cannot always get over them. Your mother taught us how to. Today, I apologize to you for every bit of pain I have caused you, and I plead with you. Give us a chance. Let us try ... please.'

Hearing all this, Trishala began to weep. Before Sia knew it, she went and sat beside her and hugged her tight.

Having Trishala in her arms emboldened her. She stretched out her arm to Tarun too. He came over and began to sob. The three of them stood huddled for a long time.

It was Sia who finally broke away. She wiped their tears and Trishala extended her hand and wiped Sia's.

'Trust us, Raj and me, just this once. I promise, we will move heaven and earth to never let you down.' Tarun nodded his head. He was beginning to see a different side to the diva, who sat there crumpled and who, until now, could not think beyond herself. She seemed genuine. Maybe they could trust her.

Trishala said, 'I guess we could try.'

Her reply made Sia smile. Children were so honest, never worried about being politically correct. She liked it, much to her own surprise. Then she said, 'So when your Papa ...'

Tarun said, 'We will try.'

Sia's heart felt lighter than it had been in a long, long time.

That evening onwards, there was a noticeable change in the children's attitude towards Raj. They were initially wary of him, but soon his invitations to a drive or a snack at a restaurant were accepted. In their attitude towards little Manvi too, there came a shift. Without anyone having to tell them, they had taken on the role of her older brother and sister. Like Soham and Aanya, they too began to pamper her.

Sia's heart sang. Her daughter would have people who would care and love her after all. She won't be alone and friendless like her mother.

Raj's joy knew no bounds. Sia had achieved the impossible, and Raj promised himself that he would never forget that. Soon after, Raj apologized to his children for all he had done. It only served to bring them closer. Bhupinder and Kamla noticed the change and their hearts swelled with pride. They must have done something right after all, to be able to witness happiness after such monumental disappointments. Even Ashima had to acknowledge that Sia was not a bad sort. One day, she addressed Sia as 'Bhabhi'. Sia was over the moon. She was finally being accepted by the family.

Kavita too had been observing Sia keenly since Simran's children had come home. Although she had never liked her, Kavita now, grudgingly, admired the way Sia conducted herself with the kids. She was amazed that the woman she had considered superficial and morally deficient had broken the barriers between Raj and his children.

Perhaps this family did have a happy future after all.

Things had settled down in Kavita's life too. After Karan's short stint in jail, he had resumed work. Initially, it was at a small scale, but eventually, the trickle turned into a steady flow of work again. Karan gladly went back to his multi-starrer movies. At least he could sleep peacefully at night. He wished his older brother would do the same.

30

Nikhil was working very hard. The film was set to release in a couple of days. He was a very private person, choosing to avoid interviews or other interactions with the media as much as he could. But since Simran was not around, he had to actively participate in the promotion campaigns. Raj also made himself available as the lead of the film, as did the heroine. And the last minute inclusion of an item number by Ashima was already being admired. So she too participated in promoting the film as a gesture of love for Simran.

One day, Raj, Nikhil and Ashima were getting ready to go on air for an interview in front of a live audience. It was to begin in five minutes. Backstage, Nikhil impulsively blurted, 'I hate this. I wish Simran was here.'

Suddenly, Nikhil found Raj and Ashima looking at him searchingly. Embarrassed, Nikhil tried to smile his comment away.

Raj asked, 'For the promos?'

Nikhil nodded.

But Raj did not believe him for an instant. He could sense another man encroaching on his former territory, and it felt strangely unnerving. Ashima knew how Nikhil felt. She had seen it in the way he looked at Simran.

They were called on stage and, in the interview, bizarrely and rather childishly, Raj made it a point to contradict everything Nikhil said. *Producer be damned! He is out to get Simran!* thought Raj. But, despite Raj's behaviour, Nikhil refused to take it personally.

Very soon the film was out and, partly due to Simran's stellar debut, but mostly due to a job beautifully and lovingly done, it broke records. In the first week itself, the film recovered its cost and was still going strong. The critics raved about Simran, about how she was the woman with the Midas touch. She was hailed as one of the most talented, new directors on the block.

This success had not come overnight. It had taken all of Simran's grit to reach here. Nikhil knew that, and he felt bad she was not around to savour the rewards of her hard work. He felt it would be disloyal to celebrate the film's success in Simran's absence.

But the one man who could not stop grinning like a Cheshire cat was Raj. He was back in the game and how. He finally realized what Simran had said was right. He really needed to start playing roles that were appropriate for his age. He was back in the media's reckoning once again, with everyone wanting to interview him.

He generously gave sound bites to anyone who wanted them. He did not hold back his appreciation for Simran. He gave her due credit for making such a film at a time when no one wanted to work with him. Raj hoped Simran would somehow hear his comments.

With the second film a runway hit, Simran had no dearth of assignments being offered to her. Nikhil diligently kept all the work proposals filed away for her to see once she returned. He had never done this before for anyone. It was increasingly becoming clear to him that he could not go on without regularly seeing her. She had been gone for about two months now, and he missed her a lot.

31

Simran had lost track of time. Ever since she arrived at the hospital in Seattle, she had been at her mother's side from one surgery to the next. It was exhausting to eat, breathe and sleep with only Shammi's condition in mind.

The only thing that kept her going was that Shammi had shown improvement and, if they continued treating her at the same pace, she would eventually recover. Caring for her mother took all of Simran's strength and left her emotionally drained. The other source of her misery was the worry about how her children were coping. She would speak with them at least once a day, and of late, she was surprised at how Trishala had taken to appreciating Sia.

Even Tarun made it a point to mention how Raj had begun to spend a lot more time with them. They mentioned how adorable Manvi was, in between mentioning how well Simran's film had done and how Raj had begun to get a lot of film offers again. While the fact that her film had done well immensely gladdened her heart, Simran would often get upset on hearing about Sia and Raj. The fact that her children were appreciating them made her feel a little betrayed, as if her kids did not love her any more.

Despite the maturity she had reached, she certainly did not want to play second fiddle to Sia in her children's life.

Had Simran had someone to reassure her, she would have perhaps felt happy that her biggest fear—her children's discomfort, rather, comforts—was being taken care of. But for Simran, who had not stepped out of the hospital in weeks except to shower and change, all such fears were monumental.

Every time she spoke with Tarun and Trishala, inadvertently the names of Raj or Sia or even Manvi cropped up, leaving her distraught and unhappy.

Then, one day, when Simran walked into her mother's room at the hospital after a few hours' break, she was shocked to see another person sitting there, reading a newspaper. They did not know anyone there, so a visitor ... It took a second to recognize him.

'Nikhil!' she ran and hugged him. 'When did you arrive? I've only been gone two hours.'

'I reached just an hour ago. I came here directly from the airport.'

Simran looked at him. 'Oh, you've made my day. So nice to have you here. I could do with some company.'

Nikhil teased her, 'Some company? Say my company.'

Simran laughed it off and said, 'Shall we get something to eat?'

Over piping hot lunch in the cold weather, Nikhil said, 'Simran, the film is a huge hit. People are praising you no end. Raj's career has got a new lease of life, and people are lining up to work with you.'

Simran nodded, feeling good. 'Believe me, Nikhil, it is the biggest high in life when one knows one's work is appreciated. My kids keep telling me over the phone that the film has generated a lot of buzz. But my place is here right now. I need to be with Mamma.'

Nikhil said, 'I know. That is why I got you a present. Something that will tell you what everyone is saying about you.' Nikhil expected Simran to be delighted, but he suddenly saw a tear roll down her eye.

Nikhil immediately held her. Simran wept uncontrollably. Nikhil let her cry, soothing her gently with caresses. She wept like a baby. Instead of asking her what the matter was, Nikhil just let her express her grief. He wanted her to know he was there for her and, no matter what it was, he would help her get past it. Once her sobs subsided, Nikhil handed her a glass of water. Then she hesitantly said, 'I am so sorry. You must think I'm such a fool.'

Nikhil shook his head. 'Tell me, what's the matter?' he asked gently. 'How is mum?'

Simran, glad at being able to talk to someone, said, 'I don't know, Nikhil. She is very slow in responding to the treatment. With cancer, time is of essence. I don't know.'

Nikhil then said, 'I spoke with Dr Kahn on arriving. He told me that recovery will be very slow due to her age, but she will be well. Don't worry, Simran. You need all your energy now and worrying will only sap your strength.'

Simran sighed. She was glad Nikhil had spoken to the doctor and asked him the one question she had been afraid to ask all along. It was like a burden had lifted off her now. But Nikhil knew there was also something else bothering her. Simran was not her usual self. She looked strained and worried. If he had his way, he would take her in his arms yet again and kiss all her cares away. But this was no film and if he really wanted her to be a part of his life, he would have to wait for the right moment.

While he was musing, Simran said, 'I don't know. I hear so much about Raj and Sia. The kids, they can't stop praising them all the time. Nikhil, here I am alone and struggling. Instead of missing me or bothering to call me up, Tarun and Trishala are getting carried away. I call them up every day only to hear about some new thing Sia did for them that blew them away. They have forgotten. They have forgotten the pain and the struggle we went through because of them. Instead, it is as if they like it more in their old house than with me. Am I going to lose my kids, Nikhil?'

Nikhil's heart went out to her, but he did not interrupt. He listened.

Glad to finally voice her fears, Simran went on, saying, 'I feel really jealous, Nikhil. I mean, I worked so hard for my children. And then I hand them over to Raj and Sia, and they simply usurp my position. What do I do? I cannot even think of leaving Mamma alone right now. I'm so angry, unhappy and confused. Sometimes I feel so suffocated.'

Nikhil let her talk. He did not want Simran to feel like she were alone. So she went on and on, and finally, when she was drained, he ordered some coffee.

Once Simran was calmer and Nikhil gauged her to be more receptive, he spoke, 'First of all, let's get some perspective. Can you leave from here and go to your children right away? Would you be okay with that?' Simran shook her head.

Nikhil said, 'So it's clear that you cannot leave. Then tell me, Simran, why torture yourself about what's going on in Mumbai? Tarun and Trishala are your children. They are not babies any more. They have seen you and Raj through the ups and downs. You have been the one close to them in their darkest hours. Do you think anyone can forget that? It that possible, Simran? A person will never forget the people who were with him in his hour of need. These are your children we are talking about. They have seen their mother suffer but never let them near the heat. They have seen how you have nurtured them when all the odds were stacked up against you. They have also seen their father walk out of their lives when they were at such a precarious age. That is something very hard to get over. Those scars take time to heal.

'But now they are with their father, someone they obviously did not want to be with. But circumstances have placed them there and they have done the sensible thing, Simran. They have tried to get over the bitterness. You know there is a wonderful saying that bitterness is like drinking poison and waiting for the other person to die! One just has to let go in order to leave no place for bitterness in one's life. Your children have demonstrated their values, the ones you have taught them. They have gone ahead and faced their biggest fears, and they have come out successful. By choosing to praise Raj and Sia, they are letting you know that they have chosen to not be bitter; they have truly moved on.

'Does that mean they love you less? No. It simply means that they have learnt the lessons you have taught them well. They deserve a pat on the back, Simran. They want you to be happy; they have done this for you. They have turned out well, Simran. You should be proud of them.'

Nikhil paused. He saw Simran was in deep thought. Then, she looked at him in wonderment. She asked, 'Really?' Nikhil nodded his head, letting it all sink in. Then she hugged him very tight. 'Thank you. Thank you so much, Nikhil. I never saw it that way. I guess ...'

Nikhil said, 'Don't beat yourself up with it, Simran. When one is in your situation, away from home, worried sick about your mother, things do seem more difficult than they are. The only thing you can do is to refuse to get flustered. Just stay calm.'

Simran said, 'Nikhil, you have always been such a stress-reliever.'

Nikhil feigned a hurt expression and said, 'Is that all I am to you? Ouch, that is a blow to my ego!'

Simran started to laugh. Nikhil liked seeing her this way. He said in all seriousness, 'You know, you have beautiful dimples. When you smile, they really are a sight worth seeing. Stay this way, Simran. Always.'

Simran stopped laughing. Inexplicably, she felt drawn to Nikhil. Maybe it was the relief, maybe it was the benefit of having someone she could talk to. There was magic in the air suddenly and, before either of them knew what was happening, they kissed.

It was a long, sweet kiss. Nikhil said everything he wanted to say to her in that one kiss. For Simran, it was a moment she was not going to forget. She knew she shouldn't have kissed him, but then why did it feel so right? They awkwardly pulled away. Simran was very self-conscious. Had she just made a huge mistake? Nikhil did not want her to feel bad about it.

Gently, as if nothing out of the ordinary had happened, he suggested they go back and look up Shammi. Evening arrived and Nikhil told Simran he was booked on the flight to Mumbai that very night. 'You came all the way only to see me for a day?'

Nikhil grinned. Before leaving, though, he handed Simran a small package wrapped in a brown bag. He told her it was a file of media reviews of Simran's directorial debut. She did not unwrap it, and Nikhil did not ask her to either. An awkward hug later, he left. Simran was all alone again. But there was a major difference now. She had Nikhil's thoughts to keep her heart warm.

That night, once Shammi feel asleep, Simran opened the package. On opening the file, lots of cuttings fell out. She was thrilled to read about people's comments and, by the time she had read the first ten, she was already over the moon. *Let me enjoy this.* The next article was by a critic with a stellar reputation. Just as she picked up the page, an envelope fell down. Simran picked it up and was surprised to see her name scrawled on it in Nikhil's hand. There was a note inside:

> *'Dear Simran, after the release of the movie, lots of people have had lots of wonderful things to say about you. Don't believe a word of anything they say, because you are far stronger and more wonderful, exceptional, sensible and unique than that. You are truly one of a kind. I thank God for the day you walked into my life. Help me keep you in it forever. Be mine.'*

A thrill ran down Simran's spine. She could not believe he felt this way too. If he did, why did he not say as much to her when he came here today? Simran realized that she must have seemed so agitated about everything that Nikhil knew she was not in the right frame of mind to focus on anything else. A wave of sadness washed over her. She wished Nikhil would have told her how he felt in person. And now, he was on a plane and would not be reachable for the next twenty-four hours. She let out a sigh. This felt so right. Nikhil was everything a husband should be.

Then she held her breath. What was she doing? Her first responsibility, as a mother, was towards her children. Would Tarun and Trishala accept this? Would they want to make another major adjustment in their lives? For Simran, a relationship with a man could only mean one thing—marriage. And she did not know if Nikhil would want that. Besides, she did not want to put her kids through the same pain Raj had dragged them through. Raj could do it without a care but she could not. She had to put her children and their happiness above all else.

She felt suffocated now, and stepped out into the balcony to get some air. As she looked at the busy city below, she realized there was no future in it. She was being stupid by getting her hopes up. In the lives of women like Simran, there was no place for love. She thought of Kabir. She would always wonder about him. But she could not bear the heartache of her children. She would have to tell Nikhil there could not be anything between the both of them. She quietly went back into the room, kept the letter back into the file and closed it.

It had been a couple of days since Nikhil had returned. He couldn't stop smiling ever since. His employees at the office were thrilled with their boss's sudden sunny disposition. They wanted him to make more frequent trips to Seattle if this is what one-day trips to the place did to him.

Nikhil was on a high. Simran liked him too. The kiss had told him all he needed to know. There was just one dark cloud on his horizon though—she had not called him after he reached Mumbai, and he had been anxiously waiting for her call. Surely, she must be as eager to talk to him as he was. But four more days passed and Nikhil had still not heard from her. On the seventh day, Nikhil picked up the phone and finally took the initiative to call her.

When she answered, she sounded strained. 'Hey!' was all she said. Nikhil asked her about the weather and she told him about other things, but never once did she mention the letter. After making small talk, they hung up. Nikhil wondered if she had got the letter, and yet, it was impossible that she had not. Nikhil wondered if he should directly ask her about it or wait for her to bring it up. Had he made a mistake? It didn't feel like it. So he decided to wait. He hoped time would find him a solution.

32

Days turned to weeks. Nikhil had still not heard from Simran. He was beginning to lose patience.

Simran didn't know what to do. She read Nikhil's letter at least a hundred times over, and every time she read it, she fell deeper in love with him.

Nikhil had helped her through such a tough time. A man like him was hard to come by, but Simran had had the good fortune of meeting someone like him and the bad luck to feel compelled to pass him up.

After days of polite conversation, Nikhil decided to be persistent. After all, it was the question of his entire life. He was certain that Simran was the person he would find happiness with.

He had to give this chance his best shot. So he called her up one evening. When Simran saw Nikhil's name flashing on her phone, her heart skipped a beat. Realizing that she was behaving like a teenager, she collected herself and answered the call.

Try as she might, she could not disguise the glee in her voice as she said, 'Hi, Nikhil.' Nikhil suddenly felt like he were back in high school asking the girl of his dreams out for coffee. All the nervousness and anxiety was back. He had to talk about a lot of things, and so he pushed those thoughts out of his head and said, 'Where have you been, Simran? It's been ages since I heard from you. Are you all right? I have been worried sick about you.'

Simran's heart melted. She nodded and said, 'I'm fine, just ...'

'It is because of my letter, right?'

There was silence.

'Simran, look, if you don't like me, you can tell me that to my face. Don't withdraw yourself like this from me.'

Simran thought for a bit and said, 'Nikhil, what gave you the idea that I do not like you? I like you too and a lot.' Nikhil's heart suddenly grew wings.

Simran continued, 'But ...' Nikhil hated that word. It always imposed conditions. He let her continue haltingly as she said, 'But, Nikhil, we are not young any more. I mean, I have two kids. The decisions I take are not for my life alone. My children are directly affected. And after the debacle with Raj, I don't know if I can subject them to getting used to another man in their father's place. Nikhil, for me, a relationship with you can only mean marriage. And I don't know if my children, or even you, are ready for that.'

Nikhil was stumped. He had only just let his feelings be known to Simran and she had already thought of marriage and the possibility that he might not be up to it. He was ready, so ready for Simran to be a part of his life. With a woman like her, there was no way he was not going to make it legit. He wanted to shout it out from the rooftops that he loved this woman.

Marriage was the answer to all his prayers and he made it known to her by saying, 'Marriage? Simran you are so wonderful that I would be a fool to not propose marriage to you. Please say yes now and relieve me of my misery.'

Simran felt sad. She wanted to tell him that she would gladly marry him, she could spend the rest of her life loving him. But she could not. She had Tarun and Trishala to think of. She said, 'I can't. I cannot do it to them, Nikhil. Their father has already replaced their mother. They would be heartbroken if they realized that even I have subjected them to the same humiliation. They will feel like I have made them second best in my life, like they do not matter to me. So, Nikhil, it is best if we give up on this idea right now. There cannot be anything but friendship between you and me. I am really sorry, Nikhil.'

When Nikhil heard Simran's words, he was angry. So angry, in fact, that his secretary, who had entered his cabin just then for some signatures, decided to withdraw immediately. Nikhil was usually a calm person. There was only one thing that annoyed him the most—unreasonable people. And right now, Simran was being very unreasonable. He decided to show her a few facts and then she could makeup her mind.

He said, 'Simran, you have become so obsessed with your children that you have forgotten that even you deserve some happiness. I know you like me too, otherwise you wouldn't have kissed me back when you did. Why don't you realize that even Tarun and Trishala are mature young adults now? Like you want them to always be happy, it is possible that they could want the same for you. Believe me. At least tell them and see what they say.'

'Nikhil, you will not understand.'

Nikhil was angry now. 'Why won't I, Simran? Because I don't have children? Because I never got the chance to have them? Or is it because I don't have a heart, or even feelings?'

Simran tried to calm him down saying, 'Nikhil, I did not mean it like that. All I meant was ...' He was not in a position to hear any more and so he said, 'Save it, Simran. I have got my answer. Even though I do not agree with it, this is your decision. I promise, I will never bother you again. Goodbye.'

Simran heard the line go dead. Something inside her died too.

'You are a fool. And that too of the first order,' Simran heard a weak voice say to her suddenly. She spun around to see Shammi saying that to her. She was overjoyed as she rushed to her mother: 'Mamma, how are you feeling?'

'Not too good.'

'Is it the medicines or the drip? I'll call someone right away.'

Shammi shook her head. 'It is your stupidity that is making me ill.'

Simran was stumped. 'So you err ...'

Shammi nodded her head and said, 'I may have been dopey and near unconscious, but I'm not dead yet. Simran, you may have just made the biggest mistake in your life. Nikhil is a very good man. I like him too and I think he will always keep Tarun, Trishala and you happy. Trust me, I know it.'

All this talking had sapped Shammi's energy and she began to cough.

Simran quickly gave her water. Shammi drifted off to sleep holding her hand. When Simran thought over what her mother had said, she began to doubt her own actions and marvelled at how her mother was so sure about Nikhil.

Had she really made a big mistake? Could she do anything about it or was it too late now?

Shammi had closed her eyes but she was thinking too. She was very happy for Simran. She was not a woman who had always felt the need for a man in her life. But this was her daughter's life. She knew a keeper when she saw one. And Nikhil, he was a truly good man, a kind and sensitive person who would nurture Simran and would cherish her in his life forever. She had always noticed Raj's condescending attitude to Simran and, as much as she resented it, she had desperately wanted her daughter's marriage to work. As a result, she had urged Simran to put up with Raj. Shammi felt guilty about it to this day. Surgery can fix one's brain but not one's thoughts. Shammi never forgave herself for asking Simran to continually adjust in her marriage.

She decided that, before she left earth, she would at least tell this much to her granddaughter: adjusting was right when it was practised by both the people in a marriage. If done just by one, it meant compromise!

Shammi no longer wanted Simran to adjust. She wanted her to choose what was right for her. And Nikhil felt right. Shammi had seen him around Simran a few times. She had heard Simran gush about him after her shoots. It was a mother's intuition and nothing else that told her this was right for her daughter. While Shammi wanted Simran to think of Nikhil, she was worried about many things. She realized that no matter how right a man seemed, it wasn't wise to put blinkers on when it came to a daughter's future and leave things to time and fate alone.

The next day, when Dr Kahn came to see Shammi, she was awake. He said, 'She is looking much better. If this is the rate at which she improves, you should be on your way home in a week's time.'

Simran could not believe her ears. They both smiled as Dr Kahn said, 'And please, tell Mr Nikhil Patel that too. He was the most concerned and curious relative I have ever seen. Do tell him about your progress.' Simran blushed.

After the doctor left, she looked at Simran and said, 'Wonder how the poor boy is doing now.' Simran looked at her quizzically. 'Simran, try as hard as you can, but you won't find a guy willing to risk serious jet lag just to come and inquire about his prospective mother-in-law's health.'

Simran did not know what to say.

Shammi signalled Simran to come close to her and when she did, Shammi pulled her in an embrace. Then, softly she said, 'Don't be scared. I know a diamond when I see one. Frankly, my dear, the guy is as rare and precious as they come.'

Simran nodded, tears falling from her eyes. She did love Nikhil.

33

After hanging up on Simran, Nikhil was very upset. On an impulse, he called Raj and asked to see him at a hotel. Raj was happy to comply, hoping it was about another film he was being offered.

As he entered the bar, he found Nikhil nursing a drink. He sat down on the sofa facing him and said, 'Just five in the evening and the party has already begun?' Nikhil put down his drink and after Raj had ordered, he said, 'I wanted to see you today about a personal matter.'

Raj's ears perked up. 'Personal' could only mean Simran. Nikhil came straight to the point. 'I like Simran a lot, Raj. She is really special to me. When I went to Seattle to see her and tell her that, she seemed to like me too. But as soon as I came back, she told me it can't happen.'

Raj was surprised. 'What? You went all the way to Seattle to see her?' The way he said it almost made him look like he regretted not thinking of going there himself. Raj hesitantly said, 'Look, Nikhil. If she says she does not want to be with you, drop it at that.'

Nikhil now insisted, 'Raj, she likes me. I know it and I can feel it. But she does not want to upset Tarun and Trishala. She says she cannot drag them through the whole phase of adjusting with someone new in their father's place.'

Nikhil expected Raj to say something comforting, but Raj surprised him by saying, 'If the mother feels this way about her children, you probably should let it be. You should respect Simran's feelings and walk away.'

Nikhil was aghast. He said, 'What part of what I said did you not understand, Raj? She likes me. I feel it, I am sure I am right. I just hoped you could help us out with the children part, but I guess you wouldn't want to.'

Raj was shaken. He was not prepared for Simran to move on so soon. Although he had wanted so desperately for Simran to let go of him, he was not able to do so in turn.

He suddenly felt an urge to talk to Simran first. He got up swiftly and said, 'Nikhil, I need to leave. Sorry.' And then, without waiting for a reply, he left. Nikhil was left sitting there, flabbergasted. Raj could dump his wife and move on with another woman. But he obviously did not want Simran to do the same. *How stupid of me to think this man would help anyone but himself. What double standards!*

Raj was at the wheel of the car when he finally got through to Simran. As soon as she answered the phone, he said, 'Simran, I heard about Nikhil and you. Do you like him too?' Raj had hoped she would deny it, that she would say she did not care for him, or even say that Nikhil was harassing her. What he heard instead was an eye opener.

Simran calmly said, 'Raj, if you have asked me this question in the capacity of an ex-husband, I do not need to give you any reply. But you will always remain the father of our children and, therefore, my friend. And in that capacity, I will answer this question with all honesty. The truth is, yes, I do like Nikhil. In fact, I love him, Raj. He is the one person who believed in me when no one did. He trusted me and my integrity. He never tried to make me feel inferior in any way, and went out of his way to make things work in my favour. He has made me believe in myself. But, Raj, I cannot put Tarun and Trishala through any more pain. They took a long time to recover the last time. I need to think of them and not just of myself.'

She was crying and Raj was teary-eyed too. He did not know what to do. On one hand, there was Simran's happiness, and on the other, his. He said, 'Fine. Let me get back to you on this one. I need to go now.' Without waiting for any response from her, or giving her the chance to ask anything, Raj hung up.

That night, he did not sleep.

He remembered how Simran looked when he left her. He remembered how she looked while she was on the sets. He remembered how she had looked when he had first met her.

He was restless. He rose from the bed and went out into the garden. How could all of this have happened to him? He realized that, somewhere in the deep recesses of his heart, he still felt Simran belonged to him. Nikhil. Raj needed to distil his feelings about this powerful, rich man. Nikhil had always looked at Simran with so much respect. He seemed to want to know what Simran thought about anything. Raj used to wonder why Nikhil wasted his time asking Simran for her perspective. Worse still, he didn't just give her a hearing, he also gave her autonomy to take decisions, and acted on what she said.

He had wondered why, then. Now, he knew.

On listening to Simran, one thing was clear: she liked Nikhil too. So, could he actually do something to help the two? Nikhil certainly seemed to think so. Raj's first instinct was to shove Nikhil aside. But ... he needed to be a better human for once. The women in his life had both shown largesse in extenuating circumstances. Perhaps it was time for him now to rise above his sense of self.

When Sia came to know, she was more relieved than happy. She had long suspected Raj's interest in his ex-wife. Now that he had decided to help them, she felt a wave of relief wash over her. Her husband would remain with her after all. She promised to help him in any way she could.

But, this time around, Raj realized she had done enough already, and it was time he learnt to talk to his kids.

The next day, Raj took Tarun and Trishala for a drive in the evening. When they reached a secluded spot, Raj pulled over and said, 'Kids, there is something I want to talk to you about.'

Tarun and Trishala looked at him attentively.

'Nikhil uncle likes Mamma a lot. He likes you two a lot too. So much so that he wants to be a part of your family. He wants to be with you both and Mamma.'

Tarun looked surprised and he asked, 'You mean he wants to marry her?'

Raj nodded. He wished they would react but they sat quiet. Then, Trishala said reluctantly, 'I like him ...' Raj realized he had been holding his breath. *This was not going to be so tough after all.* But what Trishala said next shocked him. 'But that does not mean he can become our Papa.'

Tarun jumped in immediately, saying, 'That's true. We had one Papa, who left us. We do not want to go through that ordeal again.'

Trishala began to cry, remembering the pain, the tough times, Simran's nightmare, the taunts at school. Raj felt helpless. He had never known how to handle sentiments. He had hoped the children would understand.

He wiped Trishala's tears and said, 'Beta, why do you feel you will have to go through it all over again?' Tarun, visibly shaken, said, 'Papa, we never thought you would leave Mamma, but that happened, didn't it?'

Raj realized he had really scarred his children.

There are no shortcuts to success, and Raj knew that he would have to work on this. He went and sat in the backseat with the kids and then said, 'Children, what I did was wrong. Your father left you; worse, there was no one to explain what was going on.'

Trishala then said, 'And now Nikhil uncle–'

Raj cut her short saying, 'But this is what you don't understand. Nikhil is not like that. He will never do what I did. He is not going to put you two through so much ...' Raj's eyes welled up. He had to admit it. There was no other way to put it. He had been wrong. Why was he ashamed to admit it to his own flesh and blood? He realized that he would have to be brave, braver than he had ever been.

With a lot of trepidation, Raj said what he should have a long time ago. 'I will always be thankful to you for forgiving me. I want to tell you that your mother faced the toughest times; she had no one supporting her. And yet, somehow, she made it. And she helped me too. All the while, her prime concern was both of you. She never wanted you to feel abandoned. When happiness finally knocked on her door in the form of Nikhil, she refused. Did you know that? She said, she could not think of marriage again because she did not want you both to suffer in any way.'

He now stroked Trishala's hair. He said, 'It's in your hands. I would say, let's all make sure that Mamma gets the happiness I could not give her. Also, I cannot promise you, but I don't think Nikhil will do what I did to the three of you.'

Tarun had been listening intently. He slowly nodded his head. If his mother could find happiness after so much sorrow, she should have the right to keep it. He said, 'In that case, Papa, I hope even I can be a man like Nikhil uncle someday.'

Raj felt ashamed on hearing his son speak that way.

Trishala, however, objected saying, 'Bhaiyya, what are you saying? Are you saying that Mamma should marry Nikhil uncle? Have you forgotten what we went through?'

Tarun looked tenderly at his little sister. 'Trish, why are you so scared? He is nice. And Mamma's not going anywhere. She is going to be with us. Besides, if anything goes wrong, Mamma and I are there for you.'

Raj was moved.

Trishala now said to Raj, 'If Bhaiyya and Mamma are okay with this, I guess, so am I.'

Raj hugged his children. They had grown up so much in such a short while.

Tarun said, 'Papa, if it makes Mamma happy, we will be happy too.'

Trishala said, 'She really deserves to be happy. I think Nikhil uncle is a good man.'

Raj felt relieved. This felt right. He put the children on the phone with Simran.

When Simran heard them tell her they wanted to see her happy, she began to sob uncontrollably. When had her little babies become so mature and sensible?

That day, after a long time, Raj felt good about himself. He had done the right thing, and it felt great. When Simran rang off, she said, 'Thank you, Raj.' Her words echoed through his heart.

By the time they got home, he was surprised to see Nikhil waiting outside for him in his car. Raj knew immediately that Simran and he had spoken and sorted things out. As soon as Raj and the children got off, Nikhil rushed and hugged them. Once the kids went inside, Nikhil said, 'Thank you, man. I owe you one. You proved Simran was right in placing her faith in you, even when I had objected. You are a good man, Raj Mehra.'

Raj was feeling embarrassed. Nikhil's phone rang. Raj could see that it was Simran on the line.

He walked away.

The next day, Raj revealed the turn of events to the entire Mehra family. He realized how much everyone loved Simran when even Bhupinder said, 'God bless, Mori. She deserves every bit of happiness.' Kamla could not stop smiling when she said, 'Our Mori; she has finally found happiness.'

Ashima joked that she knew something was up when, on the sets, she would catch Nikhil staring at Simran while she was busy directing the shot. Kavita and Sia hugged each other in delight and Kavita said, 'The perfect thing to happen to a very wonderful human being. I am so happy for her.' Karan smiled and said, 'Bhaiyya, this is fantastic news!'

For once in his life, Raj was glad about his stance in the entire matter. This would, more or less, be how he would feel giving Trishala or Manvi away in marriage: a little possessive, but knowing it was for the best.

He had been a fool to leave Simran. She had always been good to him. The least he could do now was value what he had: Trishala, Tarun, Manvi, Sia, his Mom and Dad.

And that was quite a lot. Yes, that was quite a lot.

Simran, on the other hand, could not believe her luck. Nikhil was going to be the man in her life. And, surprise, surprise, she had Raj to thank for it, for the ease with which Tarun and Trishala had taken the news.

She had a long journey ahead. Shammi—recovering but weak—was with her on the flight. They were heading home—tired but victorious. They had much to look forward to.

The thought of home gave Simran goose bumps, and her heart raced. Her children and a new life awaited her. She had started out as a gauche, young girl who wanted to act in the movies. Then followed her marriage to Raj and her life as Mrs Raj Mehra. People bowed and pandered to her every wish and yet, it had somehow been such a hollow life.

Now, a new lease of life was in the offing, hopefully for both her mother and her.

A beautiful anticipation overcame her. As she helped Shammi into a wheelchair at the airport, even Shammi, frail as she was, seemed to read her mind and gave her a conspiratorial wink. Simran laughed with her mother, realizing, for the first time, that she was not self-conscious about it any more. Happiness had sought her, or maybe it was the other way round—she had sought happiness.

Either way, it felt great.

Author's Note

Most of our actions stem from our subconscious mind, say the experts. My decision to write this novel, too, may have been rooted in childhood memories, which flood my mind sometimes.

My initiation into media coverage of the film industry came through my mother who was a bureaucrat. She was no movie buff. In fact, we as a family based in Delhi never really had the time or the inclination to go to the movies. We were as far removed from the world of Bollywood as anyone could possibly be. Yes, we knew the names of famous actors but hadn't watched most of their films, except those that were telecast on the national television on Sunday evenings. To us, my mother's name summed up exactly what the big screen was—Maya—an illusion.

Twice a month, however, the glitzy world of cinema would make an entry into our house. The informal circulating library in Mum's office let her take home, albeit just for one day, copies of some fortnightly film magazines. The nights she would bring them home, we understood that it was our turn to do the dishes and clear up the kitchen!

I believed that Mum would use this rare time off to dive into those pages full of gossip, glamour and the lure of a world larger than life, in order to break away from her own mundane existence. At least that's what I thought until I found out that she used to skip all the gossip and go straight to reportage about heartbreak, rejection and the sorrows of spurned industry-wives, who would then be in the spotlight. Having been through heartbreak, pain and rejection herself, she later told me that when she read the stories of star-wives, she realized how lucky she was. At least, unlike them, she didn't have to cope with her pain in the constant glare of the media; her hurt and anguish were allowed privacy.

Years later, when I worked for a society magazine and even later when I turned into a scriptwriter, I saw at close quarters many celebrities who had no place to hide their crises and sorrows. In the show-biz, the first casualty of success is one's privacy.

Readers may be able to identify many of the characters in this novel from among the fraternity that lives under the arc lights. They may not be entirely correct, for the truth is never really that simple and obvious.

The acknowledged truth is that I am grateful to many of my friends and well-wishers for their help and advice in making this book a reality. I owe a debt of gratitude to my writing associate Ridhi Sarda, editors Vinitha Ramchandani and Minakshi Thakur for exercising their craft in fine-tuning the manuscript, and Krishan Chopra for his valuable guidance at many points along its evolution, right from the concept to the finished novel. And, of course, my husband Sailesh, who believed in the book even before I started writing it!

Gajra Kottary
Mumbai
September 2014